"SOMEONE PLANTED [...] SULU ASKED. "WHO?"

Sulu dropped to his knees to open a small storage carton, but Chekov's hard grip on his shoulder stopped him. "It could be rigged to blow when we open it."

Chekov pulled out a small sensor and ran it across the carton's surface. Sulu immediately recognized the security code: EXPLOSION IMMINENT.

"Out!" Chekov dragged Sulu to his feet and shoved him toward the door. "Get out of here!"

"But—"

"Sulu, don't argue with me! Even if I manage to get this blast contained, it's going to breach the corridor. And with all the physical evidence gone, the captain's going to need your report to catch the murderer. Now get *out!*"

Logic warred with loyalty inside Sulu and won. He cursed and tore himself away from the cabin. The last memory he took with him was of Chekov's intent face as he worked the blast foam over the small white carton . . .

Look for STAR TREK Fiction from Pocket Books

Star Trek: The Original Series

Star Trek: The Next Generation

Most Pocket Books are available at special quantity discounts for bulk purchases for sales promotions, premiums or fund raising. Special books or book excerpts can also be created to fit specific needs.

For details write the office of the Vice President of Special Markets, Pocket Books, 1230 Avenue of the Americas, New York, New York 10020.

STAR TREK®

DEATH COUNT

L.A. GRAF

POCKET BOOKS

New York   London   Toronto   Sydney   Tokyo   Singapore

An *Original* Publication of POCKET BOOKS

POCKET BOOKS, a division of Simon & Schuster Inc.
1230 Avenue of the Americas, New York, NY 10020

This book is published by Pocket Books, a division of
Simon & Schuster Inc., under exclusive license from
Paramount Pictures.

ISBN: 0-671-79322-5

First Pocket Books printing November 1992

10 9 8 7 6 5 4 3 2 1

POCKET and colophon are registered trademarks of
Simon & Schuster Inc.

Printed in the U.S.A.

DEATH COUNT

Chapter One

AN UNEXPECTED BLAST of neutron radiation clawed across Sulu's helm display, obscuring his fix on the binary Beta Herculani star system for a crucial moment. The distress beacon from the crippled shuttlecraft he'd been tracking faded into static, overwhelmed by the fierce gamma ray emission of the neutron star coming up close on their starboard side.

"Chekov!" Sulu's fingers raced across the board in a desperate attempt to restore their heading. He felt an ominous lurch as the ship slid into the binary's gravitational pull. "Get me a fix on the major star."

"That's what I'm trying to do." The blood-red glow of ionized hydrogen filled the navigation screen, casting shadows onto Chekov's face as he bent over his panel. "I can't find it."

"What do you mean, you can't find it?" Sulu spared just enough time from piloting to give his companion an incredulous glance. "It's a red giant! How can you miss a star that big?"

"By having something go wrong with the ship's sensors, that's how!" Chekov sounded as irritated as the upward-slanting light made him look. "Our last fix was two eleven mark six. Try that."

Sulu tapped the heading into his computer, then groaned when he saw the arc of their trajectory begin to build on the display. "Bad guess, Pavel."

He swung his chair around to aim a punch at his navigator's shoulder. The fist rebounded from such tightly clenched muscle that he wondered if the Russian even felt it. "We're going down the gravity well."

"Maybe we can slingshot ourselves back out." Chekov glanced up, scowling, as radiation alarms began to howl around them. "It would help if you'd pay attention to your screen."

"No, it wouldn't. We're dead." Sulu leaned back in his cushioned chair, watching the main screen fill with the searing blue-white fire of pulsar emissions. "As long as we're doing a swan dive into a neutron star, I at least want to see what it looks like."

"Sulu, that's not funny—"

Without warning, the lights on all of their display screens went dark. Air hissed into the chamber, and the door of the space simulator popped and swung open. "Haven't you two managed to rescue that lost shuttle yet?" Uhura asked from outside. Her dark face gleamed in the mercury-orange glow of the space station lights, looking both amused and resigned. "You've been in here for half an hour."

"We've rescued it five times." Sulu saw her baffled look and smiled. "Chekov keeps bumping us up to the next level of difficulty. If you ask me, I think he just misses working navigations."

2

The security chief swung his chair around to glare at Sulu, a trace of red just visible on his neck above his dark shirt collar. *"You're* the one who noticed that the *Exeter* broke our old scoring record on its last shore leave here. Do you want to set a new one or not?"

Sulu opened his mouth to reply, but the bone-deep roar of an arriving ship interrupted him. "Announcing arrival of ATS *Shras* at Space Station Sigma One," said the crisp, metallic voice of the traffic control computer. "Passenger transport *Shras,* of Andorian registry, is now docking at berth 416C."

"This is our last day of shore leave on Sigma One," Uhura reminded them after the docking noise had faded. "You're not going to spend all of it in the simulator, are you?"

"Why not?" Chekov looked surprised.

Sulu snorted. "Because it's also our *first* day of shore leave on Sigma One, thanks to the Federation Auditor General and his on-site efficiency audit!" He spun his console around to watch their score click up on the control panel behind them. The number steadied in the low hundred thousands, and he heard Chekov grunt with disappointment. "Hey, what do you expect?" Sulu continued, "I've spent the last three days running so many efficiency drills for the Federation auditors, I've forgotten how to actually pilot a ship."

"I hope you regain your memory before we leave port," the Russian retorted. "Otherwise, I'm staying here."

"With the auditors?" Uhura asked mischievously.

"Hmmm." An answering smile tugged at Chekov's face. "Maybe I'll take my chances with Sulu, after all."

"I'm flattered." Sulu unhooked his safety harness,

stretching the tightness from his shoulder muscles. "So—is it my turn to pick where we go next?"

Uhura nodded, and Chekov threw him a hopeful look. "We could keep playing," he suggested.

"Not a chance." Sulu scrambled out of the simulator chamber before Chekov could prompt it to start again. He never failed to be amazed by how persistent the Russian could be in pursuit of a goal. "I'm not going to spend my entire shore leave piloting a starship. I can do that when I'm on duty."

"I can't," Chekov pointed out.

"Tough." Smiling at his friend's frustrated look, Sulu swung through the narrow hatch and straightened, brushing wrinkles out of his sleek gray jumpsuit. "Come on. There's one more place I want to go before we head back to the *Enterprise.*"

Chekov groaned and hauled himself out in turn. "We're not going to eat again, are we?" Around them, a crowd of mixed commercial spacers and off-duty Starfleet personnel surged through the station gallery, ducking in and out of storefronts. A few bulky forms in dark red police armor circulated among them, looking out of place amid the sparkling lights and signs. "I'm tired of trying to find restaurants you two haven't visited yet."

"Don't worry, you won't have to." Uhura brought her hands out from behind her back and waved a steaming pastry under Sulu's nose. The spicy smell of baked fruit wafted through the overfiltered station air. "I found a new bakery while you were playing with neutron stars. Here, I bought a pie for each of you."

Sulu took the fruit pastry from her, smiling. "Uhura, this is why I like to go on shore leave with you. Mmmm, this is great!"

Chekov lifted the pastry to eye-level, inspecting it suspiciously. "What's the yellow stuff inside?"

"I'm not sure." Uhura reached in her bag for a third pastry. Her robe swirled when she moved, its dappled African colors almost as vivid as her fine-boned face. "I couldn't quite make out what the baker called it. I think he said Elysian cloud-apple—hey, watch where you're going!"

A red-suited policeman shoved his way between them, paying no attention to Uhura's protest. The small communications officer was forced to skip sideways to avoid being trampled, losing her pastry in the process. "Hey!" she said again, more angrily, as bright yellow filling splattered across the pavement. "Didn't you hear me?"

"Apparently not." Sulu reached out to steady her with one hand as the armored officer swept past them. He used the other to hang on to Chekov. "This isn't the *Enterprise*," he reminded the security chief. "You're not in charge here; they are."

"No, they're not." Handing Uhura his pastry, Chekov turned to watch the policeman disappear into the crowd. Sulu could tell from the set of his back that he wanted to follow. "Sigma One security guards wear black, not red. And they don't walk around dressed as if they're expecting a riot. I don't know who those people are, but they're not station security."

"If you'd checked the station newsboards before you jumped into that simulator, you'd know who they are," Uhura informed him, swiping at the fruit stain on her robe. "They're Orions."

"Orions?" Chekov swung around with a scowl. "What are Orions doing on a Federation space station?"

5

"What are Orions doing in uniform?" Sulu turned to stare in surprise after the suited figure. Up until now, the only Orions he'd seen were the scruffy pirate variety, the ones Starfleet kept chasing out of the far corners of Federated space. These riot-suited aliens with their phaser rifles and grimly visored helmets were a different breed entirely. "Did Starfleet let an Orion military ship dock here?"

Uhura shook her head, making her earrings jangle. "It's an Orion police cruiser, on some kind of search-and-seizure mission. The newsboards said Sigma One had granted it a temporary writ of authority, but I think the Orions just had the station outgunned."

"Then they came in before the *Enterprise* did," Chekov said flatly. "How long have they been on board Sigma One?"

"I'm not sure." Uhura glanced around as another outburst of indignant shouts marked the policemen's path through the crowded gallery. "I gather it's been long enough for them to be annoying. Of course, with Orions, that's not saying much."

Quietly enjoying the tavern's collage of well-mannered patrons, his feet stretched beneath the table to rest on the chair across from him, James T. Kirk took note of the moment the wicked clock-spring of tension inside him uncoiled and melted away. He closed his eyes and sighed deeply of the place's anachronistic smells—wet wool, warm oil-wood, the distinctive sting of the brandy he held cupped, untouched, between his hands. This wasn't the sort of place he'd have enjoyed on shore leave twenty years ago, but for an administration-badgered starship captain of just over forty, it more than fit the bill.

"Mr. Scott," he sighed aloud to his chief engineer, "this is the best idea you've had in ages."

"Aye, sir." He could practically hear the smile in the engineer's thick brogue. "I thought it might be."

A good-natured snort from beside Kirk made the captain crack one eye. "I could stand it if they served some real food," Leonard McCoy complained as he scowled over a printed menu card. "What the hell is 'bubble-and-squeak'?"

"Something my father used to threaten us with when we were children." Scott scooted his chair around next to McCoy's and tipped the card so he could read it. The red-and-black splash of wool tartan over one shoulder stood out brightly against his white cardigan. "Not all Scottish food is something to be proud of, I'm afraid," he cautioned the doctor, looking worried. "We gave the world haggis, too, you know."

"Oh, good Lord. . . ."

Kirk laughed, pushing up the sleeves on his summer-weight blazer. He was already regretting having left the ship in something so light—he'd forgotten how chilly space stations could be with only one ship's worth of crew wandering around on board. "Be daring, Bones. Bubble-and-squeak is just a name."

"Sounds like boiled mice." McCoy flipped the card to the wood table with a sigh. "Next time, I'm going on shore leave with Uhura. At least, she knows where all the good restaurants are."

Kirk grinned and closed his eyes again. "Man does not live by bread alone."

"Man doesn't live by bubble-and-squeak, either," the doctor retorted.

The captain laughed, but didn't answer. Personally,

he hadn't thought about eating for a while—and wasn't surprised to find the thought still didn't interest him much. After spending the last three days chewing up his stomach in frustration over four nosy Federation efficiency auditors poking through his ship, he didn't think he'd want to put food down again until the *Enterprise* was well away from Sigma One. He intended to start that departure just as soon as the last shore leave personnel returned to the ship this evening—himself included.

"Jim, are you going to drink that brandy or just stare at it?"

"You're the one that keeps telling me that staring at it is healthier, Bones."

McCoy swatted the bottom of Kirk's foot with one hand, and Kirk had to jerk fully upright to keep from sloshing brandy all over the lap of his trousers. "Don't get smart with me, Captain. You're supposed to be here to relax."

Pursing his lips around a half-hearted scowl, Kirk brought both feet to the floor and set his brandy on the table. "I am relaxing." He sniffed the brandy again, decided he still didn't want it, and pushed it toward McCoy. "What's the matter? Aren't I relaxing efficiently enough?"

Scott chortled appreciatively, and McCoy's leathery face opened into a sly smile. "Aha! Do my trained medical senses detect some lingering hostility here?"

"What lingering?" Kirk folded his arms, decided that seemed too defensive and settled for leaning his elbows on the table instead. "I haven't even *expressed* enough hostility to be down to just 'lingering.'"

"That's all right, sir." Scott raised his glass in ironic salute. "I think my lads have expressed enough hostility for the lot of us."

Kirk acknowledged his engineer's sentiment with a tip of his head. "What is it with these people, anyway? The *Enterprise* needed an efficiency inspection like Spock needs a psychologist." He thumped back in his chair, arms folded after all. "I've got the best, most efficient crew in the Fleet, and the Auditor General knows it as well as anyone. Eating up our leave time with interviews and inspections was a waste of everybody's shore leave."

"They had auditors down in sickbay, too." McCoy sounded dangerously close to placating, and Kirk slid him a warning look to stave off the worst of it. The doctor acquiesced by throwing his hands up between them. "I'm just saying the irritation was mutual, Jim. But orders are orders—it's not like you could have done anything to keep them from coming on board."

Kirk thought that he could have told Chekov to position guards at every transporter station and use phasers on anyone carrying a clipboard and inspection manual. That probably wasn't what McCoy had in mind, though. "At least it's over," Kirk sighed, willing his muscles to relax and his irritation to bleed away. "We won't have to worry about it again in my lifetime."

Scott ruined the moment by glancing over his captain's head and aiming a dark, Scottish frown at the doorway. "We might be speaking just a wee bit too soon, I'm afraid. . . ."

"Kirk?" Heavy footsteps thundered up behind him, followed by a sharp rap on the shoulder. "I need to talk with you, Captain. As usual, your people are causing me problems."

Dropping his head, Kirk rubbed his eyes with one hand instead of turning to growl at John Taylor. "Mr.

Taylor, I am on shore leave. Mr. Spock is on the ship if you have questions—"

"Damn right I have questions!" Taylor stepped into Kirk's peripheral vision, obviously waiting for the captain to look up at him. He'd be waiting a long time, Kirk decided. "Your Commander Spock says we've been barred from reboarding the *Enterprise*. Is that true?"

"Vulcans don't lie, Mr. Taylor." Kirk finally swung his chair to face the man, and couldn't help lifting eyebrows in surprise to find all four auditors fidgeting impatiently behind him. He focused on the taller of the two men, knowing from three days' hard experience that Taylor was both mouthpiece and motor for this unit. A more offensive and prickly mouthpiece, Kirk couldn't have easily imagined.

"You've been barred from the *Enterprise*," Kirk said, "because your business there is finished. I was told to assist in your inspection while we were in port. You said last night you were done with that inspection, so, as of this morning, you have no further authority or need to inspect either my ship or my crew. I'll thank you to leave us our remaining shore-leave time in peace." He nodded to the other three auditors, and moved to turn his back on them in the hopes they'd all take the hint and drag their boss away.

"Not so fast, Captain." Taylor stopped him with a hand on his chair and a hard copy film of Federation letterhead under his nose.

Kirk took the film in both hands, refusing to recognize the boarding permit or the official-as-hell signature beneath it. "What's this?"

"My orders." Taylor crossed his arms, lips curled in a sneer of satisfaction. "I found a number of discrepancies while compiling my people's reports on your crew. The Federation Auditor General thought it a good idea to observe your ship in the course of a normal mission. That way, we can decide who's at fault before my final report is filed."

Kirk clenched his fist until the permit crumpled to near-unreadability.

"At fault?" McCoy's blue eyes snapped with a disapproval Kirk had learned to recognize well over the years. "You turn people's jobs and experience into sets of little numbers, then you think somebody has to be *at fault* when those numbers don't match up to some desk jockey's idea of efficiency? Good God! How are we supposed to be efficient with you people sticking your noses into everything all the time?"

"Lingering hostility," Kirk reminded the doctor. McCoy only made a face and fell silent.

"You can't come with us." Kirk turned his chair to face Taylor again, suppressing a guilty swell of satisfaction when the auditor danced back a few steps to avoid colliding with the captain. "No matter what the Auditor General thinks, you're still civilian personnel. The *Enterprise* is scheduled to conduct three separate planetary explorations in the Canopis sector on our next assignment. As captain, I have the right to declare any of those explorations too dangerous for civilians." He spread his hands and smiled his most painfully charming smile. "I am hereby declaring them so."

Scott leaned across the table to shrug apologetically. "You can't very well study a crew's efficiency when you aren't even able to be with the crew, now, can you?" He sounded as reasonable and contrite as any man ever could. "Maybe next time."

Taylor narrowed dark eyes to peer back and forth from one to another of the three officers. Kirk honestly couldn't remember if Taylor's every expression and gesture had irritated him from the beginning, or if the rare degree of enmity they shared had developed along the way. It probably didn't matter anymore. "What if you weren't going to Canopis?"

"But we are," Kirk said. "Even you can't change that."

Taylor snapped a finger against the flimsy in Kirk's hand. "I don't have to. Commodore Petersen already did."

That clock-spring of tension came back with annoying facility. Kirk flipped the printout in his hand, frowning down the long chains of legalese until words like "Orion" and "surveillance" popped out of the morass. "They can't do this." He shot a glare up at Taylor, and wanted suddenly to slap the hauteur from the auditor's face. "Why wasn't I told?"

Taylor shrugged, snatching back the flimsy. "I'm sure there's a message waiting back on board for you. Maybe you don't check your mail prompts often enough."

And maybe this was all some stupid misunderstanding, and the Auditor General wasn't really trying to push some starship captain into murdering a team of his investigators. Standing, Kirk pulled the flimsy from Taylor's hand much more politely than the auditor had taken it from him.

"Where are you going?" Taylor asked when Kirk stepped past him.

"To talk to Commodore Petersen. There has to be some mistake." Kirk stopped in the doorway to glance behind him. "Bones, Scotty—I'm afraid I'll have to take a rain check on that lunch."

They were already out of their chairs and headed after him. "Are you kidding?" McCoy grumbled while auditors parted before him like a flock of flustered pigeons. Taylor turned an irate circle, mouth agape even though he didn't try to stop the doctor. "If I have to eat anything called bubble-and-squeak," McCoy declared, "the last thing I need is somebody criticizing the efficiency of my digestion." He bumped Scott with one elbow, favoring the auditors with a withering glare. "Come on, Scotty—let's go find someplace that's a little more discriminating about who it lets inside."

Chapter Two

"THOSE WERE the rudest policemen I've ever met." Uhura's voice still smoldered with indignation. "Look at them—they're shoving everyone around!"

Sulu nodded, frowning as he watched the dark red figures weave through the crowd. Their spacing seemed too carefully measured to be the random result of shore leave. "I think they're looking for someone. Or something."

"Well, I hope they don't find it." Uhura took a bite of the pastry she held, then looked at it in surprise. "Pavel, did you give me your cloud-apple pie?"

The security chief looked over his shoulder at her, his frown fading down to one worried line between his eyes. "No, my pie was the one that dropped," he assured her. "That one's yours."

Uhura gave him a dubious look. "Are you sure?"

"Positive."

Sulu grinned. Knowing how much Chekov disliked trying any new food made it even more fun to watch him wriggle out of it. "Coward," Sulu said, licking the last pastry flakes off his fingers. He glanced around, looking for a directional marker. "Come on. We've only got an hour of shore leave left, and the store I want to visit is at the other end of the Galleria."

"It would be." Despite his sigh, Chekov followed Sulu readily enough down the gallery's curving tunnel, merely pausing to let Uhura fall into step in front of him. Sulu noticed that the Russian kept a wary gaze on the red-suited figures moving through the crowd. "So, what hobby is it this week?"

Sulu blinked, startled by the accuracy of the question. "How did you know—I mean, what makes you think I've got a new hobby?" He glanced back over his shoulder, hearing Uhura's soft ripple of amusement join Chekov's deeper laugh. "What's so funny?"

"Sulu, there are some things we always do when we're on shore leave together," said Uhura with a smile. "Chekov always cajoles you into playing simulator games—"

"Uhura always finds some strange food for us to eat," added Chekov wryly.

"—and you always find a new hobby to bring back to the *Enterprise.*" Uhura glanced back at the security chief as they passed the wide gate leading to the station's docks. "What was it last time? Arcturian yoga?"

Chekov shook his head. "That was the time before last. Last time it was carving replicas of famous starships in Iotian crystal."

Mild embarrassment prickled across Sulu's cheekbones, and he lifted a hand to scrub the feeling away.

"I'm still working on those starships," he pointed out. "And how was I supposed to know you need two sets of arms to do Arcturian yoga?"

"Sulu, anyone who ever watched an Arcturian doing yoga would have known that!"

"Details, details." Sulu spotted the store he'd visited earlier, its painted sign almost hidden by the riot of ivy and flowers cascading through the open lattice front. "This is the place I want. Come on in."

Inside the plant-filled shop, the pleasant chime of falling water mingled with the chirp of something like crickets. Sulu paused on the threshold and took a deep breath. The mingled smells of soil, leaves, and budding flowers moistened the air to almost planetary freshness. "Isn't this great?"

"It's just like your cabin." Chekov came to stand beside him, frowning as the chirping sound grew louder. "I thought insects weren't allowed on class-four space stations."

"Those aren't insects." Sulu lifted a curtain of Denebian lianas for Uhura to duck under, ignoring the spray of fragrant pollen they showered down on him. Beyond the screen of vines, water bubbled in a curved black marble pool, gently rocking the moss-green pads of water lilies. Translucent sapphire flowers rose out of the water on fragile, bending stems while small gold-speckled lizards curled catlike on the leaf pads. Their throat sacs fluttered with their chirping.

"Oh!" Uhura's musical voice softened with delight as she sank down beside the pool. "Sulu, they're beautiful! What are they?"

"Halkan water chameleons. Watch." Sulu bent and flicked the water with his fingers. The chirping soared into a chorus of alarm, then fell to total silence. On each leaf, only a moss-green shimmer marked the places where the small lizards had been. "Pretty neat, huh?"

"You're going to raise lizards now?" Chekov ducked through the lianas and stood looking dubiously down at the lily pond. "What's the point of owning animals you can't even see, much less play with?"

"I like the noise they make. And, besides, you need them to pollinate the flowers." Sulu dipped a hand into the pool to cup one of the translucent lilies in his palm. As soon as his fingers touched the petals, a pale firefly radiance sprang to life inside. After a moment, a shower of phosphorescent pollen puffed out from the heart of the flower. The tiny sparks settled across Sulu's hand and glowed there briefly before winking out. "I've only seen these in books—they're Halkan fire-lilies. I thought I'd add them to my plant collection."

"I'd like to know where—" A fierce crash from the front of the store interrupted Chekov's question. The security officer spun around, then dove through the curtain of vines with Sulu and Uhura at his heels. They emerged from the screen of plants in time to see a figure in familiar dark red armor sweep a potted cycad off its stand. Ceramic shattered violently against the tile floor.

"Hey!" A burly gray-haired man burst from a door in the side of the shop, holding a broom like a quarterstaff in his hands. He looked in disbelief at the heaps of dirt and trampled leaves on his floor, then up at the armored policeman. "What the hell do you think you're doing?"

The Orion turned his dark-visored face toward the

shopkeeper, one gloved hand already curled around another plant. "Standard search procedure," he said in a curt monotone, and sent the plant crashing to the ground.

"The hell it is! This is the Federation!" The shopkeeper tried to shoulder between the Orion and his merchandise. Sulu drew a tense breath, seeing Chekov move to intervene. He dropped a restraining hand on the security officer's shoulder just as the Orion flung the burly shopkeeper across the shop with the ease of someone used to a much higher gravity. The chirping from the back of the shop went silent with the crash.

Chekov paused warily, an arm's length from the Orion while Uhura darted forward to crouch beside the groaning shopkeeper. Sulu drew in a tense breath, watching the armored policeman turn to stare down at the slighter figure of the *Enterprise*'s security chief. "Chekov," Sulu said softly, "just let me say three words before you decide to start something here— two Earth gravities."

"I remember." The Russian's left hand twitched behind his back, fingers clenching and unclenching twice. Sulu blinked and took a slow step backward. "Uhura, is the shopkeeper all right?"

"It looks like he hit his head," she said, sounding concerned.

"Don't worry about me." The burly man levered himself up on one elbow as Sulu retreated another step. "Just go get station security. I want them to arrest this ape."

"That won't be necessary." Chekov's hand jerked again, and Sulu promptly yanked down a handful of lianas. He doubled the vines into a loop, then flung them up to catch around the Orion's neck. The armored man grunted and tore away with a jerk, but in the brief moment that his hands were occupied, Chekov ducked forward to grab his phaser pistol from his belt. The security officer had to dive sideways to escape the Orion's swift clutch, but he rolled and came up with the phaser pointed directly at the policeman's chest. The Orion stiffened as if the joints of his suit had suddenly locked.

"Get out of here," Chekov ordered. "Now."

The Orion's gloved hands twitched as if he wanted to grab for the phaser rifle slung across his back, but Chekov's fierce stare—and steady grip on the phaser pistol—must have convinced him not to try it. With a wordless growl, he swung around and headed for the door.

"Uhura, call station security." Chekov rolled to his feet without taking his eyes off the retreating red-suited figure. "Tell them their Orion visitors are breaking station regulations down on Deck Five."

The communications officer nodded. "Of all times not to have a communicator with me. Where's your station intercom?" she asked the shopkeeper.

"Inside my office." The burly man jerked his chin at the door he'd come out of, then grunted and gingerly lifted a hand to his forehead. While Uhura scrambled up to look for the communicator panel, Sulu found a clean cloth near a plant-watering faucet, then came over to press it against the shopkeeper's forehead.

The man gave him a quick, tight smile. "Thanks. You folks handled that Orion real good—better than station security would have. I take it you're from the starship that came into port the other day?"

"That's right." Chekov still watched the door, the phaser pistol ready in his hand. "What's wrong with your station security? They shouldn't be letting Orions get away with this kind of behavior."

The shopkeeper sighed. "They weren't this bad when they first hit port." He heard the dubious noise Chekov made and grunted. "Well, they were rude, but they didn't do anything this destructive. Just looked around the shop two or three times and left."

"What were they searching for?" Sulu asked, crouching back on his heels beside the older man.

"Beats the hell out of me." The shopkeeper sat up, wincing. "They said it was for Orion deserters, but that doesn't make any sense. No Orion in his right mind would head for a station this deep in Andorian space. Not after that Haslev incident."

Chekov glanced over his shoulder. "Haslev incident?"

"One of Andor's genius physicists skipped out on its space research program a few months ago, taking some kind of top-secret technology with him. The Andorians seem to think the Orions had something to do with it. If you ask me, they're both just spoiling for a fight." The shopkeeper struggled to his feet, using Sulu's shoulder as a prop. "Come on into my back room. I want to give you something for chasing that Orion out of here."

"You don't have to," Chekov assured him, tucking the Orion phaser discreetly into the pocket of his dark leather jacket. "It's our job to enforce Starfleet regulations."

The burly man shook his head stubbornly. "I insist." He tugged at Sulu's shoulder, and the helmsman allowed himself to be led into the cluttered storeroom, noticing that Chekov paused in the door to keep one wary eye on the front of the store. The burly shopkeeper reached into one corner, pulling a dust-sheet off a bulky object there. Black marble glittered in the refracted light. "There—what do you think?"

"Uh—" Sulu blinked at the curving oval pond, a smaller cousin to the one out in the shop. "You want to give that to me?"

The store owner nodded. "A little thank-you present for saving my shop."

Sulu glanced over his shoulder at Chekov, silhouetted in the doorway. "But I'm not the one who saved it."

"No, but you're the one who brought your friends here." The burly man's smile was surprisingly warm. "If I'm not mistaken, son, this is the third time you came in today to look at those water chameleons. I figure you must want some, and you're going to need something to keep them in."

"I was just going to put them in an old fish tank I have." Despite himself, Sulu stepped forward to run a hand over the marble pond's sleek surface. Metallic flakes glittered inside the jet-black surface, giving it a shimmer like fine mica. He stepped back with a wistful sigh. "It's beautiful—but I'm afraid Starfleet regulations won't let us accept gifts this expensive."

The store owner grunted and began to pull the container out of its corner. "Don't worry, this thing's not worth a Tellurian nickel. I make these ponds myself, out of marble-epoxy, and this one's a dud." He tipped the container back to show Sulu its supporting column. "See that streak across the base? Too much silver flake leaked into the mold there, and ruined the whole thing."

"Are you sure?" The small imperfection didn't seem like much of a flaw to Sulu.

"Why do you think I have it back here, instead of out in the shop?" The shopkeeper tossed an honest

21

grin at Sulu. "And I'm only giving you the pond. I figured I'd let you buy the lizards and the lilies."

Sulu chuckled appreciatively. "Well, in that case—" He helped the storekeeper carry the pond back into the main room, finding it less heavy than it looked. Chekov stepped back to let them past, eyes narrowed dubiously.

"Are you sure you have enough room in your jungle for a swimming pool?" he demanded, following them back out to the larger lily pond.

"I'll make room." Sulu raised an eyebrow as Uhura pushed through the curtain of lianas to join them. "What took you so long?"

"Station security kept putting me on hold." Her lips tightened. "I finally pulled rank on the communications officer and made him put me through. The security chief said she'd be down as soon as possible. I get the impression she's gotten a lot of calls about Orions recently." The communications officer glanced over at the small marble container. "What a nice pond!"

"Thanks. Chekov got it for me." Sulu grinned when the Russian scowled at him, then turned to watch the shopkeeper lift a potted lily out of the water with a long-handled scoop. A dozen invisible chameleons came with it, chirping anxiously, and the man expertly shook them into two small plastic bags.

"I'm still not sure this is a good idea." Chekov came to stand beside them, frowning. "What happens if your lizards get loose? The last thing we need is a bunch of invisible reptiles running around on the *Enterprise.*"

The burly man grunted, knotting the bags so a bulge of air remained in each. Muffled chirps came through the plastic as the chameleons tried and failed to blend with the transparent walls. "Don't worry, son, Halkan chameleons never go very far from their home ponds. And they don't need anything special to eat, just standard fish food. That'll be twenty credits."

Chekov grunted. "That's a lot to spend for one plant and a bunch of singing lizards who'll keep you up all night."

"Oh, Chekov, stop being so grumpy." Uhura took the bags the shopkeeper handed her, cradling them against her robe as Sulu paid the bill. The chameleons promptly turned a dozen sunset colors. "I think this is the best hobby Sulu's ever had."

"That's easy for you to say," observed the Russian dourly. "You're not the one who's going to have to carry this swimming pool back to the ship."

"Hey, you're the one who lifts weights, not me." Sulu picked up the water lily, careful not to touch the pollen-dusted petals, then thanked the burly man with a nod. The shopkeeper nodded back at them, smiling as he watched them go.

"That's what you always say when we have to carry something heavy." Despite his protest, Chekov lifted the marble pool easily enough, balancing it against his shoulder. Sulu exchanged smiles with Uhura as they followed him out the door. "Remind me never to take shore leave—"

The Russian's voice broke off when he stepped out into the station gallery, but with the glare of the mercury lights in his eyes, Sulu didn't see the reason why until he and Uhura had emerged in turn. A stark black wall of Sigma One security guards ringed the shop door, phasers aimed straight at them.

"Don't anyone move," said a clipped female voice.

"This is station security—" She leveled a damning finger at Chekov. "—and you, sir, are under arrest."

Kirk couldn't help thinking that Maxwell Petersen didn't look—or sound—particularly sympathetic to his situation.

"I'm sorry, Jim," the commodore sighed, tossing his hands up in the universal gesture of surrender. "There isn't anything I can do." He waved Kirk into the chair across from his own. "You know I would, if I were able."

Kirk glanced at the offered chair from habit, then found he couldn't quite make himself give up on his pacing and sit down. "You can keep them on the station," he suggested. Then, anticipating Petersen's objection, "You're the officer in charge of this sector, Max—you can do anything you want, and we both know it. That includes detaining four Federation auditors long enough to let me get out of port."

Petersen laughed. "Jim, for Starfleet's brightest captain, you can be awfully dense at times."

Kirk stopped at the edge of the commodore's desk, but swallowed the first unkind thing he thought to say. Being sarcastic with a commodore—even one he'd helped promote to that position—wouldn't do much toward saving his crew from six weeks of annoyance. "I'm glad you think this is funny."

"I don't think it's funny; I think you're overreacting." Petersen leaned forward in his chair, reaching out to poke at the perpetual motion sculpture on the table in front of him. The new infusion of energy hurried the sculpture's movements, flashing little splinters of reflected light all around the commodore's office. "It's politics, Jim. Somebody in the

Auditor General's office is up for reelection—yours is just the ship lucky enough to be in port when it happened." He grinned up at Kirk and folded his hands. "Recognize that it's bigger than both of us," he half-teased, dark eyes still a bit serious for his words. "Accept it. Move on."

Kirk drummed his fingers on Petersen's desk. Two-bit philosophy rarely did much for his moods. "Does the Auditor General know his people are going into the Andorian sector?"

Petersen shrugged. "I assume so."

"And that doesn't bother you?"

When the commodore only rolled his eyes, Kirk strode forward to confront him. "That's about as close to leaving Federation space as you can get without actually doing it, Max! On top of that, political relations there aren't exactly friendly right now. I'm not sure we should send a starship into that kind of powder keg to begin with, much less a starship full of civilians." He threw himself into the chair after all, glaring at Petersen across the dancing sculpture. "You know the Andorians are almost ready to declare war over this Muav Haslev thing?"

"Which the Orions," Petersen countered, "swear they had nothing to do with."

Kirk snorted. "And why would the Orions lie?"

"Look, Jim—" Petersen pushed the sculpture to one side, leaning his elbows on his knees to peer across at Kirk as though they were discussing a deep and common goal. The captain stayed seated just as he was, loath to lie with his body language any more than he would with his words. "The Andorians are exactly why we're sending you in there," the commodore explained. "The Orions on Rigel VIII may be neutral, but Andor isn't. We can't have the Andorians running around threatening wars that could involve the entire Federation. We're hoping a little Starfleet presence will remind everyone not to start anything we'll all regret."

Kirk knew halfway through the commodore's speech that what to do with four Federation auditors was too far outside Petersen's present concerns to get much of a hearing. "If the Andorians are close enough to war that you need a starship to dissuade them," he tried anyway, "I think that's all the more reason not to send civilians into the area."

"Starfleet is confident the *Enterprise*'s presence is exactly what will keep things safe for civilian traffic."

"Dammit, Max—"

"We're short a ship, Jim." Something in the commodore's voice silenced Kirk, something grim and rough, like the tearing of overstressed metal. "The *Kongo* suffered a containment field breach," Petersen said into the tight silence between them. "Two days ago, a half-day from here at warp four. She lost nearly one hundred crew in her secondary hull, has at least another fifty who might follow due to radiation exposure."

A sharp, burning image suddenly slashed across Kirk's mind—a combination of memories, knowledge, and fears. It was easy to paint in mental details of the accident, only this time it was Kirk's ship with her engines blown wide, Kirk's people reduced to radiation shadows on the corridor walls. "My God—"

"This Andor expedition was the *Kongo*'s assignment. Now, her captain isn't even sure he can get her into port without assistance. I've sent a brace of tugs to locate her, but we can't say if she'll ever be spaceworthy again." Petersen sighed, and the honesty of it prickled Kirk with guilt for having badgered the man.

"Is there anything the *Enterprise* can do to help?"

"Yes." Petersen looked at him, no longer smiling. "You can take this Andor run and try to prevent a local war between the Andorians and Rigel VIII. You can quit griping about four efficiency auditors as if they were the worst thing that could happen to a starship crew. Understand me?"

Surprisingly enough, Kirk found his earlier irritation more than willing to resurface. "Yes, sir. I understand." He understood he'd be stuck with four number-conscious pencil-pushers for six agonizing weeks, and it wouldn't do either the *Kongo* or the *Enterprise* any good.

Damn.

The intercom on Petersen's desk shrilled, and a strident female voice cut across their conversation. "Station Security to Commodore Petersen."

Petersen leaned far to his left to punch the answer button, still watching Kirk as though not trusting the captain to just sit there and behave. "Petersen here."

"Chief Brahmson here, sir. We've had an altercation in the Galleria on Deck Five, something about weapons being stolen from Orion PD. As near as we can tell, no shots were fired, but the Orions are insisting we prosecute."

"Oh, hell." Petersen surged to his feet. "Five'll get you ten the Andorians are involved. Tell the Orions I'm on my way. We'll work something out."

"Aye, sir."

27

Petersen snatched up his jacket from the back of his chair, glaring at Kirk when the captain stood as well. "Andorians and Orions, Captain," he sighed. "It's like mixing antimatter with matter." He shook his head and started into the hall. "Let's hope this is as bad as it gets."

Chapter Three

THE PRIVACY WINDOW in the door to Chekov's cell shuttered open, and an unfamiliar face bobbed into view. "You've still got one call you can make," the Sigma One guard offered, "if you want."

Chekov looked up without lifting his chin out of his hands. "Can I call my captain on the *Enterprise?*"

"No. You can only call someplace on station."

Shrugging, he turned his attention back to the opposite wall. Their answer hadn't changed since the first time they'd asked him this question, so neither had his. Chekov assumed that sooner or later they'd catch on and quit asking him.

After a moment, the privacy window flickered dark again, and Chekov was left alone.

Whoever had designed the Sigma One holding cells obviously hadn't intended them to be occupied for very long. Chekov assumed they housed drunks and vagrants, mostly—the occasional rowdy spacer on leave, just to fill out the bill. There was a toilet, an all-purpose bench-bed wall arrangement, and four distressingly similar corners on which to pass your time. There wasn't even enough room to pace, really, since the bed took up a quarter of the cell in one direction, and pacing too close to the door in the other invariably brought guards running to make sure he wasn't trying to escape. Since his only other option seemed to be spinning in random circles, Chekov simply waited on the edge of his bed, alternately drumming his feet and drumming his fingers for lack of anything better to do.

When they'd first brought him into Sigma One's security station, the guards had been ethical enough, if rude.

"Look at this, John! Another civilian superhero, taking guns away from Orions."

"Why don't you try and take my gun, son? If you can get it, you can go."

Chekov almost took him up on that one, fairly certain that if anyone ended up shot in that exchange, it wouldn't be him. He'd already sent Sulu and Uhura to contact Commodore Petersen's office, though, and it probably wouldn't encourage the commodore to look kindly on this whole incident if Chekov ended up holding his entire security division at gunpoint. So he'd just kept his mouth shut while they paraded him in front of various screens of paperwork and confiscated the Orion phaser.

Then they'd run the retina scan and obtained a positive ID.

"Oh, my God," the tow-headed desk sergeant had gasped, his cheeks flushing very red. "You're in Starfleet!"

Chekov wondered what the ID net said about him. "That's what I told you."

A half-dozen guards crowded around the sergeant's shoulders, and he pointed out one or two items on the screen. "Starship security," one of them muttered, as if he'd just found out their prisoner was going to explode. "Holy cow—"

After that, they'd taken Chekov's jacket, his belt, and every piece of identification he had. They probably would have taken his boots, as well, but there was apparently some disagreement about how safely they could come within kicking distance. They took everything they could reach over the counter, though, then escorted him back here, where he obviously wouldn't be a danger to anyone but himself.

It occurred to Chekov that maybe Starfleet should do something about security's reputation among civilian personnel.

A loud rumbling from the front of his cell caught Chekov's attention from the ever-enthralling wall, and he looked up just in time to see the door slide away to reveal a glimpse of nearby freedom. The guard in the hall stepped deferentially aside, replaced by a more massive figure in familiar, welcome Starfleet burgundy and gold.

"Lieutenant Chekov?"

Chekov jumped to his feet, delighted to see anyone not dressed in Sigma One black. "Lieutenant," he said, recognizing the other man's rank as he came forward to shake his hand.

"Lieutenant Lindsey Purviance, from Commodore Petersen's office." Although nearly twenty centimeters taller than Chekov and broad enough to fill the doorway from shoulder to shoulder, Purviance's handshake was nervous-hot, and remarkably gentle and shy. "I've talked with station security about what happened," he said in a voice that matched his tentative demeanor. "They understand your captain's waiting on you to leave port, so they're releasing you to my custody. If you promise you'll come back to go before their local judicator as soon as this mission's over, they'll let me take you back to the *Enterprise*."

Chekov leaned around Purviance's imposing bulk to nod at the young guard behind him. "I promise."

"All right, then." Purviance handed him his jacket, the pockets already heavy with sundry items. "I've got a shuttle waiting, and your friends are in the lobby. Are you ready?"

Chekov nodded, digging quickly through his pockets while he followed the other lieutenant into the hall, just to make sure everything was there. As they passed into the outer office, he glanced by reflex at the wall chronometer, and his heart sank into his stomach. "Oh, my God! Is that the right time?"

Purviance frowned, looking around until he found where Chekov was looking. "Well—yes. Is there some problem?"

"The *Enterprise* was supposed to leave port twenty-eight minutes ago." Chekov groaned and buried his face in his jacket. "I just made an entire starship late for departure."

"The captain's going to kill us," Sulu pronounced for what Chekov thought must be the hundredth time since their shuttle left the lock at Sigma One.

"We're only forty minutes late," Chekov said, pacing the narrow aisle while their taxi set down in the midst of the *Enterprise*'s hangar bay. "No one forced you to wait for me. You weren't under arrest, you know."

Sulu sighed and nodded. "I know." They'd been through this a hundred times, too.

"Besides, if it hadn't been for those Orions, we'd have been back on board in time to leave dock on schedule." Chekov wished he could make himself sit down, but almost two hours in that tiny Sigma security cell made even a passenger shuttle feel big enough to be worth prowling. "Surely, the captain knows this wasn't our fault."

Uhura made a little sound of disbelief, then turned to look behind her when the outside door sighed open as the signal they could leave. "But, Chekov, it *is* our fault." She stood, both arms wrapped around the pot of Sulu's wilted water lily. "If you hadn't taken that policeman's weapon—"

"I should have let him continue hitting that old man?"

"I didn't say you were wrong—"

"All right, all right—" Sulu, a plastic bag of water depending from either hand, made a wide-armed gesture to hurry his friends toward the open hatch. "I'm sure this is going to be a lovely argument, but can we have it later? I really, *really* want to get my lizards into something better than these bags so they have at least a small chance of surviving this adventure. It would be nice to report for duty sometime, too. So let's go, huh?"

Chekov levered the lily pond out of the seat, just as glad to have an excuse not to continue this discussion. He'd already been over this ground a million times while examining the confines of his cell, and he didn't need further reminding that—as trapped into his actions as he felt—he had no one to blame but himself. He stepped aside, pond balanced against his hip, to let the shuttle's fourth passenger into the aisle.

"Need any help?" Purviance asked.

Chekov shook his head. Despite his size, Purviance exuded all the symptoms of an office worker terrified of exerting himself. "It's not that heavy—I've got it."

Purviance nodded with a self-conscious, quicksilver smile, then ducked out the door behind Sulu and Uhura, leaving Chekov to bring up the rear.

Not that entering the hangar bay last did much to improve his reception.

"Mr. Chekov, glad to see you could make it." Kirk's tone, while pleasant enough, didn't lessen the severity of his frown.

Chekov felt embarrassment sting his cheeks like a slap. Bad enough to have to suffer Kirk's disapproval; having to suffer it in civilian clothes that still stank of a civilian brig only made matters unbearably worse. "Captain, I can explain—"

"I'm sure you can." Kirk flicked an equally sharp look at Sulu and Uhura. "If you two aren't too busy, I'm sure your presence would be welcomed on the bridge."

"Yes, sir."

"Aye, sir."

Sulu paused only long enough to drop both plastic bags into the lily pond Chekov held, then hurried off after Uhura and his plant without saying another word. Inside the bags, the lizards bumbled against each other in the newly turbulent water, chirped once in helpless alarm, and promptly vanished.

Chekov knew just how they felt.

"Captain Kirk?" Purviance stepped forward, one hand outstretched uncertainly in a bid for Kirk's attention. When the captain took his hand to shake it, Purviance beamed with what looked like relief. "Captain, I'm Lieutenant Lindsey Purviance, with Commodore Petersen's office."

Kirk nodded, although the faint line between his brows told Chekov the introduction didn't really hold much meaning for him. "Lieutenant Purviance—"

"Commodore Petersen sent Mr. Purviance to arrange for my release," Chekov explained. He made a vow not to flinch from Kirk's scrutiny when the captain turned back to him. "It was supposed to expedite matters, sir. We came here immediately after security let me go."

"I was late getting there," Purviance volunteered. "We had a communications mix-up at the office. I ended up with some Andorians down in Customs—" He trailed off into an apologetic shrug even before Kirk waved aside his justification.

"You're not the one who needs to explain, Mr. Purviance," Kirk said. He shot a hard-edged glare at Chekov. "When I see your report on this incident, there'd better be one hell of an explanation included."

Chekov nodded, tightening his grip on the lily pond. "I'll do my best, sir."

The captain nodded shortly, but Chekov knew better than to take that as any kind of reprieve. "Mr. Purviance—" Kirk turned briskly to the tall visitor. "I appreciate your help in returning my officer. Please give my thanks to Commodore Petersen, and tell him nothing like this—"

"Oh!" Purviance broke in with eyes wide in surprise. "I'm not going back to the station, sir." He seemed suddenly awkward again, and caught off-guard. "Commodore Petersen has assigned me as liaison officer to the efficiency team. To sort of acclimate them to appropriate ship behavior, and to keep them out of trouble for you. So I'll be along for the duration—" He peeked a bit timidly at Kirk. "—if that's all right with you, sir."

Kirk's mouth pressed into a line that might be either annoyance or chagrin. "I wish the commodore had called me," he admitted. Then with a shrug, "What's one more passenger? Welcome aboard."

Purviance flushed darkly. Chekov couldn't tell if that meant he was embarrassed or pleased. "Thank you, sir."

"In the meantime, we all have work to do." Kirk rapped his knuckles against the outside edge of the lily pond, and Chekov nearly jumped at the loudness of that hollow sound. "See if you can't find someplace to stow that souvenir ashtray, then put Mr. Purviance together with the auditors. I'll talk to you about this other matter after the ship is under way."

Chekov was perfectly willing to let the other matter simply drop, but knew enough to nod. "Yes, sir."

"Carry on."

Once Kirk had turned away, Chekov forced himself to relax his shoulders, and thanked God there'd been a visitor here to discourage one of Kirk's more searing lectures. As if able to read the Russian's thoughts, Purviance released a pent-up sigh big enough for both of them. "Is he always that intimidating?"

Chekov glanced up at him, smiling wryly. "That wasn't intimidating. That was incredibly well-mannered and reserved."

"Wow."

Chekov nodded the liaison officer toward the exit, more than ready to find somewhere to dispose of the pond. "Wait until you see him with the auditors."

* * *

Sulu heard the muffled whisper of turbolift doors opening outside his cabin, and groaned, grabbing for his uniform jacket. When you knew Kirk was waiting for you on the bridge, even the brief interval between turbolifts could seem like an intolerable delay. He stamped into his boots and dove through his cabin door, yelling, "Hold the lift!"

"Don't worry, I've got it." Unlike Sulu, Uhura had managed to get completely dressed, but her hair spilled down her neck in spiky disarray. She held the lift controls with an elbow until he got in, then let the doors slide closed.

"Bridge," she said through a mouthful of hairpins, and the turbolift from Deck Six sang upward. Sulu struggled into his uniform jacket and did up the fastenings, then watched the communications officer bundle her hair into a neat bun and clip it into place. It amazed him that anyone could perform such a complicated operation without the aid of a mirror.

He ran a hand through his own ruffled hair and smiled wryly. "Is it just me, or does being late for duty make you feel like a cadet again, too?"

"Now that you mention it, yes." Uhura checked her earrings to be sure they were straight, then threw him a suspicious look. "Why do these things always seem to happen when I go on shore leave with you and Chekov?"

Sulu tried to smooth his face into its blandest expression of innocence. "I was just about to ask you the same thing."

"Right." The turbolift doors whisked open on the bridge before Uhura could say more. Sulu stepped onto the busily humming deck, feeling Captain Kirk's glance rake across him as he took his seat at the helm. He winced, and suddenly found himself wishing he were assigned to a nice inconspicuous bridge station, like communications.

"Prepare for departure from Sigma One, Mr. Sulu," Kirk said mildly, then swung his chair around to watch the status reports scrolling across the engineering station's screens.

"Aye, sir." Sulu let out a trickling breath of relief while he tapped his security clearance into the helm computer and began running a standard systems check. The captain must have decided to place the blame for their delay squarely on the Sigma One liaison officer. Either that, or on Chekov.

Around him, the *Enterprise*'s other bridge officers were running similar checks on their stations, sharing updates in quiet voices as they geared up the massive starship for flight. Sulu finished running through the helm checklist, then brought up Sigma One's outboard schematic. The main docking lane glowed fiery white across the screen between the rippling gold of station gantries and the blue dots of docked ships. One of the blue dots was moving down the docking lane, already halfway out to open space.

Sulu glanced over at the dark-haired woman who shared the flight console with him. "Who's running the lane ahead of us?"

Lieutenant Bhutto glanced at the schematic. "An Orion police cruiser—I think traffic control called it the *Mecufi.*" She pointed up at the viewscreen with its wide-angle overview of Sigma One's ecliptic docks. The gantry lights at the far side of the port flickered as a slim shadow floated across them. "There it goes now."

"Captain Kirk." Uhura pitched her voice to cut through the murmur of preparation. "Sigma One station control has cleared us for departure."

"Very good." Kirk swung his console back toward the main viewscreen. "Take her out, Mr. Sulu."

"Aye, sir." Sulu took a deep breath, submerging himself in the meticulous routine of piloting a starship out into space. He brought the impulse engines to one-quarter power to avoid blasting Sigma One's delicate gantries. The dim starlit bulk of the space station dominated the interstellar night, aglow with glistening spiderwebs of red and green approach lights. The *Enterprise* slowly nosed away from its dock, steady as a gliding swan under Sulu's hands. "We should be clear of the station in approximately five and one-half minutes, sir."

"Very good. Mr. Bhutto, lay in a course to sector nine-eighteen mark three along the Andorian border. And look sharp to keep us inside Federation space." The bright intensity with which Kirk scanned the space ahead of them belied his wry tone. "After all, they tell me we're here to stop a war, not to start one."

Chapter Four

CHEKOV STOPPED by the mirror in his quarters only long enough to verify that the seams on his burgundy duty jacket lined up, then ducked out the door while still finger-combing his hair into order.

It hadn't been easy finding room for Sulu's lily pond in the helmsman's cabin. Chekov had finally given up and moved a half-dozen potted plants to the floor beneath Sulu's worktable so he could balance the pond on the end, retrieving the Halkan lily from the bathroom counter so it could sit in its new home until its owner returned. It looked remarkably dejected, drooped all over the marble-epoxy bottom for lack of water's buoyancy, but Chekov didn't dare fill the thing until Sulu had put it where he'd want it for good. Chekov knew perfectly well who would be recruited to help empty and move the monstrosity when that time came.

The plastic bags of lizards, then, he'd taken back to

his own cabin. He didn't know for sure that being left in the plastic would hurt them, but watching them bump their little noses against the transparent sides of their confinement reminded him too much of spending time in Sigma's tiny brig. Chekov's office was less than twenty meters from his quarters, so he could at least look in on them after dumping them into a sink filled with lukewarm water; if he left them in Sulu's cabin all alone, he was afraid the water would get too cold, and they'd die. At least this way, if they died, they would die from good intentions, not from suffocating in a plastic bag, or freezing in his best friend's quarters. Chekov left them chirping quietly in his darkened bathroom, splashing about with a sponge and a clean soap dish to keep them company. At least they sounded happy.

The same thing couldn't be said for the security division.

Voices from the squad room carried clearly into the main corridor despite continual reminders to the guards to either close the section door or keep their voices down. Chekov caught a fragment of sentence in Ensign Lemieux's fur-soft accent, her voice sounding louder and more strident than usual. The precise tones that answered her told Chekov why. Sighing, he passed his office door and headed for the squad room, already suspecting he'd regret not just locking himself in his office and pretending he hadn't heard.

"This isn't optional, I'm afraid," the other voice was insisting. "I have my orders."

Efficiency Auditor Aaron Kelly stood just inside the squad room door, his back to Chekov and his clipboard held at his waist in both hands. Just over his shoulder, Chekov could see Barrasso and Jagr busying themselves with weapons maintenance while Lemieux and Sweeney held the trim black man at bay. "I have my orders, as well," Lemieux said.

"I see." Kelly ran one hand down the front of his dark civilian suit. "Then can you tell me when Lieutenant Chekov will return, so I can speak with him?"

"I'm here." Chekov planted his hands on his hips while Kelly turned, feeling suitably impervious to the auditor's wiles now that he had showered and was back in ship's uniform. "Mr. Kelly, can't this wait until morning?"

"Lieutenant Chekov." Kelly glanced nervously behind him when Jagr and Barrasso hurried to their feet upon Chekov's arrival. The lieutenant waved them to continue with what they were doing, not taking his attention off Kelly. "Your people told me you were on shore leave."

"I was." Stepping past Lemieux and Sweeney, he keyed into the table-mounted station behind them. "Any developments while I was gone?" He hoped Kelly would give up if they looked too busy with other things.

"Nothing on board, sir," Sweeney reported, dragging a handful of blond hair away from his eyes. "But station security did report a brawl with Orions stationside."

Chekov hid his blush by not looking up from the screen. "Yes, I know." System announcements were unremarkable: a larger-than-normal number of personnel calling in sick, a prompt to access loaded data on the *Enterprise*'s new assignment, a handful of Starfleet bulletins. The last were usually more administrative than useful. He flicked past another two screens to the sectional prompts.

"Lieutenant," Kelly finally ventured, "I appreciate

that your people are only trying to do their jobs, but—"

Chekov frowned at the list on the screen, then turned the monitor toward Kelly and tapped it with his hand. "What's this?"

Kelly came forward a few steps to toss the screen a cursory glance. "Oh. That's what I was just discussing with Ensign Lemieux."

"Mr. Kelly is concerned with the efficiency of our duty schedules, sir."

"Oh?" Chekov raised his eyebrows. As though he needed this kind of silliness after everything else that had happened today. "I wasn't aware of any complaints. Barrasso? Jagr? Sweeney?"

"No, sir."

"None, sir."

"Of course not, sir."

Chekov turned a shrug on Kelly, and the auditor responded by grinning sheepishly. "People don't always know what's best for them, Lieutenant. That's why regulations exist." Kelly flipped his clipboard up into one hand and called up something on its screen. "According to your records," he read, "you have three officers who have worked nothing but night shift for the past six months. That's expressly against regulations, which state that no officer can be made to work third shift for more than four weeks out of every twelve."

Chekov turned the terminal back to him. "If you're talking about Tocchet, Robinson, and Trottier, no one's forcing them to do anything. Each of those officers has requested they be kept on night duty. They prefer those hours."

"Crew members' preferences don't have any bearing on regulations." Kelly's relaxed politeness was almost harder to bear, Chekov decided, than Taylor's frantic rages. "You have to understand—"

"I don't have to do anything, Mr. Kelly." He started scanning the downloads. "When it comes to something as trivial as duty schedules, I view your regulations as a list of very good suggestions from which to base my decisions. My crew's satisfaction with their scheduling comes first." His eyes caught on a familiar name amidst a dispatch, and his attention suddenly focused tight on the screen.

"Lieutenant Chekov," Kelly stated in a stiff, almost horrified voice, "this is a matter of *efficiency*. Nothing about it is trivial."

The words, amber scrambles crawling across the black background, refused to bind themselves to a structure. Ignoring Kelly, Chekov scrolled to the top of the dispatch in search of some kind of meaning.

"*. . . as a result of a breach in the* Kongo's *containment field on stardate 8747.6. Among the one hundred seven listed dead are Assistant Engineer Christopher Dailey, First Officer David Stein, and Science Officer Robert Cecil, who assisted in an effort to save forty-seven engineering crewmen immediately following the breach. Posthumous medals of honor will be awarded at a ceremony . . .*"

The words continued their steady march toward nowhere, dissolving into nonsense again. Chekov watched them without seeing, his memory having flown ten years away—to Starfleet Academy, and the wet-gray San Francisco winters spent in classroom simulators and training rooms. To a squadron bunker shared with forty other cadets, including a brilliant American boy named Robert Cecil.

"We're going to be heroes," Robert had told him

once. Robert, with his ash-blond hair, pale eyes, and quirky North American habits—Robert, who somehow always seemed to irritate Chekov as often as he amused him. Chekov trailed his fingers down the screen as if he could make the awful words more real by touch. They stayed just as distant, and just as hard to believe.

Robert was a scientist. For him, being a hero meant proving some new theory, or opening investigations on some new and different world. Chekov's job description was the one that included dying, and even that could be avoided if he were lucky enough, and careful. It wasn't supposed to have worked out this way.

"It isn't fair. . . ."

"It's more fair than what you have right now," Kelly countered. Chekov jerked a look up at him, momentarily fractured from the conversation at hand. "More efficient, too."

"Efficient?"

"Efficient," Kelly echoed. "The schedules."

The schedules. Who in hell cared about the schedules? Chekov ran a hand through his hair and switched off the terminal screen. "Mr. Kelly, if you don't get out of my department, I'll have you arrested for entering a restricted zone without authorization."

Stung, Kelly drew his slim frame up as tall as he was able. "But I *am* authorized."

"Get out!" Chekov kicked the chair back under the terminal desk, and Kelly jumped a good foot in the air. As Sweeney hurried to usher the auditor out the door, Chekov looked around at the startled guards surrounding him and felt a sting of guilt for his outburst. "I'm leaving," he told them. The first shock of reading the announcement was fading—now anger and grief were rushing in too fast to keep at bay. "If anyone else wants to see me . . ." He backed through the door, at a loss for how to excuse himself. ". . . tell them I have something more important to do."

"Captain's log, stardate 5711.12," Kirk said crisply. "The *Enterprise* has been assigned to patrol the Andorian-Orion border following an exchange of diplomatic hostilities—"

It wasn't the whir of the turbolift doors that interrupted him—it was the distinctive snarl of Federation Auditor John Taylor's voice bursting through them. Sulu exchanged gloomy looks with Bhutto. As head of the auditing team, Taylor had spent much of the last few days running the bridge crew through a battery of efficiency tests. In Sulu's opinion, the last thing they needed was his critical presence during a station departure. "—authorized by Starfleet! And I'm not going to put up with this kind of interference." Taylor stalked out of the turbolift, trailing Lieutenant Purviance behind him like a large, reluctant satellite. Captain Kirk looked up when they came in, then sighed and tapped off the console recorder.

"Mr. Taylor." For all its even tone, the captain's voice stopped the auditor in his tracks. "Do you have a reason to be on the bridge right now?"

"Yes, I do." Taylor drew himself up to his full, towering height. His scowl carved deep brackets in his aquiline face, making him look older than he was. "I'm here to lodge a formal protest, Captain. Commander Scott has locked me out of engineering."

"He has?" Kirk glanced past the auditor to Purviance, who nodded in glum confirmation. The liaison officer's stocky fingers drummed uneasily on the bridge rail, as if he weren't looking forward to the next few minutes. "Did he say why?"

"I didn't even get to see him!" Anger fountained in Taylor's voice again. "He left two technicians blocking the doorway, with orders not to let me pass!"

Purviance cleared his throat, pitching his voice to the soothing tones of a practiced diplomat. "Commander Scott said it's too dangerous for civilians to visit engineering while the ship's on active duty. I tried to explain that to Mr. Taylor, but he insisted on coming to see you about it, Captain."

"Hmmm." Kirk rubbed a hand across his mouth, not quite managing to hide the smile that tugged at it. "Well, Commander Scott's order sounds reasonable to me. What do you think, Mr. Spock?"

The first officer glanced up from his science console, his lean face impassive in the reflected reddish light. "The engineering decks do constitute the most hazardous sections of the ship, Captain, apart from the nacelles. However, I would calculate the probability of a random accident to be—"

"—more than Mr. Scott thought civilians should be exposed to," Kirk finished smoothly. The Vulcan raised one eyebrow, but didn't contradict him. "Mr. Taylor, I suggest you move your efficiency inspections to another part of the ship."

"What other part?" Taylor demanded, taking a step closer despite Purviance's restraining hand. *"You* refused to let us station anyone on the bridge, or in any of the weapons banks; Mr. Spock asked us to stay out of the science labs; now we aren't allowed into engineering—"

Purviance tapped on the auditor's shoulder. "Dr. McCoy said he wouldn't mind you examining sickbay," he reminded Taylor.

The head auditor's scowl grew deeper. "Provided we leave all our equipment outside, because it's not Starfleet-approved and might interfere with his medical sensors. He's got Chaiken and Gendron taking notes with manual pens!"

"That certainly doesn't sound very efficient, does it?" Kirk cleared his throat. "Well then, how about security?"

Taylor's expression eased a little. "We have made some progress there," he admitted. "Aaron Kelly says he can probably improve the scheduling efficiency by—"

"Mr. Taylor." Despite her polite tone, Uhura's voice cut through the conversation. The head auditor swung around, blinking down at her in surprise. "You have an urgent message coming from Deck Seven."

"I'll take it here," Taylor said without bothering to ask Kirk's permission. Purviance rolled his eyes, and Uhura pointedly glanced at the captain, waiting for his reluctant nod before she patched the contact through.

"Mr. Taylor, this is Kelly." Sulu recognized the agitated voice of the other male auditor. "We've got a problem in security."

"What's the matter, Aaron?"

"I'm not sure, sir, but Lieutenant Chekov has thrown me out and told me never to come back."

Sulu bit his lip, exchanging amused glances with Uhura. It was too much to hope that Chekov would manage to get rid of the auditors with Spock's urbane politeness or Scotty's shrewd maneuvering. The Russian simply attacked the problem head-on and with blunt force.

"What should I do, sir?" Kelly asked, after a moment's silence on the intercom.

Taylor's aquiline face hardened with determination. "Proceed to the next stage of operations, Aaron. I'll be down to join you shortly." He turned back toward Kirk, swaying slightly when the *Enterprise* cleared the last of the station gantries and swung out into open space. "Captain, it's clear we're being systematically stonewalled by your crew. I demand—"

Wheeling stars traced fiery strands of light across the viewscreen as the *Enterprise* came around to her new course. Sulu ignored the familiar pitch and roll, instead checking some last minute course adjustments that Bhutto had relayed to his console. He heard the navigator gasp, and looked up in time to see the viewscreen burst into fire-bright static. An instant later, every station on the bridge erupted with alarms.

Chapter Five

SULU COULD BARELY HEAR the captain's voice above the battering roar of warning sirens. "Spock," Kirk shouted, "what's going on?"

The Vulcan bent over his panel, eyes narrowed against the chaotically strobing light it threw back at him. "It appears we have been hit by some kind of subspace radiation pulse, Captain. It has disrupted all computer circuits."

"What about these alarms?" Kirk demanded. "Have we taken that much damage?" Sulu heard the howl of decompression alerts amid the other jolting noises, and realized why the captain sounded so urgent.

"I do not believe so." Spock glanced up at the hissing explosions of red and violet fire on the screen. "Even what we see now on the viewscreen does not reflect outside reality, only the interference from the radiation pulse. The alarms are reacting to electromagnetic surges within the bridge stations, not to structural damage elsewhere on the ship."

Sulu wrenched his eyes away from the meaningless static on the viewscreen to find a similar dribble of electronic nonsense crawling across his helm monitor. With a shock of very primitive horror, he suddenly realized that he was blind, deaf, and dumb to the outer world—and still piloting the *Enterprise* through it. "Captain, I've lost helm control," he said sharply. "I'm cutting impulse power—no, wait a minute. I think the helm's back." He looked up to find the normal diamond-fires of stars sprinkling the dark screen again. "What happened?"

"The radiation pulse appears to have faded." Spock toggled his panel controls and several of the alarms fell silent. "The ship seems to have returned to normal, Captain."

"Then let's see if we can't get the rest of those alarms off." Kirk watched the screen with intent eyes, as if defying it to misbehave again. "Mr. Sulu, is our course still set for sector nine-eighteen mark three?"

Sulu glanced at his console monitor and saw reassuringly familiar figures there. "Yes, sir."

"Then let's get out of here." Kirk's voice got easier to hear as a few more alarms went quiet. "Warp six, Mr. Sulu."

"Warp six." By habit, Sulu tossed a look up at the viewscreen for one last verifying glimpse of stars before he engaged the warp engines. His fingers froze on the controls, then jerked back as if the dark metal had seared his skin. He flung a hand out to slam off the impulse drive. "Captain, we're off course!"

"What?" Kirk sprang down to stand beside him, scanning the monitor's display. "Mr. Sulu, what are you talking about? This heading reads correct."

"But it's not." Voice sharp with disbelief, Sulu watched the stars drift toward them, then tried to give the helm another course. The monitor display never changed. He spared one glance up at Kirk, just long enough to read the comprehension on the captain's face, then went back to fighting with the controls. A moment later, he heard Bhutto gasp again and looked up to see the lights of Sigma One swing back onto the viewscreen. The *Enterprise* drifted slowly toward them, running on the slight inertia of her cut-off impulse drive.

"Captain!" Uhura's voice was urgent. "Inquiries coming in from Sigma One, sir. They want to know why we've changed our course."

"According to the helm computer, we haven't." Kirk glanced at the navigation screen to watch their present trajectory build across the screen, a line of red fire that ended abruptly at a solid white square. "Navigation shows us on a direct collision course with Sigma One, but helm insists we're still on our original heading."

"Helm's not responding to reprogramming orders, sir." Sulu fought an urge to drive his fist through the piloting panel that had locked them onto this heading. "I don't know what's wrong with it."

Kirk swore and glanced over his shoulder. "Spock, can you bypass helm control?"

"I am endeavoring to do so, Captain." The first officer's voice was as imperturbable as ever, but Sulu could tell from the high-speed whirring of his console that he was inputting commands to the ship's computer at a speed no human could have matched. "The radiation pulse we experienced has apparently caused a complete failure in that sector of the computer."

"Captain, Sigma One is hailing us again." Uhura

paused. "If our equipment malfunction is not repaired, they say we'll impact with the station in two and a half minutes."

"Damn." Kirk glanced up at the screen, hazel eyes narrowed with concentration. "If the helm computer won't let us change our heading away from the station, then we'll have to find some other way to change it." He spun and went back to his command console. "Bridge to engineering."

"Scott here." The background sound of alarms must have told the engineer that something was amiss. "What do you need, Captain?"

"I want to change direction, Scotty, and I can't use the helm to do it. Is there any way we can maneuver the ship with just the impulse engine controls?"

Scott sounded doubtful. "Well, I could flip the polarization of the impulse engines so that they'll thrust the ship in reverse. But that won't give you any maneuverability, sir—that'll only put you one hundred eighty degrees off the heading you're already locked onto."

Sulu scanned his helm screen, then swung around to glance at Kirk. "That would get us clear of Sigma One, Captain."

Kirk pursed his lips and nodded. "Get to work on it, Scotty."

"Aye-aye, sir." There was a pause, and the murmur of distant orders given. "We've started on it now, Captain. It'll take a few minutes to get to all the switches."

"You have two minutes, Mr. Scott." A thread of laughter flared unexpectedly in Kirk's voice. "Be efficient."

Sulu glanced at the warp drive controls he had almost touched, and shivered. Even a fraction of a second at warp speed would have sent the *Enterprise* crashing into Sigma One, given the course setting they were locked on. When he looked up again, it was to find Lieutenant Bhutto staring at him. "How did you know the helm computer had malfunctioned, sir?" she asked below the shrill blare of the last remaining alarm.

"I'm not sure." Sulu frowned at the viewscreen. Sigma One blinked its spidery lights at them, then suddenly went dark. The station commander must have started emergency procedures, closing bulkheads and shutting down power lines to minimize damage from the impact. "A course of mark three should have brought us around toward the Orion nebula, but I didn't see it cross the screen."

Kirk gave him a noncommittal look. "Mr. Sulu, at this distance, the Orion nebula should look like any other star out there."

"I know, sir," admitted Sulu. "I'm not sure how I recognize it, but I usually can."

"One and a half minutes to impact, Captain," Uhura reported quietly. Kirk grunted and turned his back on the blackness of the station with a calm that amazed Sulu. Behind him, John Taylor had retreated to the turbolift doors, his face ashen and his hands clamped on the bridge railing as if he didn't quite trust the ship on which he rode. Beside him, Purviance just looked worried.

"Any luck with reprogramming, Spock?"

"I have made some progress in restoring computer functions, Captain, but I have not yet managed to restore helm control to the bridge." The Vulcan never took his eyes from the computer codes scrolling across his screen. "We remain locked on a collision course with Sigma One."

"That won't matter if we can throw the impulse engines in reverse." Kirk hit the ship communicator again. "Scotty, have you repolarized the engines?"

"We're almost there, sir." A faint quiver ran through the *Enterprise,* whatever noise it made lost beneath the drone of the last alarm. "Engine polarization complete, Captain. She'll run in reverse of whatever your helm setting is now."

"Good." Kirk spun on his heel, striding back down toward the helm. "Three-quarters impulse power, Mr. Sulu."

"Aye, sir." Gritting his teeth in silent prayer, Sulu brought the impulse drive on line. With the slightest of jerks, the *Enterprise* reversed course, pulling away from the station with her usual swift power. Sulu let out the tense breath he'd been holding as Sigma One dwindled from a massive presence in the sky to a retreating patch of darkness against the stars.

"Sigma One is back on line, Captain." Even as Uhura spoke, Sulu could see approach lights blossom across the space station's outflung gantries. "They want to know if we require assistance with our helm malfunction."

Kirk glanced inquiringly at his first officer. "Do we require assistance, Mr. Spock?"

"I do not believe so, Captain." Spock tapped a final command into his console, then turned toward Sulu. "Mr. Sulu, if you check your helm computer, I think you will find it is now operational."

Sulu toggled one course adjustment switch and watched the piloting panel respond with a swift flicker as it changed headings. "Affirmative, sir. We can engage warp drive now."

"Not yet." Kirk swung around in a slow circle, scanning every panel on the bridge. "Before we go anywhere, I want to know why that last damn alarm is still active." He paused, facing the security panel and its stubbornly flashing screens. "Well, Mr. Howard?"

The tall security guard looked desperately over his shoulder. "I can't seem to make it turn off, sir. I've tried everything I can think of."

Kirk's eyebrows rose. "Then maybe it's not a false alarm. What seems to be triggering it?"

"According to this, it's—" Howard checked the screen and his voice faltered briefly. "—it's an intruder alert, sir."

The *Kongo*'s primary engine room glowed in the sickly plasma-light of core overload. Ripples of superheated gas blurred the central warp chamber, and the trans-steel alloy of the engine room walls was pitted and strained by radiation flares. Alarms howled like tortured souls; only the dim black shadows of engineers remained to hear them, trapped forever against the blasted walls in a tableau of startled inaction.

"The core's pretty hot, but I think we can reach it." The face on the comm screen—seared shiny red, with eyes burned a deep, unforgiving black—was fractured by washes of static. If he'd been calling anywhere farther away than the *Kongo*'s bridge, no one would ever have seen his transmission at all. "I'm going out the lock in the Number Two Jefferies tube, Mr. Stein's going out the lock in Number One." A bloom of brilliant light swelled up in the chamber behind him, and the man ducked reflexively, not even turning around. "We'll call back as soon as we're finished. Cecil out."

Almost on cue, the lights in the narrow communications booth went black, and the comm picture in front of Chekov snapped down to a pinprick, like a star left behind at warp speed. Chekov shook himself out of the morass of horrid images—a corridor-long pile of charred bodies, the twisted engine breaches revealed by the *Kongo*'s diagnostics, his friend's face still open to hope even as he turned away from the comm screen to die.

We'll call back as soon as we're finished.

Chekov knew now it had been a mistake to call the *Kongo* for details.

Power flooded back into the comm booth's system, and, with it, the raucous squall of the ship's intruder alert. Still too close to secondhand memories of the *Kongo*'s disaster, Chekov had to fight down a wave of dread as he punched the intercom next to his terminal. "Chekov to Lemieux."

"Deck Six," she reported without having to be asked. "Sector thirty-nine."

Barely around the corner from the booth in which he sat. "Send a team. I'm on my way."

"Aye-aye, sir."

The empty corridors enlarged the alarm's voice, battering sound all over the section. Chekov cut down the corridor to section ten while the noise would still cover the sound of his approach. The automatic systems would shut down deck exits, but it would shorten pursuit if he could get the intruder in sight as soon after detection as possible. Chekov rounded the last corner just as a lean, dark figure spun to meet him, the small device in its hand swinging to center on his chest.

Adrenaline seared through him at the sight of a potential weapon. Twisting aside, he threw his shoulder against the intruder's outstretched arm and pinned it tight against the wall. He blocked a wild swing to his head, and struck back in the same moment Aaron Kelly's voice yelped in panic.

Chekov felt every muscle in his left arm twinge as he stopped his blow just short of a full extension. He knew even before Kelly hit the deck that he'd broken the auditor's nose, but hoped for both their sakes that he hadn't done anything worse.

"Get up, Kelly." Chekov caught Kelly by the front of his dark suit and hauled him to his feet, wishing he had time to be more gracious. "You've got to get out of here."

Kelly slumped groggily against a doorway with his hand clamped over his nose. "What are you doing here?" he slurred in confusion. Blood dripped from under his hand to splatter all over the deck and his shoes. He seemed almost as interested in those Rorschach patterns as in Chekov's attempts to push him back into the doorway's relative safety. "Did you come from Deck Seven?"

Leaning an arm against Kelly to hold him still, Chekov hissed the auditor into silence. "There's an intruder alert," he whispered, peering up and down the hall for signs of movement. No one, and probably no chance of surprising anyone now, intruder or otherwise. "I was down the hall when it went off."

"Oh—" Kelly surged unsteadily against Chekov's hold, trying to swing his right hand up in front of his eyes. "Oh, Lieutenant Chekov, this is terrible!"

Chekov glanced irritably at Kelly, and at the bright metal device in Kelly's hand. A stopwatch, he realized. He'd just broken a man's nose on account of a digital stopwatch.

The sound of running feet reached them ahead of the small security squad that appeared at either end of the corridor only an instant later. "This'll probably ruin everything," Kelly lisped as the guards came to cluster around him. He sniffed a little, then winced and depressed one of the watch's buttons with his thumb. "Mr. Taylor isn't going to like this at all when he hears."

Chekov had a feeling *he* didn't like this already. "Mr. Kelly, what are you talking about?"

Kelly blinked at him with pain-watered brown eyes. "The test." He swayed a little when Chekov released him to stand on his own. "I'm fairly sure your being here invalidates the test, Lieutenant."

The guards exchanged uncertain looks, but Chekov only braced his hands against either side of the doorway and asked grimly, "Did you set off that intruder alert, Mr. Kelly?"

The auditor nodded limply.

Suddenly deprived of any real emergency, Chekov's tension flared inside him as cold anger. "You falsified a shipwide alert? For what?" He snatched Kelly's wrist and jerked the stopwatch up between them. "To time security's response?"

He could feel the auditor trembling through his grip on Kelly's wrist. "It's an essential component to determining efficiency," Kelly offered in a tiny, blurry voice.

"Damn your efficiency!" Chekov sharply released Kelly's hand, resisting an urge to reach out and shake the man. "Is efficiency worth endangering personnel with false security alerts? Is it worth getting yourself killed? My God!" He pounded both hands against the jambs, then pushed away from the doorway to pace in frustration. "Why is it that we have people lining up to waste themselves just to prove they can?"

"But Mr. Taylor—"

Chekov spun to glare at Kelly, and the auditor choked down into silence. "Did Taylor put you up to this idiocy?"

Kelly, eyes wide behind his hand, nodded. "He needs some sort of data for his recommendation, and you won't let me into anywhere else in your division."

"Recommendation?" Chekov came to stand in front of him again, hands kept carefully at his sides. "What kind of recommendation?"

"His recommendation to the Auditor General." Kelly's eyes darted back and forth among the collected guards, finally coming to rest on Chekov as though terrified of what was coming. "About when and how to restructure your department when we get back to Sigma One."

"You're telling me this entire investigation is because you don't like the way I run my division?"

"That," Taylor admitted from one of the sickbay's diagnostic tables, "and other things. But mostly that." He waved irritably at Purviance to silence whatever the liaison officer had opened his mouth to say. "Frankly, Lieutenant," Taylor said, sitting up and glaring across the foot of the table at Chekov, "your division is a mess."

As near as Chekov could tell, the only advantage Taylor had at the moment was that they were all in sickbay, so there'd be a medic team nearby when Chekov decided to tear the auditor limb from limb. "Captain Kirk has had no complaints."

"Of course he hasn't," Taylor said through a sneer. "For a ship as highly regarded as the *Enterprise,* an awful lot around here could stand redefining. Your captain is no doubt the main reason." He hopped to his feet, chin high. "That's why I'm here."

"You're here to audit ship efficiency," Purviance intervened.

Chekov tried to appreciate the awkward good intentions that made Purviance step in front of Taylor, but instead found himself resenting the other's intrusion. "Maybe if you kept your people to their official duties, unfortunate run-ins like this wouldn't happen."

"Maybe if you minded your own business," Taylor snapped, "we could spend more time working and less time kissing up to Captain Kirk."

At the edge of his vision, Chekov saw McCoy glance up from setting Kelly's broken nose; he made himself repress his temper before the doctor interfered. Being scolded by the ship's chief medical officer wouldn't do much for his credibility in Taylor's eyes. "Have you ever served in Starfleet, Mr. Taylor?"

The auditor crossed his arms with a frown. "Of course not. But—"

"No," Chekov cut him off, "no buts. Until you've served on a starship and faced the things that come up here every day, you haven't any idea what constitutes a well-run department."

"Ah, but that's where you're wrong." Arms still crossed, Taylor paced slowly to his right, moving from behind Purviance and forcing Chekov to either turn to face him or wait for the auditor to circle back around in front of him. Chekov decided to wait for him. "Regulations tell me everything I need to know, Lieutenant. When I see personnel exhibiting continual, flagrant disregard for regulations concerning duty assignments, scheduling, division of responsibility— well, it's my job to ferret out whatever causes those problems." He planted himself in front of Chekov and poked the lieutenant once in the chest. "Take a guess what that cause usually is."

"Mr. Taylor," Purviance objected weakly.

Chekov curled his hands into fists so tight his wrists ached. "If you really care about efficiency," he said slowly, "you should be judging us on our performance, not on our adherence to every minor regulation."

Taylor gave a short bark of laughter. "Performance such as nearly killing one of my junior auditors?"

"Yes!" Turning away from Taylor's infuriating scowl, Chekov gestured to Kelly on the bed across the room. "What was our response time?"

"Fantastic!" Kelly popped into a sitting position despite McCoy's colorful protests, and leaned around the doctor to make eye contact with Taylor. "Lieutenant Chekov reached my position in just under seventy-eight seconds, and the official squad got there only about a minute later." He grinned at Chekov, the growing bruises under his eyes making him look sleepy but pleased. "That's the best time for any starship I've ever tested."

"In other words," McCoy said over his shoulder to Taylor, "if it ain't broke, don't fix it." He pushed Kelly flat to the bed again. "Lie down!"

Taylor heaved an impatient sigh, but didn't look away from Chekov. "This isn't really your concern, Dr. McCoy."

"No," the doctor readily agreed, "but it is my sickbay, and I can assure you my efficiency is not being improved by you two standing here barking at each other." He deposited his medical scanner on Kelly's chest, admonishing the auditor against moving with a finger shake Chekov recognized all too well. "Let's see if you can't make yourselves useful. Taylor!" He waved the taller man toward the door, brow furrowed with a savage frown. "I'm still trying to get my hands on the rest of your auditing team for a radiation exam. Now, unless you want your entire party to drop dead at your feet, I suggest you see what you can do about getting them in here."

Taylor bristled at the doctor's tone. "Lieutenant Purviance is the liason officer. Let him find them."

Purviance actually managed a wry little smile. "I'm the liaison officer, but you're the man in charge. I suggest you do as the doctor says and get out of here."

"You heard him," the doctor said with a smile. "Get!" When the auditor finally gave up posturing and headed for the exit, McCoy said more quietly to Chekov, "I need to see that second-in-command of yours, too. Lemieux tells me he was on the bridge during that radiation surge, and I want to check everyone who was on the upper decks just to make sure there won't be any problems."

Chekov nodded, only half-listening, and watched Taylor hesitate again at the door before finally taking his leave. *Don't worry,* he wanted to tell the man, *I'm sure we'll talk about this again later.* He wasn't looking forward to the discussion.

"Lieutenant Chekov?"

Blinking his attention back to the moment, he looked around to find Purviance studying him in that quiet, professional way that only the best career Starfleet people seemed to have. Chekov glanced across the room at McCoy and Kelly, just to have somewhere else to look.

"Nobody in his right mind could look at the way Captain Kirk runs this ship and think there's anything wrong," Purviance said, too quietly even for McCoy or Kelly to hear. "From what I can tell, security's every bit as good as a man like Kirk deserves." He dropped a hand on the lieutenant's shoulder with a surprisingly fatherly smile. "I suggest you just do your job. Let idiots like Taylor take care of themselves."

Easier said than done when this particular idiot controlled an audit sheet that might mean the dismantling of his department. "How can you work with him?" Chekov asked. "Knowing what he plans to do to this ship, how can you stand to be his liaison?"

Purviance considered a moment, his pale brown eyes turning inward for a moment of thought. "I like to think I have a higher purpose for being here," he said. Then, flashing Chekov an ironic grin: "People like John Taylor are just the price of doing business."

It wasn't much of a comfort, but Chekov appreciated the thought. "I'll try to keep that in mind." Turning, he caught McCoy's attention from across the room, and called, "Contact security for an escort whenever Mr. Kelly's finished."

"An escort?" Kelly lifted his head in mild alarm, peeking around McCoy's arm. "To where?"

"The brig." When the auditor only squeaked in reply, Chekov explained, very patiently, "Under Starfleet *regulations,* Mr. Kelly, setting off a security alert without due cause is a criminal offense. You understand."

Purviance laughed aloud.

"But I'm not a Starfleet officer!" Kelly called to Chekov's retreating back.

"I know." Chekov paused in the doorway only long enough to turn and smile thinly. "And that's the only reason I'm not going to court martial you."

Chapter Six

SULU SIGHED IN RELIEF, hearing the turbolift begin its distinctive whistling drop from the bridge down to crew's quarters. He rubbed a hand across the tense muscles at the back of his neck, then glanced over at Uhura, Bhutto, and Howard. All his shift-mates looked as exhausted as he felt. Starting the day with a crisis always had that effect.

"I think I need more shore leave," the helmsman said.

Ensign Howard's face lit with a tired smile. "We almost had some, sir. If you hadn't noticed the helm damage from that radiation pulse—"

"—we'd be back on Sigma One right now." Sulu smacked a hand against his forehead. "Why didn't I think of that?"

"Because you were too busy spotting invisible nebulas," retorted Bhutto. The turbolift sang itself to a stop at Deck Five, and she stepped out. "See you guys at supper."

"Right." The turbolift doors hissed shut, but for a long moment nothing happened. Uhura glanced up at the monitor panel in surprise. "Deck Six," she reminded it.

The computer chimed acknowledgment of her command, but it took another long moment of silence before the turbolift whistled to life again, resuming its downward journey.

"That's odd," Sulu commented. "I wonder what caused that delay."

The tall security guard shrugged. "It happens on space stations all the time—the computer programs too many lifts into one shaft, and some of them have to wait."

"But the *Enterprise* has never had that problem." Uhura's gaze met Sulu's, the same suspicion flitting into both of them. "I hope those Federation auditors aren't trying to improve the efficiency of our lift systems."

Sulu chuckled. "Mr. Scott will weld their cabin doors shut if they are." The turbolift doors slid open again, this time on the familiar curve of their own corridor. "Remind your boss he's eating supper with us tonight, Ensign," Sulu told Howard as they stepped out.

"Aye-aye, sir."

Uhura gave him an amused look as the turbolift closed behind them. "With all the emergencies we've had on board today, do you really think Chekov's going to take time to eat supper with us?"

"Hey, it never hurts to try." Sulu walked down the hall with her, pausing to punch his access code into his cabin door. "One day, that boy's going to wake up and realize he needs a social life. After all, he's—"

His cabin door slid open, abruptly slicing off Sulu's voice. Smashed plants, scattered clothes, and broken shards of Iotian crystal trailed a tornado-erratic path from the cabin door to his worktable. The sweet, wet smell of crushed leaves drifted out from the destruction.

"Sulu?" Uhura's voice from outside made the helmsman start. "What's wrong?"

He resisted an urge to keep her from seeing the extent of the chaos. That was always his first instinct in a crisis—seal off the damage, emotional or physical, so no one else could get hurt by it. Fortunately, the years he'd spent working with Uhura had taught him that her delicate exterior masked a woman who could handle a crisis better than most galactic diplomats.

He sighed and stepped aside to give her a clear view of the debris. "Somebody wrecked my room," he said unnecessarily.

"Oh, my God!" Uhura followed him in, her coffee-dark eyes widening in shock. Dirt carpeted most of the floor, with uprooted plants and tumbled shelves scattered across it. Uhura knelt to rescue a small violet fern, half-buried under its potting soil. "Is anything missing?"

Sulu sighed and squatted down beside her, finding the fern's pot and scooping in some soil for her to slide the bare root stem into. The small bud that had been about to curl into feathery blossom now dangled on a broken stem. He plucked it off with gentle fingers.

"Actually," he said, glancing around, "it's kind of hard to tell. The only thing I know is, the water chameleons are gone."

Uhura scanned the room in dismay. "Are you sure they're not just hiding?"

"If they are, they're not making any noise."

"But they don't when they're scared." The communications officer picked her way gingerly through the trail of debris, patting at the rumpled clothes to feel for lizard-sized lumps. "They could be anywhere."

Sulu looked at the trail of crushed plants the intruder had left through the room and winced. "Oh, God, I hope not—"

The door to his quarters buzzed, bringing him to his feet in a nervous surge. Fortunately, Sulu was still close enough to the wall to trigger the release without having to step on any chameleons. Chekov stepped in, his eyebrows climbing when he saw the scattered wreckage. "*Shto bardachnaya dyela!*" His gaze swung around to snag on the helmsman. "What happened?"

"What does it look like?" It was amazing how often you had to restate the obvious in a situation like this, Sulu thought wryly. "Someone demolished my room."

Chekov scowled at him. "While you were here?"

"Of course not!" Sulu said indignantly. "Do you think I would have let it happen if I were here? And watch where you're walking—you might step on one of the water chameleons."

"I doubt it," Chekov said, "since they're still in my cabin." He colored under the force of their astonished looks. "I just thought someone should keep an eye on them, that's all."

"Well, that's one mystery solved." Sulu picked up one of his favorite plants, a pale red ginger palm, and carefully tamped the soil in around it to hold it straight. Somehow, knowing the little lizards were all right had lifted his spirits enough that he could actually undo some of the damage, not just survey it. "I guess that's why you're the security officer, and I'm the pilot. Now, if you can find out who threw all my plants on the floor, I'll owe you a supper back at Sigma One."

Chekov's cheeks turned darker red. "I didn't *throw* them on the floor," he said stiffly. "I put them there, very carefully."

Uhura looked up from gathering shirts over her arm. *"You* put them there?"

"Well, there wasn't enough room for the swimming pool, otherwise." Chekov gestured at the marble lily pond, now upside down and embedded in a heap of spilled potting soil. "And I didn't know where Sulu wanted it."

Sulu gave him a skeptical look. "So you threw some dirt down on the floor to set it on?"

Chekov snorted. "No, your visitor did that. I left it on the end of the worktable."

"Well, that's good to know. I was wondering why you left it upside down." Despite himself, Sulu felt a grin surface through his distress. It was impossible for him to resist teasing Chekov. "I figured even you would know the water would run out of it that way."

The Russian gave him an exasperated look. "Do you want me to help you with this or not?"

"Sorry." Sulu went back to picking up plants while Chekov examined the trail of debris, tracing it backward toward the door. He paused there, tapping some sort of security clearance into the locking mechanism and watching it flicker with color-coded information.

"So, Sulu," he said absently, "when did you leave your door open today?"

Sulu cursed as his fingers tightened a little too hard

on a Denebian lemon cactus. "I didn't! I locked the door when I left for my shift on the bridge, and I didn't come back until just now, when I found the place like this." He pointed an accusing finger at his friend. "If anyone left the room unlocked, it was you."

Chekov's dark hair ruffled with the vehemence of his headshake. "No, I locked it when I left. Trust me."

Uhura threw Sulu a reproving look as she hung clothes back in his wall closet. "Security guards don't tend to forget things like that," she reminded him.

"I know." Sulu let his irritation drift out with his sigh. He picked up a pot of half-wilted star orchids and put them back on the table to be watered. "Someone must have broken the door code."

"Impossible," Chekov said curtly. "The locking unit in your door is designed to keep anyone from using random codes to break in—three wrong code entries in a row locks the door until someone from security resets it. And, according to its record, the only code entries it got today were the correct ones." He drummed his fingers thoughtfully on the door frame. "Whoever got in here knew your code number."

"Well, that's impossible, too," Sulu retorted. "No one who knows my code could have done something like this to my plants!"

Uhura shook a flattened moss rose out from one of Sulu's uniform jackets and frowned. "I can't think of anyone on board ship who would have wanted to do something like this," she admitted. "Can you?"

Chekov grunted. "Maybe the auditors wanted to see how efficiently we clean our rooms. And pick up our clothes—" His eyebrows lifted quizzically as he watched Sulu put another shirt away. "Do you always hang your shirts in groups by color?"

Sulu felt his cheeks prickle with embarrassment. "Don't you?"

Uhura's chiming laughter sparkled through the room. "How can he? His shirts come in one color: Starfleet gold."

"I have a black one for wearing on shore leave," Chekov said defensively.

Sulu gave that remark the silence it deserved. "You really don't think it was one of the auditors who did this, do you?"

"People who would set off an intruder alert just to see how quickly we respond would do anything," Chekov said gloomily. "But no, I don't think they did this. There's no way any of them would have known your code number." He bent over the locking panel again, as if the remark had reminded him of something. "That's one thing we can do something about."

Sulu watched him warily. "What are you doing?"

"Programming a new code number for your door."

"No!" Sulu scrambled to his feet in alarm. "Don't do that! The last time we changed it, I kept locking myself out for a week."

Predictably, Chekov ignored him, and when Sulu looked at Uhura for support, all she gave him was a shrug. "Don't look at me," she said, while she closed his closet. "I've never understood why a man who can recognize star coordinates at a glance can't remember a four-digit access code."

"But that's exactly the problem," Sulu argued. "Whenever I try to use coordinates as a code, I can never remember which star I picked."

Chekov grunted. "I have a suggestion. Let me pick the access code for you. I can come up with something totally meaningless—"

"Yeah, you're good at that," Sulu agreed with another irrepressible grin.

The Russian scowled at him. "Do you ever want to see your water chameleons again?"

"All right." Sulu spread his hands in defeat. "Make up an access code for me."

Chekov tapped a programming prompt into the lock. "How does 7249 sound?"

"Like a number I'll never remember." Sulu swept up the last of the potting soil and crushed leaves, dumping them both into the waste disposal unit. "Will *you* remember it?

"Of course," said Chekov. "It's the first four digits of the serial number on my phaser."

"Oh, great." Sulu tossed him a mocking look. "So now, anyone who wants to know my access code can read it off your hip?"

"I don't walk around armed with a phaser at all times—"

Uhura cleared her throat and headed for the doorway. "I'm going to dinner," she announced. "Are you boys going to come with me, or are you going to stand and argue with each other all night?"

Chekov sighed and shook his head. "I've got to tell the captain that we've had a violation of ship security. Even if Sulu left his door wide open, the fact that someone did so much damage to his room makes it an act of premeditated vandalism. Captain Kirk will want to know about it immediately." He opened the door for her. "I'll join you later, if I can."

"I know what your 'laters' mean—usually that we won't see you again for a week." Uhura paused in the doorway as he went out, glancing back at Sulu. "Aren't you coming, either?"

Sulu shook his head. "I have to water and repot a bunch of these plants if I want them to survive. You guys can bring me back something if you're feeling generous."

"It's a promise." The door slid shut behind her, then opened a moment later to let Chekov lean back around the jamb. "I almost forgot—Dr. McCoy said you missed your radiation scan today. He wants you to stop by sickbay tonight."

Sulu glanced down at his drooping plants and shook his head. "It'll have to wait until tomorrow morning."

Chekov offered a warning frown. "He won't like that."

"I know." Sulu shrugged. "But it's just a medical check. How annoyed can he get?"

"Mr. Sulu." A breakfast tray slammed down on the rec room table with an irate clatter, followed by a thump as Dr. McCoy dropped into the empty chair on the other side. "Do the words 'permanent genetic damage' mean anything to you?"

Sulu flinched and looked up guiltily from his half-eaten stack of lingonberry pancakes. "Um—that I'm going to get yelled at?"

McCoy snorted and began to butter his toast. "Damned right you are." The background hum of food processors delivering a steady stream of meals to the first shift crew could not disguise the exasperated snap in the doctor's voice. "That was an emergency radiation scan you missed last night, young man, not a routine physical. It would have served you right if you'd woken up this morning looking like a giant carrot!"

Sulu ducked his head, trying to avoid Uhura's

amused glance from farther down the table. McCoy would never forgive him if he started to laugh right in the middle of a scolding. "I'm sorry I missed my appointment, sir. I had a slight crisis—"

"Doctor." Spock looked up from the table's other end, setting down the electronic reader that usually accompanied him to meals. "I am not aware of any cases of severe cellular mutation resulting from subspace radiation exposures as brief as—"

"Dammit, Spock, it was just a figure of speech." McCoy gave the Vulcan a disgruntled frown while he stirred his coffee. "How the hell am I supposed to intimidate anybody aboard this ship with you constantly contradicting me?"

"If you did not indulge in such extreme exaggerations, Doctor, contradiction would not be necessary."

McCoy snorted. "If the line officers on this ship would show up for medical exams when I tell them to, intimidation wouldn't be necessary, either." He shot Sulu a glare as he started to pick up his tray. "Don't you try to sneak out of here, either. I'm going to haul you down to sickbay for that scan as soon as I'm finished with breakfast."

Sulu grimaced as he checked the time display on the nearest wall monitor. "Dr. McCoy, if I'm late for two bridge shifts in a row, Captain Kirk will—"

"—make you stop eating breakfast with longwinded doctors." The captain set his own steaming tray down on the table beside Sulu, a smile tugging at his hazel eyes. "Bones, I could hear you yelling clear across the room. What's the matter now?" He cocked an eyebrow at the bowl of steaming yellow mud on the doctor's tray. "Food processors malfunctioning?"

The Southerner gave him an incensed look. "I *asked

for grits," he informed him in dignified tones. "And if you didn't set such a bad example for your officers, I wouldn't have to yell at them. Do you, by any chance, think you're immortal?"

Kirk picked up his fork, trading long-suffering looks with Sulu. "Bones, we've been over this before. The food processors remove all the saturated fat from bacon and eggs when they're synthesized—"

"I'm not talking about the coronary bypass special," McCoy retorted. "I'm talking about your DNA. For all you know, it could be even more scrambled than those eggs." He swung around to point a spoonful of grits down the table at Spock. "Don't say it."

The Vulcan lifted an austere eyebrow. "If you insist on using inappropriate analogies for complex scientific concepts, Doctor, I certainly cannot stop you. However, I would like to point out that—"

"Was the radiation pulse really that bad?" Kirk demanded, cutting through the argument with the ease of long practice.

McCoy shrugged. "How should I know? According to Spock, all the bridge stations were too busy throwing off false alarms to record anything useful." He threw a challenging look at the Vulcan, who, as usual, ignored it.

"Our data record is fragmentary, Captain, but computer analysis suggests a short-duration, low-frequency event, most likely from a distant neutron star. It appears to have been confined to the upper decks of the ship."

Memories of long-ago astrophysical lectures nudged at Sulu, and he gave the science officer a curious look. "Isn't that odd behavior for stellar subspace radiation, sir?"

"Indeed." Spock steepled his fingers thoughtfully. "I suspect that gravitational lensing from Sigma One—"

"It doesn't matter where it came from or how it got here, Spock." McCoy dropped his spoon into his empty bowl with a impatient clink. "As long as it contained unknown levels of subspace radiation, I want to scan everyone who might have been exposed to it. It's like rabies—if you don't catch the dog, you've got to take the shots."

Kirk sighed again, clearing his plate and reaching over to help himself to the last of McCoy's toast. "All right, Bones, you've made your point. You can run me through your DNA descrambler."

The doctor blinked in surprise. "Right now?"

"Why not?" Kirk picked up his tray and slid it into the nearest waste disposal unit. "Mr. Spock can take command of the bridge until I get there."

"How about your helmsman?" McCoy persisted, dropping a hand on Sulu's shoulder when he rose to clear his breakfast tray. "Can I scan him now, too?"

"Anything to make you happy, Bones."

"Well, hot dog." Smiling broadly, McCoy dumped his own tray and herded them to the door. "Now, if I could only get that big liaison officer from Sigma One—what's his name?"

"Purviance," Sulu said.

"Right, Purviance. He snuck out of sickbay yesterday before I could get him—might as well catch all my fish at once." McCoy's face brightened when he spied John Taylor's tall form emerging from the turbolift opposite the rec room door. "Hey, Taylor. Where's your liaison officer?"

The head auditor threw him a suspicious look, as if he didn't trust what might be behind the question.

"He's assisting Gendron today. I sent them down to check dispatch records on the Deck Seven transporter."

"Good. We can stop by and collect him on the way to sickbay." McCoy followed Sulu into the open turbolift, reaching back to tug at Kirk's elbow when the captain paused to frown at the auditor. "Come on, Jim. Radiation scan, remember?"

Kirk's mouth tightened, but he allowed himself to be pulled into the lift. "What the hell are Federation auditors doing checking our dispatch records?" he demanded once the doors had closed. "I thought they were supposed to be improving our efficiency on this trip."

"Deck Seven," McCoy told the lift, then turned back toward the captain as it began to move. "Jim, as far as I can tell, their idea of improving efficiency means enforcing every regulation some Federation bureaucrat ever dreamed up."

Sulu frowned, visions of red tape and endless paperwork groaning through his head. "Hasn't anyone ever told them that some of those regulations weren't meant to apply to Starfleet?"

"Apparently not." McCoy's eyebrows knitted in a scowl. "They've already threatened to report me because I let my doctors conduct medical research while they're on duty. I can't seem to make them understand that we're not some factory ship hospital, dealing with daily accidents." The turbolift hissed to a stop. "Hold the lift here," the doctor told them while he waited for the doors to open. "It should only take me a minute to—"

"Bones—" Kirk's swift yank brought McCoy to a halt before the doctor could step out onto the deck. Sulu followed the captain's gaze down to the corridor floor and felt his stomach lurch with dismay. A iron-dark trickle of blood crawled across the clean bright metal, inching its way out through the closed transporter room doors.

"What the *hell*—?" McCoy demanded.

Footsteps pounded down the hallway. "Sir!" A transporter technician rushed up breathlessly beside Kirk, his arms full of record disks. The young ensign's eyes widened with horror when he followed their gaze toward the blood-stained floor. "Sir, I swear—I was only away from my station for a minute! The auditors said they needed more dispatch records—"

"Don't worry about that now." Kirk motioned the technician toward the transporter chamber. "Just open the doors."

"Aye, sir." The technician stepped forward, his hand shaking slightly as he lifted it to activate the door. Sulu took a deep, steadying breath, and immediately wished he hadn't. Despite the busy whine of the ventilating system, the air that rolled out the open transporter chamber smelled like rotten meat.

"Oh, my God—" McCoy pushed past Kirk to stand locked on the threshold of the room, his shoulders jerking as if someone had hit him. Sulu forced himself to take one reluctant step closer, peering over the doctor's shoulder. He choked and turned away, overwhelmed by the glaring evidence that they had arrived too late.

Everything inside the room was red.

Chapter Seven

CHEKOV LEFT the transporter room only ten minutes after having gone inside. He didn't know how McCoy and the medics could stand it—how he could expect his guards to clean up the area as though they were mopping up a coolant spill in engineering. Environmental suits, maybe. Pretend it wasn't blood that made the flooring so tacky, force a separation between themselves and this awful reality by shielding themselves inside layers of plasfoam and plastic.

Folding his arms on the corridor wall to rest his head against them, Chekov wondered if the engine room on the *Kongo* had smelled this bad.

The transporter room door whisked open behind him, and a coppery feather of stench ghosted into the hallway. "You going to be all right?" McCoy asked quietly as the door drifted shut again on the smells.

Chekov nodded, turning to lean back against the bulkhead instead. Just outside the transporter room,

McCoy looked slim and professional in his green sterile jumpsuit, blood flecks and tricorder only adding finishing touches to his medical image. "I just feel a little sick," the lieutenant admitted. He crossed his arms, embarrassed by what felt too much like weakness. "I guess I'm not used to this."

McCoy shook his head and came a few steps farther into the hall. "It's not an easy thing to get used to." He rubbed a thumb across the screen on his tricorder. "I don't know if it's good that we can."

Survival meant getting used to things, Chekov reminded himself. You had to keep moving, had to go on. "Do you have an identification on—the body?"

McCoy nodded, and Chekov knew what McCoy would say from the way the doctor kept his eyes on his tricorder. He tried to make things easier by anticipating the news. "It's Ensign Sweeney, isn't it?" Thanks to Kelly's new schedule, Sweeney had gone on duty at midnight last night, then hadn't signed off at 0800 this morning. No one had seen him, he wasn't in his room, and his post had been observed unattended as early as 0700. Try as he might, Chekov couldn't ignore where that kind of evidence pointed.

When McCoy finally looked up, the gentle regret in his eyes was as good as an answer. "During a normal transport, the system would have made a record of whom we were trying to beam out. In an accident like this, where the equipment apparently went off without any preparation or destination, it makes things harder." He shook his head sadly. "I went over the DNA scans myself. I'll have to send to Sigma One to verify the match on Lindsey Purviance, but there's no doubt that one of the victims is Roberta Gendron and the third is Dennis Sweeney." He sighed, like a doctor who feels he should have done something more. "I'm sorry, Chekov."

Chekov nodded, not sure what he should say. At least he was past being shocked by the news. That helped, at least a little.

"So we've definitely got three victims?" Kirk's voice sounded clearly from halfway down the corridor. Behind him, Scott followed with a diagnostic kit in hand. Chekov didn't envy the engineer his upcoming job.

"As near as we can tell so far," McCoy said in answer to Kirk's question. "I'm afraid the transporter didn't leave us a lot to go on. Most of their cell structure was completely denatured, but enough DNA fragments are left to play medical connect-the-dots. So far, we've been able to reconstruct chains from three distinct humans. I'm hoping we don't find any more."

Kirk cast a short, grim glance at the closed transporter room. "Do we actually have enough mass to account for all three people?"

McCoy snorted, scowling. "How the hell am I supposed to know?"

"Well, you're the doctor, Bones, you seemed the logical one to ask."

Clearing his throat, Chekov moved a little away from the wall to stand beside the doctor. "Security will be taking care of cleanup, sir. Once we've had a chance to—" He hated having to pause and search for words to disguise the awfulness of their task. "—assemble everything, we'll have a better idea how much is there."

"Och, this is a sorry business." Setting down his diagnostic kit, Scott stepped close enough to the door to trigger it. Chekov was forced to glimpse the thickening sheen of red again when he didn't glance aside quickly enough, and Scott made a gruff noise of disgust before turning away.

"I've seen it before at public cargo transporters," the engineer said as the door slid shut behind him, and the hideous smell slowly drifted away. "The lads there don't always wait to get verification that a ship has dropped her screens; they try to send the payload through—" He slapped his hands one against the other, mimicking a payload ricochet. "The shields bounce back the transporter beam, usually along its transmittal path, and you end up materializing the cargo all over the origination chamber." He scrubbed self-consciously at his face, and Chekov wondered if Scott felt as sick as he did. "It leaves you with a bonnie mess, not to mention a misaligned transporter."

"Why didn't they rematerialize as people?" Kirk asked.

"Interaction with the shield energy scrambles the signal," Scott told him. "It's the same thing that keeps phaser shots from coming through during combat." He started to glance over his shoulder, then seemed to catch himself and stopped. "The worst part about this is, the backlash probably wiped most of the system's automatic records of the accident. It's going to be shameful hard to figure out what happened."

"Oh, my God—" Taylor came down the hall toward them at a near run, his eyes fixed on the transporter room door. "It's true, isn't it? Oh, my God, it's true!"

Chekov and Kirk moved to stop him at the same time, each catching an arm and together dragging the tall man away from the portal before his presence could signal it to open. *Please, keep it closed!* Chekov prayed as he helped push Taylor back against the wall. He didn't think he could handle the smell even one more time.

"What happened?" Taylor demanded. His sallow face looked honestly frantic, and Chekov felt the first sympathy he'd ever had for the man. "Where's Ms. Gendron?"

"I'm sorry," Kirk said, "there's been an accident."

McCoy tried to take over, gentle doctor role intact. "You don't want to go in there. Ms. Gendron and Mr. Purviance tried to beam somewhere through the ship's screens."

"No, Bones." Kirk glanced away from Taylor long enough to shake his head at the doctor. "We weren't running with screens on."

McCoy only stared at Kirk in confusion, but Scott raised his eyebrows and pulled a thoughtful scowl. "We've got ourselves a problem, then," he mused. "The transporter tech said Purviance was explaining beaming procedures to Gendron when he left—he's not even sure how Sweeney got in the room. I've been assuming one of them accidentally activated the transporter and then tried to direct the beam through the screens. However, the screens were off, and without screens to bounce the signal off, somebody had to scramble the transporter beam on purpose. There's no other way we'd have gotten the matter back into the transporter room—any other malfunction would've just scattered them out into space."

Chekov felt his nerves go cold at the thought of what Scott was suggesting. "You mean murder."

"Aye, lad, I think I do."

"Where the hell was security?" Taylor shook off

both Kirk and Chekov, glaring back and forth between the two. "Aren't they supposed to prevent things like this from happening?"

"A security guard died with them," McCoy said stiffly. "What more do you want?"

"I want to know what happened," Taylor shot back. "I want to know *when* it happened!" He glared down at Chekov, and the lieutenant felt a sudden resurgence of his old dislike. "Was this guard actually assigned to help Ms. Gendron?"

Considering he'd systematically thrown every auditor out of security over the past weekend, Chekov thought this a ridiculously optimistic question. "No," he said, as civilly as possible. "Ensign Sweeney was assigned to guard a weapons locker ten meters farther down the corridor." He pointed, even though the curve of the hall would keep Taylor from seeing anything.

The auditor looked anyway, frowning. "Then what was Sweeney doing in the transporter room?"

"Gendron and Purviance must have asked him to help them with some procedure."

Chekov knew that was somehow the wrong reply when Taylor snapped his head around to peer at him. "But you don't actually know?"

"There's no one left we can ask," Chekov pointed out. "Your auditor and liaison officer were killed along with him."

"What's the point of this?" Kirk demanded before Chekov could go on.

Taylor snorted as though Kirk didn't have any right to interfere. "The guards are supposed to call in before abandoning their positions, aren't they?"

This time, Kirk deferred the answer to Chekov with a glance, and Chekov nodded.

"But Sweeney didn't, did he?"

"No."

"He didn't even request a replacement before leaving a locker full of phasers unattended?"

"No, Mr. Taylor," Chekov flared, "he didn't. And now he's dead, so I can't very well discipline him for it, can I?"

Taylor tipped his head back against the wall, and the laugh he barked sounded both bitter and sad. "My God, Lieutenant, this is exactly what I was talking about! Hasn't it even occurred to you that this boy might *not* be dead if you were stricter about enforcing these sorts of regulations?"

"Mr. Taylor!" Kirk snapped, but Chekov already spoke over him, the urge to strike Taylor nearly unbearable.

"Since I assumed command of security, department fatalities have dropped more than 28 percent! What matters more to you? That we do our jobs, or that we do them in a certain way?"

"It matters that you take care of the people entrusted to you!"

The comment stung like a phaser burn. "I would give my life for my people," Chekov grated. "They know that."

Taylor snorted. "That supposed dedication didn't do much for your ensign this morning, did it?"

"What was your auditor doing inspecting sensitive equipment that she didn't know how to operate, Mr. Taylor? Didn't she have anything better to do than call a security guard away from his post just to prove that nothing on board this ship is sacred to you?"

"Gentlemen!" Kirk pushed between them, silencing Chekov with a penetrating glare. "That's enough."

"Please don't interrupt, Captain." Taylor extricated

himself completely but didn't walk away. "I'm interested in hearing Lieutenant Chekov's rationale."

"Your interest—" Kirk began, but the intercom a few steps away slashed across his words with a shrill whistle.

"Bridge to captain."

Glowering darkly—whether at Chekov or Taylor, Chekov couldn't tell—Kirk backed toward the panel to punch the button with his thumb. "Kirk here."

"Spock here, Captain. We have detected a civilian distress beacon two parsecs off our current course. Mr. Sulu has not been able to identify the ship's registry, but Federation articles do require we render the needed assistance."

Chekov saw Kirk's attention shift bridgeward, and the captain dipped a nod toward the intercom panel. "Bring us out of warp speed, Mr. Spock, and radio Commodore Petersen at Sigma One that we're altering course. I'm on my way up. Kirk out." He punched off the intercom and waved for Chekov to follow him. "Scotty, Bones—do whatever you can here. We'll continue our discussion later. Mr. Taylor—" Kirk speared the auditor with a cold hazel stare that would have had Chekov ready to apologize for every wrongdoing since the Romulan War. "I don't want to find out that you've interfered in any aspect of this investigation. Understood?"

Taylor's jaw clenched with anger. "Completely, Captain." He scowled across at Chekov with a smugness that made the lieutenant's stomach burn. "We're not finished, either, Lieutenant. Your captain will see my report before I file it, and, I promise you, he won't like a damn thing I have to say."

Kirk tugged on Chekov's arm, glaring coldly at the

auditor. "Believe me, Mr. Taylor, I wouldn't have it any other way."

The long wail of the universal distress signal echoed through the bridge of the *Enterprise* like a child whose crying couldn't be silenced. Sulu's fingers tightened uneasily on his helm controls. He knew the distress call had been designed to pierce subspace static and shipboard noise, but that didn't make the sound any easier to listen to. Its endless cry for help kept hurling images of possible accidents and disasters through Sulu's mind, images that were all too easy for him to picture after what he'd seen that morning in the transporter room.

"Looks like some kind of freighter," Lieutenant Bhutto observed quietly. Sulu nodded, watching the disabled ship expand across the viewscreen as the *Enterprise* came closer. The blue-white glare of Cygnus Eridani made details hard to see, but the blunt sausage shape of multiply-linked segments clearly belonged to a hauling ship. "I wonder why they haven't responded to our hail."

"I don't know." Across the bridge, Sulu could hear Uhura trying to open a hailing frequency, still to no avail. "They must have subspace radio capability, or we wouldn't have heard their distress call."

Bhutto's eyes narrowed. "Maybe there's no one left to talk to."

"I was trying not to think about that." Sulu gritted his teeth, repressing memories of a charnel-splattered room. "What is it about navigators that always makes them so gloomy?"

The turbolift doors slid open before Bhutto could reply. Sulu didn't have to turn around to know Kirk had come on deck—he could feel the decisive crackle of energy that ran through the bridge crew. From the corner of his eye, Sulu saw Chekov stride past the captain's console to take his place at the security station.

"Update, Mr. Spock." The captain's chair whispered on its hydraulic bearings as he swung it around to face the viewscreen.

"We are approaching the distressed ship now, Captain," Spock said calmly. "She either cannot or will not respond to our inquiries. Sensors indicate only that she is an interstellar freighter of somewhat antiquated design."

"Current distance, Mr. Sulu?"

Sulu glanced down at the white line blinking across his monitor's display. "Twenty thousand kilometers and closing, sir. Our estimated time of contact is four and a half minutes."

"Hmm." Kirk's fingers drummed a speculative tattoo on the arm of his console. "Mr. Spock, can you find any physical evidence of damage to the ship?"

"None, sir. Judging by the output of ionizing radiation from her engine banks, her field generators appear to be in working order."

"Captain." Chekov's voice was grim. "Weapons scan shows probable phaser banks in both port and starboard hulls."

"Phasers on a freighter?" Kirk vaulted out of his chair and came down a level to lean over Sulu's board. "Bring us to a full stop, Mr. Sulu, just out of phaser range."

"Aye, sir." Sulu shot a glance at Chekov, and, a moment later, the approximate radius of fire rippled across his monitor display, transferred from the security officer's computer. Sulu floated the *Enterprise* to a stop just outside that dark red sphere. "Full stop, Captain."

"Keep us there." Kirk swung around. "Uhura, I want you to stop trying to hail our friends over there."

"*Stop* trying, Captain?" The communications officer sounded startled.

"That's right. I want them to wonder about *us* for a change." Sulu risked a glance over his shoulder, and saw Kirk settle back into his chair, eyes glinting with intensity. "Now, we wait."

Silence fell across the bridge, the tense but trusting silence of people who had seen their captain's maneuvers work time and again. Against that disciplined quiet, the shrill cry of the distress signal seemed even more grating. One moment crept past, then another.

"Orion freighter *Umyfymu* calling Federation starship." The dark, growling voice sent a shudder down Sulu's back, reminding him of previous encounters with Orions. The viewscreen stayed suspiciously dark. "Federation starship, can you hear us?"

Kirk nodded at Uhura, and the communications officer tapped open a channel for him. "This is the USS *Enterprise,*" the captain said crisply. "What seems to be the problem, *Umyfymu?*"

A long pause sizzled across the open channel. "Engine difficulties," the Orion on the other end said at last. "Partial destabilization of field control has crippled our warp drive."

Sulu heard Spock quietly clear his throat behind them. Uhura toggled her controls without being ordered to, then said, "I've closed the audio channel, Mr. Spock, so the Orions won't hear you."

"Thank you, Commander." The science officer turned to face Kirk. "Captain, even a partial field destabilization should have left a trail of subspace radiation behind the *Umyfymu* when she decelerated from warp speed. Our sensors detect no such trace anywhere in the vicinity of Cygnus Eridani."

"So the Orions are lying. But why?" Kirk tapped one fist reflectively against his chin. "They can't possibly hope to take out a Constitution-class starship, even if they are pirates—"

"They're not pirates, Captain." The knowledge welled up inside Sulu before he even realized how he knew it. "No Orion pirate I've ever met spoke English that well."

"No," Chekov said soberly. "But Orion military officers do." His gaze darted back to the viewscreen, and Sulu's followed, fueled by the same sudden suspicion. "Look at the shape of that hull—"

"—without the extra radiation shielding," Sulu added. "Then take away those cargo sections—"

"—and it's an Orion T-class destroyer!" Chekov finished triumphantly.

"A military vessel!" Kirk leaped to his feet, scowling. "Mr. Chekov, I want full shields—now!" A phosphorescent shimmer ran across the viewscreen as the security officer obeyed. "Mr. Sulu, take us back another ten thousand kilometers, out of photon torpedo range. Uhura, put the ship on yellow alert."

"Aye, sir." Strobing golden light splashed across the normal soft blue of the bridge, accompanied by the tense whir and click of console chairs locking into battle positions. Sulu took a deep breath, feeling the sharp kick of adrenaline through his blood as he sent the *Enterprise* racing back to a safer position.

"Federation starship, you are abandoning a ship in distress." The growling Orion voice on the bridge startled Sulu, until he remembered that Uhura had left their communication channel open to reception.

The viewscreen showed no changes in the apparent freighter's position. "This is a first-degree violation of interstellar conduct. We demand an explanation."

Kirk snorted, motioning Uhura to re-open their channel. "If you know interstellar codes so well, Orion *destroyer Umyfymu*," he snapped, "you may recall that misuse of a universal distress signal is also a first-degree violation, punishable by exclusion from all Federation space ports for up to a standard year."

Blank silence hissed after his words, then shattered with Uhura's tense voice. "Captain, the *Umyfymu* is signaling on another subspace channel. The message is coded, but I think they're calling for help."

Spock bent over his sensor display, already tracking the path of the Orion transmission. "Long-range scan indicates another ship approaching, Captain, at warp three. She has just entered detector range." He tapped thoughtfully at one of his controls. "Scans also register a sensor ghost behind her—possibly a smaller companion ship, traveling in her shadow."

"Is the main ship Orion?" Kirk demanded.

"According to initial readings, yes. However—" Spock glanced up from his monitors with lifted eyebrows. "—she appears to be approaching from Federation space."

"Captain, I am receiving a transmission from the second Orion ship." Uhura paused, eyes widening as she listened to her board. "They've identified themselves as the Orion police cruiser *Mecufi*, sir—and they say they've been sent from Sigma One to arrest us."

Chapter Eight

KIRK SCRUBBED A HAND across his face. "I feel like I just fell down a rabbit hole," he complained. Sulu nodded silent agreement as he turned back to watch the viewscreen. Beyond the luminescent shimmer of their shields, the blue light of Cygnus Eridani now glared off two ships: *Umyfymu*'s deceptively ungainly sprawl and the sleeker wedge of the *Mecufi*. Neither had ventured within the *Enterprise*'s firing range. "Uhura, can you make direct contact with the Orion police commander?"

"I'll try, sir." The communications officer bent over her board for a moment, dark face intent as she spoke to her counterpart on the Orion ship. "Contact coming through now, sir."

"Put it on the main screen." Sulu heard Kirk's chair hiss behind him as the captain stood to face the image now rippling into focus. The Orion police commander's broad form, heavy with high-gravity bones and muscle, seemed stuffed into his crimson uniform. His thick black beard had been razored off with military precision across his chin, leaving two long plaits braided with silver grommets below his ears. Bronze eyes glittered against dark green skin.

"Starship *Enterprise,* this is Police Commander Shandaken." Like the Orion aboard the *Umyfymu,* the commander spoke stiff but flawless English. "You will permit us to immediately board and search your ship."

"Request denied." Kirk's mouth hardened as he frowned. "Neutral police forces have no authority over Starfleet vessels."

"But you are carrying Orion criminals." The commander lifted a stubby, accusing finger. "There, right on your bridge!"

"What?" Kirk swung around to meet Chekov's astonished look. "I have no idea what you're talking about, Shandaken. This man is one of my line officers."

"He's also an Orion criminal." Shandaken folded his arms across his burly chest, chin jutting with disdain. "He attacked and injured one of my police officers on Sigma One—"

"That's not true!" The sudden depth of Chekov's accent conveyed his outrage more clearly than the words themselves. "All I did was disarm him!"

"That's enough, Mr. Chekov," Kirk said quietly.

"—and then he stole an Orion weapon," continued the commander implacably. "And smuggled it aboard your ship—"

"He did not!" Sulu swung around, stung by that injustice. "Chekov handed the Orion's phaser over to Sigma One security, Captain. I saw him do it."

Kirk shook his head at him, warningly. "Mr. Sulu, I said that's enough."

"—not to mention interfering in legal Orion search procedures." Shandaken's face darkened with a scowl. "For all these offenses, we demand the right—"

"Captain, that was not a legal search procedure!" This time it was Uhura who broke into the accusation, her vivid face ablaze with indignation. "That Orion was destroying Federation property with no provocation—"

Kirk frowned. "Commander Shandaken, excuse me for a moment while I confer with my crew." The Orion grunted as his image faded back into the starfield outside. The captain promptly swung around to pin Chekov with a keen hazel gaze. "All right, Lieutenant. Remember the explanation I asked you to put in your report about Sigma One? I think you'd better give it to me now."

"Yes, Captain." The security officer sat rigidly at attention in front of his bridge station. Even from the helm console, Sulu could see the way the Russian's knuckles had whitened around his controls. "We came across an Orion policeman physically assaulting one of the merchants on Sigma One. All I did was take his phaser. He must have reported me to station security; I turned his phaser over to them when they arrested me." A trace of red tracked up his cheekbones. "You know the rest."

"Hmm." Kirk didn't bother to glance at Uhura or Sulu for confirmation; he obviously knew his security chief. "That doesn't seem like a very good reason to come chasing after you, Mr. Chekov."

"I know, sir." Chekov threw a baffled look at the ships glittering on the viewscreen. "I don't understand it."

"Orions are known for holding grudges," Sulu offered. "Maybe they thought they could make an interstellar incident out of this, and embarrass the Federation."

"Maybe." Kirk motioned to Uhura. "Get the Orion police commander back on line."

"Yes, Captain." The screen rippled back to the bridge of the *Mecufi*. Shandaken looked up from a handheld communicator, blinking in surprise.

"Your conference is over already, Captain?" he demanded.

"Yes, and I have one question for you." Kirk's voice was bland. "Since the altercation with your policeman occurred on a Starfleet space station, I presume you're aware that any prosecution of Lieutenant Chekov would fall under the jurisdiction of the Federation?"

The Orion's bushy eyebrows yanked together. "That is not acceptable—"

"It is, however, the only legal recourse available to you," Spock pointed out calmly.

Shandaken brought a fist down on his command chair. "We refuse to—"

The screen rippled without warning, and the red-uniformed Orion was replaced by one in bronze and black—obviously from another ship. His broad face wore an even more severely plaited beard than the police commander's, with a captain's medallion dangling from one beefy, dark green ear. A busy military bridge gleamed behind him, stark contrast to the ancient cargo holds visible through narrow windows.

"Starship *Enterprise,* you are on direct course for Orion space." The dark growling voice was the one that had spoken previously from the *Umyfymu.* "This is a violation of Orion neutrality."

Kirk's lips tightened. "Our course is set for the

Federation border, Commander, and our orders are to stay on our side of it."

The Orion military commander snorted. "Federation double talk! Why patrol the border unless you want something on the other side of it? I warn you—if you do not alter course immediately, we will be forced to open fire."

"Chekov." Kirk never took his eyes from the other commander. "What's the maximum speed an Orion T-class destroyer can make?"

"Warp four, Captain."

"And the police cruiser?"

Chekov shook his head after a moment's scrutiny of his monitor. "According to our records, no better than warp three." He glanced up with suspicion dark in his eyes. "If the *Umyfymu* hadn't stopped us with that fake distress call, the *Mecufi* would never have caught up to us."

"I was beginning to suspect that, Lieutenant." Kirk dropped a hand on Sulu's shoulder. "Mr. Sulu, engage warp engines. Take us out to the Orion border." He cast a mischievous smile at the screen. "At warp six."

The corridor outside was blessedly devoid of people when Kirk finally left sickbay some five and a half hours later. He took a moment to stretch his shoulders, and calculated their distance from the Orion border without really meaning to. Another day, perhaps, of travel before they had to face the tensions boiling along that troubled lane. God, it was awful to think this was all just leading up to the real action.

He doglegged down an adjacent corridor, aiming for a turbolift at random and flexing his fingers into his palms in rhythm with his thinking. Experience had taught Kirk that missions badly begun frequently ended badly, as well; the fact that none of their current problems related to Orion-Andorian hostilities didn't set his mind at ease. All that mattered to him right now was that his ship had suffered radiation damage, a member of his crew had already died, and his chief surgeon was up to his eyeballs in work thanks to both disturbing events. McCoy hadn't even supervised Kirk's radiation screening; he'd been too busy ministering to a guilt-racked transporter technician who'd sunk beyond anyone's ability to reassure. If Kirk could fix only one thing about this horrible day, it would be that.

"Mr. Taylor," a woman's voice echoed from down the hall, "I'm afraid I can't let you leave this area."

And then there were the auditors.

Kirk paused a dozen meters outside the security corridor, just beyond the junction that would take him to the turbolift and away. He listened to voices from deeper within security as they swelled in his direction, repressing a scowl of annoyance just as John Taylor popped into view at the mouth of the department doorway. Somehow, Kirk thought, it seemed only appropriate that one of the auditors would show up to ruin even something so simple as a trip back to his quarters for the night.

"Don't try to intimidate me," Taylor instructed the young Korean woman who followed him out of security. "I've been threatened by bigger fish than you, Ensign Paek, and none of them ever forced me to obey orders, either." He stood in profile to Kirk, mouth twisted into a sour line.

"I don't mean to intimidate," Paek began, but Taylor talked right over her.

"If your lieutenant should happen to miraculously appear sometime this evening, tell him I'm not im-

pressed by his strong-arm tactics. Either he releases
Aaron Kelly with all charges dropped, or the Auditor
General gets an earful about misuse of Starfleet au-
thority. Understood?"

Kirk wondered if auditors could be reported for
misuse of authority, too.

"Mr. Taylor," Paek insisted, stepping sternly behind the auditor when Taylor turned to stalk down the
hall toward Kirk, "attempting to drop a brigforce
screen constitutes a jailbreak, sir. If you attempt to
leave this area, I may be forced to shoot you." She
raised frantic eyes to Kirk, her phaser still untouched
on her hip.

Kirk nodded, not interested in finding out how
Taylor would cast this incident if Paek did as expected
and carried out her duty. "Hold your fire, Ensign."
She relaxed her shoulders in silent relief, and Kirk
ambled over to block Taylor's path when the auditor
made to hurry by him. "You seem to have this effect
on everyone," the captain commented pleasantly. "Is
it a talent, Mr. Taylor, or an acquired skill?"

Taylor stopped before he could bump into Kirk, and
sighed down at the captain. "I'm not interested in
your sarcasm, Kirk." He jerked a nod over his shoulder. "Are you aware that your chief of security has
incarcerated one of my auditors?"

Kirk made a show of following Taylor's indicated
gesture, eyebrows lifted. "I'm aware that one of your
auditors violated Starfleet regulations, and that Lieutenant Chekov reacted accordingly." He cocked his
head. "I thought you were the one with such a high
regard for regulations."

"For regulations, Captain," Taylor returned with a
scowl. "Not for using them as an excuse to harass
Federation officials. It's not as though Aaron mur-

dered someone, or sold Starfleet secrets to the Klingons."

"By setting off a false alarm," Kirk pointed out, "Mr. Kelly endangered the safety of everyone on this ship."

"Endangered?" Taylor laughed, but it was malice that sparkled in his dark eyes. "Come on, Kirk—*your* man broke *my* man's nose, remember."

Kirk laced his hands behind his back before his right fist clenched. "He's lucky Chekov didn't break his neck."

Almost immediately, the captain could have kicked himself for his quick tongue. Taylor's mouth stretched thin on a predatory smile, and the auditor asked in grim innocence, "May I quote you on that?"

Kirk wished it had been Taylor inspecting that transporter instead of Gendron. "You can do whatever you please," he said, "just so long as you do it from your quarters."

Taylor pulled his head back, blinking. "Excuse me?"

If Taylor was intent on deluging the Auditor General with complaints, Kirk figured he might just as well make the bad report a clean sweep. He wouldn't let his people go down without him, either way.

"You're confined to quarters, Mr. Taylor," Kirk said, mimicking Taylor's expression of innocence. He felt some satisfaction, at least, in the frustration that flashed across the auditor's face. "Security's been investigating three deaths, not to mention all their usual starship duties. Lieutenant Chekov doesn't need you down here interfering with his people's efficiency, and I certainly don't need you coming to me every time something doesn't go to your liking. So—" He lifted a hand to wave Paek forward without taking his gaze off Taylor. "Ensign Paek, why don't you escort Mr. Taylor to his quarters? And see that Auditor Chaiken is in her room, as well. I don't think we'll need to assign a door guard, but I'm sure that can be arranged if Mr. Taylor would prefer it."

Taylor jerked his elbow away from Paek's light touch. "I don't think that's necessary," he grumbled, glaring at the guard.

Kirk smiled tightly and nodded. "I'm glad to hear that."

"Will we be allowed out of our quarters again once your people have finished their investigation?"

Kirk shrugged. "We'll talk about that when the time comes." He nodded Paek toward the turbolift, and she hastened to obey, one hand firm on Taylor's elbow despite his squirming. "I'll warn you, though," Kirk said as they passed, "investigations don't often go the way you want them to. And Lieutenant Chekov has a lot of other things to do."

By 2300, Chekov almost wished Kirk had kept them around to fight it out with the Orions. It would have saved Chekov from joining his crew at the transporter room cleanup site, at least, and might have given him something to worry about besides a multiple murder, Scott's newly discovered petty thefts in engineering, and Taylor's plans for dismantling his department. Leaning back against the wall of the turbolift, the three infrared visors he carried clacking quietly against each other, Chekov listened to the lift slow for Deck Seven and hoped he wouldn't fall asleep in the absurdly long time it seemed to take the doors to open.

Chekov hadn't seen Taylor since their fight this afternoon. Granted, the lieutenant had been in engineering since shortly after the Orions faded from view, following Scott's people around and compiling a list of the cutters, capacitors, and meters that suddenly no one in engineering could find. The junior engineers were convinced someone had made away with the equipment; Chekov was convinced nerves had everyone scenting foul play in the aftermath of the transporter accident. "Why would anyone need all these things?" he'd asked more than one of them. They'd only shrugged, returned the visors he'd sent down days before for repairs, and gone back to their work; they weren't willing to speculate.

Too bad Taylor can't get into engineering, Chekov thought, heading down the evening-dimmed corridor toward his office. Any chance that Taylor might be a suspect in the robberies could have been excuse enough to bunk him in the brig alongside Kelly. Except that would probably guarantee the destruction of Chekov's department, so the thought really wasn't so attractive, after all. Chekov shifted the visors uneasily from one hand to the other, wondering if Taylor could actually see some structural problem that he and Kirk were missing, or if all of this was nothing more than personal bias on the auditor's part. He fervently hoped it was the latter.

Passing by the doorway to the duty desk, Chekov heard the murmur of discussion without being able to distinguish the actual words. He identified the guards on duty by the shape of their voices, by the characteristic rise and fall of their intonations and the length of their sentences: Recchi and Paek. The careless pattern of their conversation said nothing was wrong, so Chekov didn't bother interrupting them. He was supposed to be off duty anyway; he could read their reports in the morning.

He tossed the visors to his desktop amongst a scatter of waiting tapes and records, and knew he was tired when the disarray didn't even bother him. Much. He was just about to turn his back on the clutter to key open the cabinet behind his desk when his eye caught on a note beside his computer, scribbled in his own hand: *Sweeney.*

He hung his head, one hand on the infrared visors preparatory to putting them away. Oh, God—Sweeney. He still had to clear Sweeney's gear out of the squad room and get it down to cargo for transport back to Earth. Sliding the visors off the desk, he turned back to the cabinet, waited through the retina scan, identified himself for the voice ID, unlocked the doors with his key, and tried not to sling the visors into the rear of the cabinet as he thought about distilling a young man's career down to only as many one-by-one-by-one-meter boxes as could be stacked in the corner of a small civilian shuttle.

It was at times like this that he hated his job.

No one had been in the squad room for hours. Chekov turned up the lights as he came through the door, watching the darkness draw away from tables and lockers, listening to the late-night hush that was so different from the room's normal daytime chatter. At first, he didn't see the white storage carton he'd left for loading, earlier that day. Then he caught sight of the crate already stacked with three others, filling the top of a table that had been pushed against one wall. Guilt and relief mixed uncomfortably inside him. Someone else—probably Sweeney's bunkmate, Coffey—had already packed Sweeney's belongings and marked them for transport. *One less job to do,* Chekov thought, as he threaded his way between tables and chairs to look at the markings on the pile.

Still, it was a job he'd have preferred no one have to do in the first place.

On top of the first box, a hand-scrawled note covered a small pile of loose items.

Chief,
Please send with.

Chekov picked through the accompanying pieces, feeling a little like an unwelcome intruder at some other family's funeral. A disk of who-knew-what—photo images, music, text. He put it with the note and set it aside. A small spray of preserved flowers, handwritten sympathies from at least three different people, a bright, jumbled collection of pictures from a field hockey game the guards had played at their last rec stop. Chekov rearranged the photos in the order he'd found them, then placed them gently beneath the original note to hide Sweeney's smiling face from view.

"You have an alarm in your cabin," Sulu's voice croaked from behind him, "that goes off whenever someone tries to get into your office. I don't mean to be rude or anything, but does the word 'anal' mean anything to you?"

Chekov jerked around, startled, and knew the flash of irritation he felt was just a surface substitute for the embarrassment churning inside him. Embarrassment over what, he wasn't exactly sure, but he wiped at his eyes with the back of one hand as though expecting to find something there. "What are you doing here?"

Sulu leaned heavily on the squad room doorjamb, his uniform jacket unfastened and rumpled, one hand shielding his eyes against the overhead lights as he squinted across at his friend. "I think I hate you.

You're dressed, you're clean, you don't even need a shave." He tipped his head slightly to peek at the squad room clock, and groaned sleepily. "God, Pavel, do you know what time it is?"

Chekov half-glanced at the clock, even though he was perfectly aware of the time. "Sulu, what are you doing here? You work first shift in the morning."

"I don't work anywhere if I can't get into my room for a bath and clean clothes." He slid into one of the chairs, yawning. *Stop that!* Chekov thought at him angrily. *I don't have time to get sleepy!* But the damage was already done, and he caught himself echoing the helmsman's yawn. "I guess I fell asleep on your couch. Where the hell have you been?"

Trying to salvage my department, Chekov wanted to answer, but knew that wasn't entirely honest—he wasn't convinced there was anything wrong except for the auditors. Scrubbing at his eyes again, this time to clear away sleepiness, he turned to poke through Sweeney's boxes until he could find one with enough small space to stow the guards' mementos. "Trying to do my job."

Sulu made a noncommittal noise. "You know, the whole point of having subordinates is so they can do your job for you when you're off duty. Or do COs get higher efficiency ratings if they fall asleep at work?"

That struck deeper even than Chekov expected. He had to repress a sudden urge to slam the boxes against the facing wall. "Sulu, go home."

"Hey—"

"Go home!"

He heard the helmsman shift position, and hoped for a moment that Sulu had actually taken the hint for once and left him to be alone. Instead, the squadroom door slid shut and Sulu asked quietly, carefully, "Are you okay?"

"I'm fi—"

"Look at me."

Chekov hesitated, caught with the spray of flowers in his hand and nowhere in the box safe enough to keep them from being destroyed. He finally laid them crosswise atop the waiting photos and turned to meet Sulu's stare.

The helmsman always surprised Chekov with the frank intensity of his attention. It was that same superhuman focus that let him squeeze the life out of a hobby in less than two weeks, and let him pilot a starship better than any other being alive. It also made him very difficult to face when he chose to direct his attention to somewhat more personal matters. "Pavel, what's the matter with you?"

Chekov took advantage of his answer to glance away from Sulu's expectant frown. "I've just had a lot on my mind since the murders, that's all." He made the mistake of looking up to check his progress with the dodge, and his resolve unraveled like mist in a stiff breeze. Damn Sulu—if they weren't friends already, Chekov could probably learn to hate him. "Oh, Sulu, I'm so tired," the lieutenant sighed abruptly, sinking into the chair across from his friend.

"Then go to bed," Sulu said with a shrug, obviously at a loss for what else to suggest.

Chekov leaned over his knees to bury his face in his hands. The whole business of sitting upright seemed suddenly too strenuous, and he wanted nothing so much as to fastforward through his sleep period and get back to trying to invent solutions for problems he wasn't sure he could identify. "I don't know what to do," he admitted, his voice muffled against his hands. "John Taylor wants to take away my department—he wants to reassign my people and put me out of my job, and I don't know what to do to stop him."

"Can he actually do that?" Sulu asked, startled.

Chekov nodded and sat back, his hands in his hair. "So far as I know. Why couldn't he? Isn't that why the Federation sent them here—to tell us how well we do our jobs?" He looked over at Sulu, dark eyes meeting dark eyes across the empty table. "All I've ever wanted was to be a good officer. I never expected someone like Taylor to come in and tell me I wasn't."

"Don't be stupid—you're a good officer."

Chekov had a feeling even Sulu knew how close that sounded to condescension.

"I just don't know anymore," Chekov sighed. "I keep thinking that I should be more certain, more dedicated, more sure of where I'm going. I keep being a—" *Afraid,* he wanted to say. *Afraid that I'm not really good enough to have so many lives depending on me.* But the admission seemed to border dangerously on weakness, at a time when nothing but the very best would do. "I just don't want anything else to go wrong," he finally settled on, looking almost anywhere but at Sulu. "I don't want anyone else to die—not when I'm here this time, and in charge, and supposed to be able to prevent it."

Sulu didn't answer right away, and Chekov caught himself thinking, *I shouldn't have sat down,* when his muscles started lodging sleepy complaints. He was just summoning the willpower to push to his feet when Sulu asked, "What did you mean just then— 'here this time'?"

A little shot of adrenaline flashed through him, and Chekov knew that Sulu saw the startled embarrassment on his face before he could remember how to school his expression. Lack of sleep, he told himself. Talking and not even knowing what he was saying. It was his own fault for dwelling too much on the *Kongo,* and Robert, and how nothing he thought of now could save them.

"It's nothing." He tried not to seem flustered as he stood, but lying didn't come to him easily enough even to serve in stupid situations like this. "I'm just tired and not making sense."

Sulu, still seated, peered up at him suspiciously. "You were making sense before."

Chekov stopped by the doorway and shrugged with a weak smile. "It happens like that sometimes." He pantomimed shooting himself in the temple. "All at once."

"Right." Sulu didn't look convinced.

"It's late," Chekov went on, not giving his friend a chance to pry further. "You really should go home and get some sleep. So should I."

Sulu looked for an instant as though he might pursue the discussion, then relented and stood to follow Chekov down the hall. "I can't go home. Some stunningly brilliant chief of security locked me out of my cabin by picking me a door code I can't remember." He stretched, then winced and rubbed at his shoulder. "I just wish that chief of security's couch was more comfortable."

Chekov smiled—mostly for his friend's benefit—and felt a surprising twinge of gratitude that he had someone like Sulu nearby through all of this. "The chief of security picked you a nice, easy number to remember—7249."

Sulu made a face as he latched the front of his jacket. "That's what I typed."

"No, you didn't," Chekov told him patiently. "If you had, it would have let you in."

Still, when they got to Sulu's cabin on Deck Six, the helmsman hurried ahead to punch four digits into his lock before Chekov could look at the readout. "Aha!" Sulu cried triumphantly.

Chekov gave a sigh and leaned over Sulu's shoulder to look at the panel. "So what? That just means you tried an incorrect entry code at least three times and locked up your system."

Sulu frowned at the locking mechanism. "I only tried once. And I swear I did it right."

Chekov shrugged, not sure what else to tell him. "Then somebody tried to break into your cabin."

"Oh, great," Sulu groaned. "I still haven't finished cleaning up from the first time!" He stepped aside to let Chekov open the panel and manually activate the door. "What is it they want, anyway? It's not like I own anything valuable."

"It didn't look like they were interested in robbery when they were in here before." Although he couldn't imagine what else could motivate someone to harass the helmsman like this. Having no other comfort to offer, he said, "Your door system worked, though, so I don't think you have to worry. Just let me know if anybody tries this again."

Sulu nodded dejectedly and heaved a frustrated sigh. "In the meantime, could you do me a favor? Just in case someone does break in?"

"Probably," Chekov admitted, not willing to commit before he was asked. "What?"

"Keep my lizards for me?"

Chapter Nine

A NIGHTMARE HOWL wrenched Sulu out of sleep, adrenaline exploding in his blood so fiercely that he'd bolted out of his sheets and made it halfway to the door before he quite knew where he was. The fuzziness of his thinking told him it couldn't have been more than three hours since Chekov let him back into his quarters, and his gut recognized the icy bite of terror before his sleepy mind could identify the source: the ship's decompression alarm had gone off. He skidded to a stop, cursing, but it was too late—his door's automatic sensors had already hummed into motion. Expecting the other side to be cold and airless, Sulu forced himself to blow out all his breath.

The metal panels slid open, not to the devouring black rush of vacuum, but to warmth and light and a jangle of worried voices. Other crew members were emerging from their quarters along the hall, their shocked-alert faces at odds with rumpled night clothes. Sulu took a thankful breath of air, then caught Uhura's amused glance from across the corridor and blushed, ducking back into his quarters.

"—possible hull breach on Deck Six only." Spock's calm voice echoed along the hall as the ship's intercom momentarily cut through the blaring alarm. Sulu listened intently while he pulled on his uniform and stamped into his boots. "Evacuate all sectors according to standard emergency procedure, then report to damage control. Repeat, we have a possible hull breach on Deck Six only. All personnel should evacuate their quarters immediately."

Footsteps thudded outside as crew members hurried toward the nearest turbolift entrance. Sulu threw his jacket on over bare skin, spared one regretful glance for his unfilled lily pond and the small jungle of plants around it, then ran for the door.

It opened onto Uhura's concerned dark face. "Are you all right?"

Sulu nodded, still feeling the flustered warmth in his cheeks. "Nobody ever died of embarrassment," he said wryly. Farther down the curving passage, an orderly file of crew members waited to pack themselves into the open turbolift compartment. Sulu glanced around, worry swamping all other emotions. No panicked civilians were disrupting that well-drilled response.

"Have you seen any of the auditors?" he asked over the howl of the alarm.

"No." Uhura's long bronze robe rippled in a gust of wind. Sulu's pulse jumped with fear, but when he looked up he saw it was only the turbolift compartment moving away without closing its outer doors. Another lift slid into place, and the evacuation continued with barely a pause. "Maybe they went to a different turbolift."

"But this is the closest one to their quarters."

"They may not know that," she pointed out.

"They were told how to evacuate their area in an emergency. They must have been!" Sulu turned to look down the empty corridor, tension crawling up his back. He made his decision abruptly. "Wait here—I'll be right back."

"Hey!" Uhura grabbed his arm with surprising strength, dragging him to a halt. "Where do you think you're going? The turbolift's that way."

"I'm going to go look for the auditors. If they don't get out soon, the bulkheads will come down and trap them." Sulu shook off her hand as gently as he could. Behind them, the turbolift sped away with the last of their sector's crew, and a third empty compartment took its place. He swallowed a longing to dive into it. "You stay here and hold the lift for me. The computer may not send another one down."

Uhura's intelligent dark eyes narrowed with suspicion. "Sulu, are you trying to make sure I'm safe?"

"Yes," he said frankly. "Because if the bulkheads come down while I'm still on this deck, I want someone else on board to know about it."

"Oh." She frowned for a moment, then nodded reluctantly. "All right, you win. Go check the auditors —I'll wait for you here."

"Thanks." Sulu took a deep breath and pushed himself away from the wall, somehow feeling as if this were zero gravity and he needed the momentum. He saw Uhura watching him as he rounded the corridor's curve, her hand poised over the manual controls for the turbolift. She looked as worried as he felt.

The empty corridor felt huge and echoing, splashed with pulsing red where alert beacons lined the walls. Sulu ran to the auditors' quarters without stopping to check at any of the other cabin doors. Starfleet people knew the dangers of a decompression alert, knew how to evacuate an area before the atmosphere evacuated it for them. Civilians were the ones who had the luxury of growing complacent about their safety. "Don't worry about it," a station administrator had told him once, when a station decompression alert had sent him and seven other Starfleet officers hurrying for emergency bulkheads. "It goes off all the time around here—it doesn't mean anything."

And, sure enough, it hadn't.

Alarms didn't work like that on the *Enterprise,* though. If the ship hadn't located the hull breach yet, it would do so soon, and then nothing would be able to save the auditors from being trapped by the emergency bulkheads that would protect the rest of the ship.

The door panel on the first of the auditors' cabins refused to yield to the quick slap of his palm, its golden flare of light indicating that it was still locked from within. Sulu stepped back and toggled the internal speaker. "Ms. Chaiken! We have a decompression warning! You've got to evacuate your cabin!"

There was no reply. Sulu cursed and ran to the next door down the corridor. The auditors' quarters were connected through a shared bathroom—maybe they were having a late-night conference.

Right, Sulu, he thought. *I can just see them shouting out efficiency estimates over the noise of the alarm—*

The second door startled him with its hiss, sliding obediently open as soon as he hit the access panel.

Sulu scowled and took a cautious step into the dimly lit interior. The air inside smelled faintly metallic and stale.

"Mr. Taylor? Mr. Taylor, are you here?" Seeing no sign of motion in the darkness, Sulu reached to turn on the lights. The male body on the floor seemed to leap into sight with the sudden brightness, ruffled hair and rumpled suit dark against the beige carpet. The stilted angle of head and neck, flung back like an envelope flap against his shoulders, told Sulu there was no use in calling sickbay. John Taylor was dead.

"Oh, my God—" Sulu approached the auditor's body, not sure what he should be looking for but feeling vaguely that someone ought to examine it. There were no obvious signs of struggle in the room— the scattered notebooks and recorders around Taylor's sprawled form looked as if he'd simply dropped them when he fell. No bruises or abrasions discolored his skin, and even his face wore only an expression of mild surprise.

Sulu edged past the dead man, just far enough to dart a glance through the open bathroom door. He saw a second still form draped across the polished tiles, long hair cascading across her caved-in forehead to join the sticky red halo on the floor.

The sour warmth of sickness pushed at the back of Sulu's throat, and he spun around, desperate for clean corridor air to wash away the metallic smell of blood.

A short, insistent signal pierced Chekov's sleep, jerking him into wakefulness and bringing him bolt upright in his bed before his conscious mind had identified the sound. A throb of amber light drew his attention quickly through the dark, and he focused on the security panel by his workstation. His private alarm, telling him someone was trying to access the security office without coming to him first. He struggled out of bed, kicking sheets to the foot of his bunk, and grabbing trousers and tunic from the top of his dresser. In the bathroom, Sulu's lizards chirruped happily, echoing the alarm's strident whistle with their own peeps.

Chekov glanced at his desk chronometer while he stepped into his pants, then shouldered into his tunic on his way out the door without bothering to locate his boots. 0300 meant Davidson and Tate were the two guards manning the duty desk, and they knew better than to go into his office without first telling him—all the guards knew better. Which meant the trespasser wasn't from security, probably wasn't from the *Enterprise* at all. Chekov thought about Kelly and the bogus intruder alert, but dismissed this sort of stunt as too stupid for even the auditors. Then he thought about Scott's insistence that Sweeney, Gendron, and Purviance had to have been killed by someone else's deliberate action, and he couldn't dismiss that line of thinking quite so easily.

Chekov's office was the first door inside the entrance to security. The outer office was empty and darkened, but Chekov could just glimpse faint light from beyond the open inner doorway. He padded, stocking-footed, up to the inside door and leaned around the jamb. His activated work terminal cast an icy glow against the equipment locker behind his desk, but no one waited for him inside the tiny room, and nothing else seemed to be missing or disturbed. Grumbling about whoever had pulled him out of sleep for nothing, he stretched across the desk to power down the monitor.

He stopped when the graphic on the screen caught his eye.

The circular spiderweb of blue lines was a blueprint schematic for Deck Six of the *Enterprise*'s primary hull. A thick, white-light X obscured a portion of sector thirty-nine, and, next to the mark, someone had printed sloppily: "BOMB." Under that: "BETTER HURRY."

Chekov felt his hands go cold. Pushing away from the desk, he sprinted down the security corridor for the squad room and its lockers full of equipment. The lights came to half-power when he slapped the controls on his way through the door, but he still slid across the last meter of deck for lack of shoes or traction. When he collided with the kit locker and slammed open the door, one of the ensigns at the duty desk clambered out into the hall. "Who's there?"

"Davidson!" he shouted, tearing the bomb kit off its rack. "Put the department on standby alert!"

"Lieutenant Chekov?" She came halfway into the room, only to duck into the corridor again when he dove past her at a run. "What's happened?"

He didn't slow to explain. "Just stay here at the duty desk with Tate in case the captain needs you! I'll be on Deck Six."

"Aye-aye!"

He thundered up the access ladder to the deck above, afraid of being trapped inside a lift shaft if there really was a bomb and it detonated before he could reach it. The decompression alarms swarmed around him as soon as he threw back the upper hatch. An urge to search every cabin on the deck gripped him, and he fought it back. The closest thing he had to useful knowledge was that warning on his terminal, and he couldn't afford to ignore it if there were even the slightest chance it might be true. Sector thirty-nine, he reminded himself. Sulu's quarters. Uhura's quarters. The quarters for more than fifty crew members.

The deck was well evacuated by now. Chekov wondered with an ache in his stomach how old the decompression alert was, and how little time there might be left to find an explosive device and disarm it. Tightening his grip on the bomb kit, he wished insanely that he'd stopped to put on his boots, so that he could run full out, like he wanted to.

Chekov skidded around the last intersection in the corridor, banking off the opposite wall, and had only enough time to realize that someone had burst out of the doorway in front of him before they'd crashed into one another and gone tumbling to the floor.

Kirk shot upright in his bunk, right hand flashing out to answer the intercom's whistle before he was even awake enough to think of it. "Kirk here."

"Bridge—Spock here." The Vulcan's deep voice filled Kirk's cabin, pulling him the last quick stages into wakefulness. "Internal systems report a hull breach on Deck Six. Engineering has mobilized a repair crew, and search teams have begun assembling on Deck Three."

Kirk swept his sheets aside, crossing to his bureau for trousers while the lights slowly brightened around him. The last of sleep's fuzziness washed out on an adrenaline surge. "But?" he prompted, sensing additional information underlying his first officer's report.

"As of yet," Spock said, "there is no physical evidence of a breach. Not on Deck Six, or anywhere else. There is only the alarm."

"That's odd." Kirk jammed on his boots and snaked his arms into the sleeves of his tunic. "If we're lucky, Mr. Spock, we can keep it that way." He snatched his jacket on his way to the door. "Call Scotty on Deck Three—tell him I'm on my way."

"He has already been notified." The cabin door hissed shut on the last half of the Vulcan's reply, but Kirk heard enough to guess the rest: "He is awaiting your arrival. Spock out."

Wrenching free of the weight that held him pinned, Sulu rolled to his feet and spun to face his attacker. At first, all he saw was dark gold clothing—not Starfleet, his instincts warned him, not a crewman! He lifted his hands to lash out, then recognized the face above the tunic and felt relief slam through him. "Oh, it's you."

Chekov glared up at him, face tight with tension. His uniform jacket wasn't the only thing he hadn't bothered to put on, Sulu saw. Stockinged feet slid gracelessly on the deck as the security officer scrambled to retrieve the package he'd been carrying. "What are you doing here?" he demanded.

The decompression alarm broke off in midhowl before Sulu could reply. No reassuring message from engineering followed on the intercom—just a sudden, stifling silence. Sulu felt a shiver run down his back. Something had to be wrong—that wasn't the way a false alarm shut down.

"Sulu, what are you doing here?" Chekov repeated urgently.

"I came to find the auditors." Sulu fought an urge to look back into the room behind them. The doors whirred, kept mindlessly open by their nearness. "Someone killed them."

"Damn." The security officer spared one brief glance for Taylor's sprawled body, then ran for the next cabin door. Sulu sprinted after him, baffled by his behavior.

"It's locked," he warned as Chekov slid to a stop at Chaiken's door. "And anyway, she's not in there." The Russian grunted and palmed open the door's security panel, hitting the switch that bypassed the lock. "Chekov, what are you doing?"

"Looking for a bomb."

Sulu felt his stomach clench as if someone had punched him. "Someone planted a bomb on Deck Six? Who?"

"I don't know." The door hissed open onto total darkness, and Sulu and Chekov sprang apart by reflex, sheltering behind opposite sides of the opening. Nothing stirred inside. Sulu got a wordless nod from his companion, and snaked a hand inside to brighten the lights just as Chekov recklessly launched himself through the door. The helmsman cursed and darted in after him.

"Are you nuts?" Sulu hissed. The room was empty except for the lingering smell of blood. Chekov searched it swiftly, ducking his head to peer under the built-in bunks and desk units. "The murderer could have still been in here!"

"I don't know how long we've got until the bomb goes off." The security officer yanked open the trash disposal unit and looked inside. "The warning note on my computer screen said to hurry."

"Someone left a warning for you?" Sulu found the access plate for the wall storage unit and palmed it open. Only a few plain civilian suits and blouses hung inside, above a small storage carton labeled "Gendron." He forced himself to rifle through

Chaiken's clothes, feeling uneasily like a graverobber. "Who?"

"I don't know." Chekov levered up the cover on the food processing unit and checked the space inside, then slammed it and swung around to glare at the room again. "Damn it! It has to be here somewhere!" His gaze fell on the carton containing Gendron's possessions. "Did you look inside that?" He crossed the room in three long strides.

"No." Sulu dropped to his knees and reached for the lid, but a hard grip on his shoulder stopped him. He sat back on his heels as Chekov squatted beside him and rummaged through his bomb kit. "You think it could be rigged to blow when we open it?"

"That would explain why someone left me a warning." Chekov pulled a small sensor out of the kit and scanned it across the carton's surface. After a moment, it whistled a security code so familiar that even Sulu recognized it: *explosion imminent.*

"Out!" Chekov dragged Sulu to his feet and shoved him toward the door. "Get out of here!"

"But—"

"Sulu, don't argue with me! Even if I manage to get this blast contained, it's going to breach the corridor." Chekov grabbed at the plasfoam sprayer in his bomb kit. The searing smell of oxygen-hardened plastics tore through the air as he began to build a blast cage around the carton. "You're the only one on board who knows what happened to the auditors. With all the physical evidence gone, the captain's going to need your testimony to catch the murderer. Now get *out!"*

Logic warred with loyalty inside Sulu and won. He cursed and tore himself away from the auditors' cabin, his chest tight with frustration. The last memory he took with him was of Chekov's intent face as he sprayed a second layer of confining plasfoam over the small white carton.

When the turbolift doors opened sluggishly on Deck Three, Kirk jammed his hands between them to squeeze out while they were still half-closed. Work crews and technicians already criss-crossed the deck, assembling into tight knots of activity around their respective projects and equipment. Befuddled, half-dressed clusters of Deck Six evacuees cluttered several doorways, and Kirk had to force himself not to stop and count faces. There would be time for that later. He pushed between two engineering teams on his way to the briefing room where Scott should be setting up central control. The teams knew not to stop their work just to acknowledge his arrival; they simply moved aside to let him pass, their attention fixed on other things. Kirk was painfully glad to have such a strong, efficient crew.

Scott and his assistants proved easy enough to find. The chief engineer's brogue carried down the full length of the corridor, and his crew's environmental suits stood out like clumsy white beacons amid the rest of the storm. Kirk trotted to stand at Scott's elbow, waiting for the engineer to finish issuing orders before asking, "What do we know?"

Scott glanced back at him, then swung a suited arm for Kirk to follow him into the briefing room. "We know there hasn't been a breach," he said, his voice as loud and lyric as always. "At least, not anyplace our sensors can reach. Look here." He tapped a thick finger against a running terminal, tracing the ship schematic with its outline of glowing amber. "Even if there were enough damage at the breach itself to prevent sensors from reading the hole in the hull,

we'd detect a voltage drop across the screens anywhere there wasn't perfect integrity."

Kirk nodded, bending to read the terminal. "And
there's nothing."

"Not even so much as a dip," Scott agreed. "I've
even got lads working on a communications search of
the ship, listening for silent spots where we might be
holding vacuum instead of air." He shrugged and
straightened. "I don't expect much, though."

Kirk stood up as well. "Then if there's no breach
and no atmosphere loss, what set off the alarm?"

Scott rubbed his chin, eyebrows high with thinking.
"Maybe a who."

"The auditors?" That didn't seem likely, not with
Kelly still languishing in jail from their last little test
and the others confined to their quarters.

"No," Scott said, shaking his head. "They seem a
pesky but straightforward lot. To trigger a decompression alarm without getting Chekov down your throat,
you'd have to use a secure computer line. None of
them could even break into one, I don't think, much
less trip the alarm and erase all evidence of their visit
on their way out the door."

Kirk turned to look back into the hall, at the
growing rivers of humanity gathering outside the
briefing room. "That means we're either being distracted by a well-prepared saboteur," he mused grimly, "or we're looking at a very shy good samaritan."

Scott gave an unhappy snort of laughter. "I know
which I'd rather it be."

"Bridge to captain." Spock's voice echoed through
the crowded corridors, the open channel carrying his
words from one end of the deck to the other. "Priority
transmission, channel one."

Fighting down a wave of dread, Kirk leaned across

the briefing room table to punch the intercom with his thumb. "Kirk here. Go ahead."

"Captain." Sulu's voice sounded thin and breathless, backed up by the whine of a turbolift's anti-gravs. "Sir, there's a bomb set for immediate explosion in sector thirty-nine, Deck Six. Lieutenant Chekov is trying to build a containment housing around it—we didn't have time to disarm it." The helmsman hesitated, and Kirk heard someone else moving near that distant intercom. "I found auditors Taylor and Chaiken murdered in their rooms," Sulu went on, "apparently so the bomb could be hidden there. Both were killed by unarmed assault, with no signs of violent struggle in the room."

Kirk didn't pause to acknowledge Sulu's transmission. Opening another channel, he snapped, "Spock! Put the ship on red alert and bring us to a full stop!"

The siren shrilled out almost before he'd finished speaking, splashing the inside of the room with scarlet light. "All hands prepare for explosive decompression on Deck Six." It was Spock, a certain sharpness ringing through his voice despite his Vulcan calm. "Repeat, all hands prepare for explosive decompression."

Kirk felt the subterranean shiver of the warp drive fade, replaced by the brief growl of impulse power as the ship braked its momentum. Then the impulse drive died in turn, leaving the *Enterprise* afloat in utter stillness.

"I'll get my lads ready," Scott said, and ducked out the door without awaiting Kirk's reply. Still, the captain nodded tensely, turning to follow Scott into the hall.

Without prelude, the deck shuddered and lurched

fiercely, hurling the captain to the floor. Kirk barely had time to hear the clamor of horrified cries beyond the doorway before the noise of the explosion followed the shock wave: first the roar of shattered metal, then the unmistakable distant scream of air rushing out into vacuum.

Chapter Ten

THE DOORS TO Sulu's turbolift snapped open to the scream of multiple alarms and the pulsing intensity that engulfed the *Enterprise* during a crisis. Red alert lights seared across the faces of the crew as they pulled bulky environmental suits out of wall lockers and assembled into damage control teams. Spock's calm voice echoed from the intercom speakers overhead, asking all decks for damage reports.

Sulu scrambled to his feet inside the lift chamber, swinging around to pull Uhura up beside him. The communications officer's bundled hair had come loose, spilling down to hide her face from his concerned gaze. "Are you all right?"

"Fine." She tucked her hair back and pushed out into the crowded main corridor of Deck Three. Sulu followed her, trying to spot Kirk somewhere in the swirl of activity. It didn't look as if the shock wave had hit as hard here, probably because three layers of insulated decking separated this part of the ship from the blast. After a moment, Sulu gave up trying to see through the milling crowd and reached out to snag a passing engineer by the elbow.

"Where's Captain Kirk?" he demanded.

"Down at the emergency command center." The young woman jerked her chin portside, her hands full of metal plates and welders. "Sector twenty-six."

"Thanks." Sulu glanced down at Uhura when she stepped back. "Aren't you coming?"

She shook her head. "You won't need me. I'm going to commandeer a uniform from somebody and head for the bridge. That's where I can help most now."

"Okay." Sulu cut a swift path between repair teams, thankful that he was small enough to slide around the portable vacuum bulkheads being assembled in the hall. Halfway around the curve of corridor, he found the temporary command center: a conference room now bristling with repair equipment and engineering consoles. The door was open, but the way inside was blocked by a man in a bulky white environmental suit wrestling one last monitoring station through the door. Sulu thumped at his shoulder, hard enough to be felt through the stiff metal fabric.

"What?" Scott turned, the hard lines of his face softening behind his face plate when he saw Sulu. "Ah, it's you, lad," he said, his voice deepened by his suit communicator. "The captain wants you inside."

"I know." Sulu ducked past him, then spotted Kirk's slimmer environmental suit, the distinctive dark red of a line officer. The captain hadn't pulled on his helmet yet, and his face wore the look of focused strength that a crisis always brought out in him. He bent over the communications display on the conference room table, activating it with one metal-gloved fist.

"Spock, are those damage reports in yet?"

"Only preliminary estimates so far, Captain." Spock's lean face gave the screen an odd greenish cast. "Deck Seven reports extensive power outages and minor structural damage, but no decompression. Decks Five and Eight report only scattered power losses."

"And Deck Six?" Kirk's quick glance at Sulu told him the captain hadn't forgotten about Chekov.

"Impulse engine crews report complete power outage in their section but no decompression. The rest of the deck appears to have lost intercom capability."

"Well, see what you can do about restoring it. Kirk out." The captain looked up from the monitor as it went black. "Scotty, is the advance team ready to enter the breach?"

"Almost, sir." Scott glanced up from connecting his engineering console to the rest of the array. "We've got two more portable bulkheads to assemble and load on the turbolift."

Kirk grunted and turned toward Sulu, his eyes agate-sharp with intensity. "All right, Mr. Sulu. What kind of bomb was it, and where was it placed?"

"Type of bomb unknown, sir." Sulu felt his shoulders draw back into cadet-rigid attention while he strove to keep his answers short and informative. Getting debriefed by Kirk always had this effect on him. "It was hidden in a carton of Auditor Gendron's possessions, in the storage unit of the room she shared with Chaiken. We didn't have time to examine it."

Kirk frowned. "How did you know to look for it there?"

"Chekov found an anonymous warning note on his security computer. That's why he had a bomb kit with him."

"I'm getting a little tired of all this anonymous help." He fixed his helmsman with a keen stare. "You're sure you saw the bodies of both auditors?"

Sulu swallowed, remembering the metallic smell of the auditors' quarters. "Yes, sir. I found Taylor in his cabin, with a broken neck. Chaiken was in the bathroom. I think she died from a skull fracture—there was a lot of blood."

"So it's doubtful either of them set the bomb." Kirk drummed metal-clad fingers on the conference table. "That doesn't leave us very many other suspects." He swung around and purposefully picked up his helmet. "Get a suit on, Mr. Sulu. I'm taking a security team down to Deck Six to record blast effects for evidence before the engineers repair them. I want you with us when we examine the auditors' quarters." The captain settled his helmet on his shoulders, then added grimly through the communicator, "That is, if there's anything left of it."

It was amazing, Kirk thought, how much you could stuff into a turbolift car if you really tried. This one held four portable vacuum bulkheads including one with an airlock built into it, a dozen tall canisters of supercompressed air, an engineering console with a remote link to the emergency command center on Deck Three, and an assortment of tricorders and electronic notebooks. It also held nine crew members, all in bulky environmental suits.

The four security guards made a wall of solid black across the back of the lift chamber, packed tight as phasers in a weapons locker. Sulu and Scott had found space on either side of the portable bulkheads, but Kirk and the other two engineers had been forced to jam themselves between air canisters in order to fit inside. It was a good thing none of them was fat—as it was, every time Kirk took a deep breath, a canister valve tried to implant itself between his shoulder blades.

He shifted slightly to relieve the pressure on the laminated metal fabric of his suit, feeling the crinkle of thermal heating units under its absorbent inner lining. The suit ventilator poured a comforting hiss of air into his helmet, keeping his face plate clear of fog despite the prickle of sweat across his upper lip. Mindful of what lay ahead, Kirk ran another internal check for suit closure. "Scotty," he said across the suit's communicator channel, "is this the only turbolift access we have to Deck Six?"

"Aye, sir." The chief engineer carefully steadied the swaying bulkheads as the turbolift shifted to horizontal motion. "The main power circuit running through Deck Six got cut by the blast. So far, we've only managed to restore continuous lift power to the port shaft." He glanced up at the flashing display over the door, his helmet light sweeping the chamber. "We should be coming up on it in just a few—"

"Captain." Spock's voice broke into their communicator channel without ceremony. "Commander Uhura and I have managed to partially restore intercom circuits on Deck Six."

A little kernel of relief bloomed in Kirk, a sense of gaining control again after all this chaos. "That was fast. Patch me into whatever's working."

There was a short pause, then Uhura's quiet voice replaced Spock's. "Captain, right now I can only link to Deck Six via shipboard circuits. Can you reach the panel in your turbolift?"

Kirk struggled to half-turn, bracing himself against Sulu's shoulder as he reached for the intercom. "Barely," he said. The helmsman reached up to help him hit the button. "Am I on line now?"

"Yes, sir."

The captain raised his voice to cut through the background hum of the turbolift. "Kirk to Chekov. Repeat, this is Captain Kirk calling Lieutenant Chekov. Can you hear me?"

What answered him through the communicator wasn't silence—it was the slow, bitter cracking of metal as it cooled to absolute zero. Kirk lifted his hand from the panel abruptly, feeling as though the sound of his crippled ship had burned it.

"No reply, sir." Beneath her professional tone, Kirk heard the deep sadness in Uhura's voice.

He opened his mouth to respond, then closed it again. Grief was a luxury they couldn't afford right now. "Continue to monitor Deck Six intercoms from the bridge," he said instead. "Let me know if you pick up anything. Spock, I want you on our suit channel once we're in the breach. You may notice something we miss."

"A logical precaution, Captain," the Vulcan agreed. "With your permission, I shall monitor your tricorder output as well."

"Do that." The turbolift hushed to a halt on Deck Six and promptly began chirping in alarm, its doors locking down against the vacuum it sensed on the other side. Kirk found himself suddenly chilled by the prospect of searching that darkness for unlucky crew. "Open us up, Scotty," he said, very quietly.

"Aye, sir." It was the chief engineer's turn to try to reach past the row of air canisters and tap a command into the lift's control console to override its safety mechanism. The blurred reflections of nine helmet lights steadied against the doors, and crew members braced themselves for the illusory buffet of wind that came with decompression.

The line of shadow between the doors widened into devouring blackness as the lift doors slid apart. Kirk watched the tattered shreds of their atmosphere rush beyond the reach of his helmet light, a spray of winking ice and frozen gases. Viewed through a vacuum, the corridor ahead looked two-dimensional and hyper-sharp: abnormally bright where their shifting beams of light hit it, and utterly dark elsewhere. Kirk missed the warm diffraction of atmosphere, missed the myriad small sounds that normally go with walking. All he could hear as he stepped out of the lift was the even *hush-shush* of his own breathing and the creak of his suit joints.

He stepped to one side so the others could file out, scanning the hallway with one quick sweep of his helmet light. "Security team, circle the outer corridor first." He pointed down an adjacent hall as the engineers dragged their equipment out of the lift. "Check all turbolift exits and access shafts for signs of tracked blood, or other traces of our saboteur. He had to get off this deck somehow."

"Aye, sir." Kirk recognized Lemieux's soft French-Canadian accent and determined face as the black-suited guard emerged from the lift. "Final assembly point, sir?"

Kirk glanced across at Sulu, brows raised inquiringly behind his face shield. "The bomb was placed in sector thirty-nine," the helmsman replied. "Cabin eight."

Kirk nodded. "We'll meet you there, Ensign."

"Aye, sir." Lemieux turned, waving one of her three subordinates into the curving forward corridor and another into the aft, while she and the third headed down the central hall bisecting the deck. Their black environmental suits blended so well with the lightless deck that Kirk lost sight of them almost immediately.

"Sulu, grab that tricorder." Kirk glanced over his shoulder at the engineering crew as they began to set up their equipment. "Scotty, can you assess the amount of damage on Deck Six from here?"

"I'm getting the first glimmers of it, Captain." The chief engineer watched his scrolling monitor with a frown. Behind him, the other engineers wrestled portable airlocks into place around the turbolift doors, preparing to reflood the car with air before they sent it back for a second repair team. "The entire crew quarters on this deck have gone to vacuum, that's for sure. Judging by the voltage drops I'm getting across the sensor network, it looks like we've lost about three cabins' worth of hull. It must have been a pretty big blast."

"Estimated time for repairs?"

This time Scott did look up, the furrow between his eyes deepening. "Not less than several hours, sir. Possibly a full day, depending on structural involvement. But we should have power up and running fairly soon, and most of the deck will be back to atmosphere as soon as we isolate the breach."

"Good." Kirk swung away from the turbolift and moved carefully into the central corridor, unused to walking in a world with only two dimensions. Sulu followed less confidently, trailing his hand along the corridor wall to keep his balance.

Cabin doors crept eerily into their slanting helmet lights, only to whisper away into darkness again. They passed the larger darkness of the central corridor junction, seeing the distant firefly gleams of security guards down each intersecting arm. Kirk resisted an urge to signal open each cabin they passed, search each interior for some sign of his security chief. He didn't know what he wanted more—to delay finding out what had happened to Chekov, or to find his body immediately and get on with the pain.

Switching his suit communicator to a private channel, he said quietly, "Spock—anything from Chekov?"

"No, Captain."

"We haven't found anything here, either."

The Vulcan paused—judging Kirk's mood by his tone, perhaps, or maybe just dealing with some other fragment of emergency business. "It is unlikely that Lieutenant Chekov is still on Deck Six," Spock finally pointed out carefully.

And if he were, Kirk knew his first officer was thinking, it was even more unlikely he'd be able to answer. But everywhere else on the ship had working intercoms. "I don't think we're going to find him," Kirk admitted. It wasn't as hard to say as he had thought it would be.

Spock's answer was surprisingly gentle. "That is unfortunate. He was an exemplary officer."

"Yes—yes, he was."

A subliminal warning tingled across Kirk's skin, distracting him from his mourning. Still, it took him several more steps before he registered that the sparks of light ahead of him were actually stars and not just the scattered reflections of his and Sulu's helmet lights. He slowed to a stop at the lip of the breach, overwhelmed by a blast-torn expanse taller and deeper and wider than he had ever feared to see. "Oh, my God—"

The vertigo alone made him feel as though he stood at the very edge of the world.

Sulu braced a hand against the last edge of corridor wall, feeling disappointed when no adequate sensation made it through his heavily gloved palm. The blast had taken out not only the ship's hull, but also the partition separating the auditors' cabins from the curving outer passageway. A fractured latticework of metal was all that remained of either wall.

"Steady, Commander," Kirk warned him through the suit communicator. "Start taking tricorder readings. Spock, we're at the breach."

"Acknowledged, Captain." The Vulcan's calm voice seemed oddly out of place amid the twisted and charred ruins of the deck. He paused while Sulu scanned the breached area with his tricorder. "Initial analysis indicates that the damage was produced by a large thermochemical explosion. The pattern of destruction is consistent with that produced by an overloaded power pack, possibly one belonging to a phaser or other phase-shifted optic device."

"You mean a device like a metal cutter?" Kirk paced across the auditors' quarters, not seeming to notice the yawning gulf of space just beyond his left shoulder. He stopped near a blackened expanse on the floor, then looked up and beckoned Sulu to join him. The helmsman took a deep breath, stepping gingerly over the shock-crumpled decking to take a close-up tricorder reading of the blast zone.

"The power pack from a metal cutter could produce such an explosion," Spock conceded. "As could that of a welder or resin-caster. In fact, there are a number of specialized tools—"

Kirk didn't wait for him to finish. "What you're saying is that the saboteur could have obtained his weapon from almost any engineering section of the *Enterprise.*"

"Yes, Captain," the Vulcan agreed. "Or brought it on board himself. Our entry scanners are not designed to recognize power packs as possible weapons."

Kirk grunted. "Maybe they should be." He turned as four black-suited guards approached from the far side of the shattered cabin wall, helmet lights weaving a luminous tapestry across the destruction. "Well, gentlemen? Any luck?"

"No, sir." Lemieux sounded as if she took the failure personally. Sulu glanced up at her tight face, then at those of her fellow guards, seeing the same grim expression on each of them. He realized that he wasn't the only one mourning Chekov's loss. "We did locate the break in the main power circuit, sir. Mr. Scott says we should have power back shortly."

"Good." Kirk stepped back, drawing Sulu with him into the corridor. "I want all of you to examine this area closely before the engineers rip it apart. We're looking for evidence of two murders as well as sabotage, so report *anything* suspicious."

"Aye, sir." The guards scattered across the auditors' quarters, although Sulu noted that all of them skirted the open area in the hull as carefully as he had. His gaze lifted to the star-spattered dark beyond the frayed edges of the ship. Given a choice of fates, eternal drift through that limitless black gulf did not seem like such an awful one to him. Unfortunately, Sulu was fairly sure Chekov wouldn't have agreed.

"Sulu." Uhura's quiet voice touched his ear, as close as if she were a guardian spirit sitting on his shoulder. "I'm getting a strange interference pattern in one of the communicator panels in sector thirty-six. Could you go down and check on it for me?"

"Captain?" Sulu glanced at Kirk inquiringly. The captain nodded permission without taking his own intent gaze away from the breach in his ship. The bleakness on Kirk's face did not surprise Sulu—the helmsman knew it stemmed from the ship's injury, as well as from the loss of crew.

Settling the tricorder at his waist, Sulu turned his back on the blasted area, tracing his steps back down the central ship's corridor to sector thirty-six. Halfway down the hall, he caught sight of his own door and suppressed a mental image of the huddled plants inside, blackened and torn by the cruel frost of vacuum. At least, the water chameleons hadn't been there. Unbidden, the memory of Chekov's voice floated up inside his head, protesting, "I just thought someone should keep an eye on them, that's all."

Sulu's throat tightened. Here in the stark emptiness of the hull breach, it was getting harder and harder to resist the knowledge that he might never see his friend again. *There was enough time for him to get out,* his mind insisted, but the ache in his chest didn't believe it. The security officer would have reported to the bridge by now if he'd been able to. Sulu thought about the water chameleons, filling Chekov's silent cabin with their feathery chirping, and felt the back of his throat burn with grief.

"Uhura, which—" His voice caught unexpectedly

on the ache in his chest, and Sulu had to take a deep breath to clear it. "Which communicator panel are you having trouble with?" he asked Uhura through the suit channel.

"It's not trouble, precisely." The communications officer's soft voice was almost hesitant, as if she weren't sure how much to say. "I'd just like to know where the interference is coming from. I'm reading it in several locations, but it seems strongest just down the hall from turbolift nine."

"All right." Sulu found the panel and eyed it carefully. There were no signs of damage from the blast. "Nothing looks out of order to me. What seems to be the problem?"

"It's not exactly a problem." Uhura hesitated again. "Sulu, put your hand up on the panel, and tell me if you can feel some kind of vibration."

He obeyed her without asking questions, knowing she must have a good reason for the request. "I can't feel much through these suit gloves," he warned as he touched the panel. A faint shiver touched his skin, then vanished. "There was—something. I'm not sure what it was."

"Does it feel stronger if you move farther down the hall?" Uhura asked urgently.

"Um—yes, I think so." The vibration came and went irregularly as Sulu trailed a hand down the corridor wall, its intensity increasing with each faint thrum. There seemed to be a pattern to it, but he couldn't quite catch what it was. He concentrated on it so hard that the end of the wall caught him unaware.

Sulu stopped abruptly, peering into the dark central junction. "I've run out of wall," he told Uhura. "Where do you want me to go now?"

"To the right," she said at once. "That's where the turbolift is."

"The turbolift—" Sulu cursed and spun around the corner to slap both hands flat on the turbolift doors. Vibrations shook the double layer of plate metal, the soundless echo of some impact from inside. "Uhura, it's coming from inside the lift chamber! There's someone in there!"

"I *thought* so." The communications officer's muted voice could not hide her excitement. "Put your helmet against the door, Sulu, so I can hear the pattern. I think it's Starfleet code."

He leaned up against the metal obediently, letting the vibration rattle his face plate. Once inside his suit's small shell of air, it translated to a faint but distinct tapping sound. Sulu listened to the pattern of intervals between thumps—short, short, long, very long—and built up a message letter by letter. "K, O," he muttered, hearing Uhura echo him softly from the bridge. "V, C, H, E,—Uhura, it's *Chekov!*"

Her wordless cry of delight confirmed his guess. Sulu raised a fist to signal back at his friend, but before he could even begin, a giaring cascade of light staggered him back from the lift. By the time his dark-adjusted eyes realized it was only the wall lights, coming back on as the ship's power was restored, it was too late. His outstretched hands met only the familiar long humming of a turbolift moving away.

Chapter Eleven

THE TURBOLIFT LIGHTS bloomed warmly into being, and Chekov jerked a look up at the ceiling panels before it occurred to him that he'd be blinded. Squinting, hand over his eyes, he swayed against the closed lift doors when the anti-gravs hummed into life and dropped the car straight downward.

"Now no one's going to know I'm in here." His voice rebounded hollowly from the curved lift walls. He shivered from more than the vacuum-induced cold, thinking about how close he'd come to never getting out of this turbolift alive. Maybe he should be grateful to be leaving the breached area by any means at all. "Security," he told the computer, chafing his arms to rub away the cold. "Deck Seven."

After spraying the last layer of plasfoam over the bomb in the auditors' quarters, Chekov honestly hadn't thought he'd make it out of the blast area in time. He'd run for the turbolift opposite the one Sulu would have taken, not trusting a lift car from Sulu's turboshaft to be in range when he needed it. The doors of his lift had swished shut just ahead of the explosion—a short, flat, percussive bang that tore away the strength of its own sound as it tore away the ship's atmosphere. Chekov had felt the lift buck alarmingly, then the lights had pitched into blackness, and he'd begun pacing his vacuum-sealed coffin, doomed to passively wait. At the time, pounding his name out, over and over, on the closed lift doors had been the only action he could think to take toward his own rescue. He suspected even now that it wouldn't have been enough.

The lift he rode slewed gently sideways, then bumped to a stop. He stepped closer to the doors, ready for them to open and release him. He needed to trace who had left him that message—he wanted to see lab results on anything the search parties found at the bomb scene. He wanted to call Sulu and the captain, and tell them that he was alive. When the doors slid open to the security corridor on Deck Seven, though, they revealed only a blackness as deep and broad as the vacuum above. Chekov caught the door with one hand, holding it open while he poised nervously in the doorway. He hoped Davidson and Tate had called engineering about the blackout; he didn't much look forward to navigating his own department in the dark.

"Ensign Davidson?"

He listened into the darkness with all his might, but heard only ship sounds and distant thrummings. He had power to the turbo shaft, dammit, and the hull breach was on the starboard side of the hull. What had happened to security?

"Tate?"

Nothing.

As the duty officers, Davidson and Tate wouldn't have left their posts, he knew that. Not against his orders, and not while Kelly was still in the brig as a prisoner. Chekov's skin tingled with premonitions of disaster, and he slipped into the open corridor. The air smelled clear and warm. No breach then. Circuitry damage, maybe. But all over this area? He started around the corner toward security, sliding his feet along the deck in small, uncertain steps as he fought for equilibrium in the darkness.

A spark of yellow-white light blinked at the fringe of his vision, and instinct recognized the flash before thinking did. Chekov threw himself to the deck just as a crackling bolt of phaser fire ricocheted off the corner to spatter against the opposite wall.

In the silence that followed, Chekov held his breath to keep from being heard above the tick of cooling metal behind him. That had been a phaser set to high heat burn, not stun. Raising gingerly up on his elbows, he strained his eyes for some bit of light, but total darkness reduced the security corridor to a hard, impenetrable black expanse. He tried to remember exactly how long it had been since he'd been told about the bomb and its explosion. God, this saboteur got around. But what could he want in security? And what had he done to the ensigns on duty?

It doesn't matter what he wants, Chekov caught himself thinking. *If he's going to get out of there, he has to come through me.* He couldn't count on help from Davidson and Tate—he could only concentrate on what it would take to drive this intruder back behind the force barrier in the brig, where Chekov had some hope of containing him until help could arrive. He was already counting in his head the number of steps from here to the security isolation door, from there to the equipment locker in the back of his office, as he eased his legs beneath him and slowly regained his feet.

He froze that way for a moment, listening. Nothing came to him through the darkness except the rubbing of his uniform against his body as he breathed and the high, white-noise hissing of his blood in his ears. Deprived of every useful sense but hearing and touch, his focus zeroed down to a point so fine it made him dizzy. He put a hand against the wall to steady himself, and the ridged metal felt cold and intricately contoured.

He resisted trailing a hand along the wall when he started to walk. The faint sound of his skin against the metal seemed obscenely loud in the darkness. Vertigo bled into the void once he was moving, and the layout of his department blossomed in his mind's eye like graphics from the simulator games on Sigma One—oversimplified but accurate, with important doors and goals highlighted to supernatural clarity in his thinking. Stepping away from the wall, he kept to the center of the corridor and crept down the darkness toward his office door. There were phasers in the equipment locker behind his desk, and they'd be easier to reach than the ones kept locked in the squad room. If he could just get a weapon and stun whoever was down here, he'd be fine.

His eyes kept fooling him, warning him of movements and flashes of light that he knew he couldn't truly see. Ignoring them was hard—he caught his hands twitching with a want to do something every time a phantom shadow twinged his nerves. He finally balled his hands into fists just to keep them steady. No sounds of breathing, though. No click of hard-soled shoes on decking, no whisk of fabric brushing fabric from somebody else's movements. He stopped twice to feel the wall for the edges of a door and to listen. Once, he thought he felt the heat of someone's body very close beside him. Then the feeling passed, and he shivered from the image. He hoped that hadn't meant the intruder had somehow crept by.

The office door came up on him sooner than he had envisioned. He stretched out one arm to feel the wall beside him, and didn't realize he'd reached too far until his balance betrayed him and toppled him through the opening, into the room beyond. A crash sounded as he tumbled to the floor. He rolled, trying to scramble away from the sound, suddenly blind and lost all over again. The clash and clangor of falling equipment and slamming locker doors filled the dark sector with shards of broken sound. Something in him registered that the noise came from deeper in the department, near the squad room.

A man's voice cried out in alarm, answered by the waspish song of a phaser.

Davidson? Tate? Not calling out to them was agony.

Chekov found the door to his inner office on all fours, sensing its nearness only an instant before actually colliding with the surface. It slid aside when he stood, and seven fairly confident steps took him around to where he knew his desk must be and placed him close enough to the equipment locker to find it with both hands. *This is going to get me killed,* he thought as he poised his thumb above the trigger for the lock. But he couldn't think of any other way to stand against this intruder, and he couldn't let a saboteur leave the area.

His thumb depressed the trigger, and the lock panel exploded to life with a blast of green light and an ear-shattering chime. The computer's voice, tuned to a conversational volume, rebounded off the green-lit office walls like the sound of mortars: "Prepare for retina scan."

It was all Chekov could do to keep his eyes open when everything in him wanted to wince away from the damning intrusion of noise. He dug out the key while the scan temporarily blinded him again, fitted it against the lock while the computer requested, "Voice identification required."

He set himself to jerk the doors open as soon as it cleared him. "Chekov," he whispered, "Lieutenant Pavel A."

"Please speak in a normal tone."

God, *God,* when he got out of here he was going to memo every security division in Starfleet about redesigning this damned system. "Chekov, Lieutenant Pavel—"

A shriek of phaser fire arced white light all over the room, and a force like a light-speed missile slammed into his shoulder, throwing him against the locker. Seared flesh and burnt blood filled the room with a choking stench, and Chekov felt the horrible, deep heat in his shoulder blade that meant damage worse than being shot by a phaser set on stun. The locker doors popped open as he fell, a random collection of phasers and gear clattering out onto the floor around him. Footsteps clicked near the outside door, and he jammed his right hand in his mouth to muffle his anguished breathing as he pawed about him for a phaser, for a rifle.

His left hand closed on a slim arc of metal, and hope speared through him sharply enough to make him groan. One of the infrared visors he'd brought back from engineering yesterday. Wrenching to his knees, he bit his hand against a swell of pain, and collapsed, gasping, across the desk chair. The gunner knew where he was—Chekov heard someone push aside the visitor's chair near the corner. Slapping on the visor, he shot a frantic look around the office, already knowing he had no route of escape.

The phasers, measuring the same temperature as the deck and the rest of the room, showed up against the flooring like deep gray jigsaw pieces, faint outlines against the bigger darkness. Underneath his desk, the butt of a phaser rifle barely registered between the legs of his chair. The heat from Chekov's body showed up warm yellow through the visor; a cooling handprint in his own blood glowed sickly orange against the floor.

Only the gunman radiated outside the proper spectrum—framed and detailed in brilliant silver and white, screaming temperatures no human could have survived much less sabotaged a ship while suffering. Even the phaser in his hand showed cherry red from the warmth it had absorbed from his body.

Not human, Chekov's mind whispered urgently. He tried to connect a race with the tall, stocky body configuration even as the saboteur slowly raised his phaser, aiming it over the desk—

—and Chekov dove underneath for the rifle, squeezing off a shot without even lifting it clear of the floor.

The blast blew out the front of the desk. Chekov heard the intruder shriek and stumble back into the hall, but pain and blood loss kept Chekov from gathering his right arm beneath him with enough strength to scramble after. By the time he'd dragged himself out from under the desk, his head looped in such sick surges that he didn't make it cleanly out the doorway. Staggering against the bulkhead, he hugged the phaser rifle across his chest one-armed, and tried not to give in to the waves of dizziness crashing over him.

Something brilliant yellow stitched a splotchy trail down the corridor. *I hit him,* Chekov realized with some relief. *He can't get far.*

Unfortunately, neither could Chekov.

A movement at the fringe of his hearing shot adrenaline through him. He whirled as best he could, bringing the rifle into line with the slim heat-outline behind him.

"Davidson?" he asked, recognizing the mottled collection of orange-and-yellow as human, even though he couldn't identify a specific person.

"Lieutenant?" The tiny voice that drifted to him out of the darkness didn't belong to either of Chekov's missing guards. "I didn't—" Aaron Kelly took a shuddering breath, and his heat pattern slumped to sit on the deck. "Are you the only one here?"

Chekov lowered the rifle, trying not to notice the brittle *tick-tick-tick* of his own blood dripping onto the floor. "Are you out of your cell?"

Kelly's outline nodded, then the auditor seemed to remember that Chekov shouldn't be able to see him in the dark, and he verbalized, "Y-Yes. I think he destroyed the generator—"

"I'm going after him," Chekov cut him off, pushing away from the wall. "See if you can restore the lights. The main panels are near the turbolift, farther down this hallway. Can you find them?"

Kelly fumbled for a grip on the wall behind him, nodding again. "I can try."

From an auditor, that's all Chekov could ask.

The saboteur's blood sprinkled an uneven trail down the starship's corridor. The glowing spots—

already faded from sunburst yellow to a deep green—
were large and spaced at irregular intervals: the saboteur was moving fast, then, but bleeding hard, as well.
They had that much in common, Chekov acknowledged grimly. The lieutenant tried to flex his right
hand, and took a certain amount of comfort in the feel
of his fingers curling into his blood-slicked palm. It
hurt like hell to even think about lifting his arm away
from his side, but at least he knew he could do it if he
had to.

Blood splatters peppered the bulkhead and led
around the corner, finally coming together in a wandering puddle at the door to a maintenance ladder. A
hand-sized smear marked where the saboteur had
jerked the doorway open to climb inside.

Chekov slowed, and his equilibrium overshot him
and nearly knocked him to his knees. Breathing deep
to quiet his gasping, he made himself pause to look
carefully to all sides, to really see all the pieces of the
multihued infrared puzzle. No, the saboteur's trail
really ended here—this was no clever trick. He eased
up to the side of the access door, briefly passing the
rifle to his slippery right hand, and balanced the
muzzle across his left forearm as he reached across to
fling the door open. If the saboteur were crouched
inside, ready to shoot whoever breached his hiding
place, at least Chekov wouldn't be standing in front of
the entrance to make an easy target.

When he knocked the door aside, though, the
explosive in-rush of air jerked him into the doorway
as the atmosphere around him voided into sudden
vacuum.

Sulu slammed a frustrated fist against the turbolift's
outer door, barely feeling the impact through his

layered environmental suit gloves. "The power came back on," he told Uhura through his suit channel. "It took the lift away before I could talk to Chekov."

There was a long pause. "I'm not getting any response on the turbolift intercom," Uhura replied at last. "But Mr. Spock says it went directly to the security corridor on Deck Seven."

"That figures." A faint film of mist bloomed inside Sulu's face plate with his snort. "Knowing Chekov, he's probably gone back to work."

A vacuum-sharp shadow slid across him, and Sulu turned to see two white-suited engineers wrestling a portable bulkhead down the central hallway. "It looks like they're getting ready to isolate the hull breach. I'd better report back to Captain Kirk before they shut the permanent bulkheads down."

"Acknowledged. I'll tell him you're on your way."

"Thanks." Sulu ducked around the corner after the engineers and hurried down the corridor, his silent footsteps even eerier now that the ceiling gleamed with its usual strip lighting. Relief at finding Chekov alive fizzed through him, tempered only by the nagging worry that the security officer might be injured. *He was healthy enough to bang out his name in code,* Sulu reminded himself. *If he was hurt, he could have sent the lift down to sickbay—*

A reflected flicker of motion swam up the curved side of his face plate and Sulu spun to face it, all his instincts suddenly alert. He tried to balance himself on the edge of one foot to free the other for a kick, but the thick metal fabric of his boots refused to cooperate. Cursing, he retreated a step, then realized the motion was just a cabin door sliding closed. He relaxed with a sigh that turned into a choke when he noticed the room number.

"Hey!" Sulu launched himself across the hall, banging a fist on the security plate beside his door. The small message panel embedded there flashed a golden *locked-for-privacy* remark at him, which meant there was someone inside. "Hey, that's *my* room!"

A memory of smashed plants and scattered clothes tore through his head, jumbling his thoughts while he tried to punch his access code into the door panel. What the hell was that new number Chekov had given him? 4729?

"Mr. Sulu, is something wrong?" Kirk's voice in his ear startled him until he realized the captain was speaking over the communicator channel.

"There's an intruder in my room, sir." The message display suddenly flared red, warning him that he'd tried an incorrect access code. "I'm trying to get in to see who it is."

Kirk's voice sharpened. "Location?"

"Corridor C, sector thirty-nine. Cabin nineteen." Sulu racked his brain for the access code, trying not to think about the myriad small treasures left in his room for a vandal to destroy. Was it 4279? No, that didn't feel right—he was pretty sure the seven and the nine hadn't been that close together. How about 7429?

"We're on our way," Kirk said grimly. "Proceed with caution, Mr. Sulu. Kirk out."

Another red warning message crawled across the security display, this time informing Sulu that he had only one more chance to enter the correct code before the door barricaded itself against any further entries. His face plate misted with the force of his groan. He knew the silence from inside the room meant nothing, since sound couldn't carry in a vacuum. Right now, the invader could be obliterating everything he owned. Did 7249 sound right?

It was his best guess, Sulu decided, and punched it in with reckless haste. The message display rippled, then faded to a familiar, welcoming blue as the doors slid apart. Sulu dove through without thinking and found himself locked in gathering darkness when the doors slid shut behind him.

Dammit, he thought in exasperation, *I'm getting as bad as Chekov!* The sweeping arc of his helmet light danced across the contours of his room, an alien landscape under a glittering shroud of ice. Nothing stirred.

"Sulu." This time, the abrupt crackle of Kirk's voice in his ear made Sulu jump. "We're having a little trouble getting past Mr. Scott's portable bulkheads. We're going to have to circle the deck. Are you all right?"

"So far, sir. I haven't seen—" Something large and pale hurtled at him from the shadows, and Sulu leaped out of its way. He recognized the white gleam of an engineering suit, cursed, then let his momentum ricochet him off a wall and back toward the intruder.

The collision staggered both of them against the wall, frozen plants falling around them in a silent cascade. Sulu squirmed inside his environmental suit, trying to grapple with the bulky white form looming over him. He knew the two layers of vacuum-proof fabric between them would blunt the force of any blow he tried to deliver, no matter how well-aimed. His best hope was a wrestling hold.

His attacker simply ignored his efforts, lifting him as if he weighed nothing, then slamming him down onto the worktable. It wasn't the jolt of pain that galvanized Sulu—it was the pitiful feel of his ice-crusted plants shattering beneath him. Indignation at this final assault on his possessions gave him the strength to roll back onto his feet and hurl himself at the intruder.

They crashed to the floor in a tangle of bulky limbs, with Sulu mostly on top. He tried to keep his position long enough to pin his assailant, but the body below him exploded into a desperate convulsion of violence, awkward but powerful. The first slamming blow tore Sulu's hold away completely; the second sent him sliding across his plant-littered floor to thump against his overturned lily container. He rolled over in time to see the intruder lurch to his feet and bolt for the door.

"Dammit!" Sulu untangled himself from the marble pond and scrambled up to follow, his breath hammering inside his suit.

"Sulu, report!" Kirk's voice sounded impatient on the helmet channel, as if he'd repeated the order several times. Sulu couldn't remember hearing it. "What happened?"

"I found the intruder, sir," Sulu panted, skidding out into the hallway in time to see the white-suited form aim for the turbolift doors. He sprinted after him. "He's heading for turbolift eight now."

"The lift doors should be locked." The captain's voice sounded almost as breathless as Sulu's. Running in a bulky environmental suit wasn't easy. "He's not going to get out that way."

"No, sir." Sulu pounded down the hall in eerie silence, slowly gaining on his assailant. Sweat trickled down his face and stung at his eyes, blurring his view of the corridor for a moment. When he shook his vision clear again, he thought at first that the white-suited intruder had vanished. Then he saw him—

crouched across the hall from the turbolift, beside the red-rimmed panel that opened onto the maintenance ladders.

Sulu's breath left him in a horrified gasp. "Captain, he's trying to get into the repair shafts!"

"Stop him, lad!" Scott's voice broke into the communicator channel. "The ladderways are still at atmospheric pressure—opening them will yank the air out of the entire emergency access system!"

"Kirk to bridge, priority call!" The captain's shout thundered inside Sulu's helmet as he flung himself down the hallway at the intruder, praying he could reach him in time. "Seal off all repair shafts above and below Deck Six. Repeat, seal off all repair shafts—"

A battering wall of wind hit Sulu in midstride, hurling him back against the corridor wall hard enough to slam the air out of his lungs. He choked and dragged in a trickle of breath, just enough to let him force his way through the fierce blast of frost-sparkled air, to dive into the emergency ladderway and onto the intruder's back.

They fell together against the rungs on the far side, both scrabbling to hold on against the silent blast of wind. Something brushed across the back of Sulu's neck, tugging gently at the metallic fabric of his suit. The gusting wind slowed to a clearing whirl, then died in a final flurry of ice crystals down the dim ladderway.

Sulu's breath eased with relief. Someone on the bridge had closed the vacuum barriers across this section of the repair shafts, closing off the supply of air. He wiped the dusty film of ice from his face plate, then lifted his head to see where the white-suited intruder had gone and promptly thumped his helmet on something hard. He looked up to find a gleaming metal bulkhead directly overhead, and realized how close he'd come to being decapitated.

He pulled in one last, sweat-tainted breath and scrambled down the dimly lit passage, his vacuum-booted feet clumsy on the wall rungs. The narrow shaft curved away steeply below him as it angled down toward Deck Seven. Sulu couldn't see anything beyond the bulky control panel on his chest, couldn't hear anything except the trapped rasp of his own breath. Somewhere below him, he knew, another bulkhead would have sealed the access shaft below Deck Seven. The intruder could be anywhere in between.

When the blow came from below, Sulu's adrenaline-pumped muscles responded before he could think, kicking down viciously at his attacker's upward shove. It wasn't until his third complete miss that he realized he was kicking at air. A fierce rush of wind blasted up the shaft past him, pouring in from an opened access panel somewhere below.

Sounds bloomed in the returning atmosphere, faint at first but growing louder as the air pressure stabilized. Beyond the thud of frantic footsteps and the metallic scrape of environmental suits, the only sound Sulu could identify was the unmistakable whirring click of a phaser rifle being armed.

The helmsman froze on his wall rungs, guessing from the abrupt lack of footsteps that his quarry had done the same. In the looming silence, Chekov's voice sounded oddly fierce.

"Stop right there, whoever you are," the security officer growled. "Because even if my first shot misses, the ricochet inside this shaft won't."

Chapter Twelve

"CHEKOV?" SULU'S VOICE echoed down the narrow ladderway as though from an intercom, filtered and tinny. "Don't let him get past you!"

Relief surged through Chekov with such startling strength that the security chief nearly sank to the floor in exhaustion. "He's not going anywhere." He raised his rifle to prod the bulky shimmer of reflected heat above him. "All right, you—climb down. *Slowly.*"

The prisoner hesitated only a moment before awkwardly disentangling himself from the ladder and shuffling out into the hall. Chekov knew without asking that this wasn't his saboteur—the heat reading wasn't nearly high enough, even taking the environmental suit into account. The only strong primary heat sources were the suit's power packs and a bright square of brilliance at the top of his helmet. Chekov realized this must be the helmet lamp when Sulu came down to meet him and the same bright white spot swept across the visor's spectrum.

"What are you doing down here?" Chekov asked, lowering the rifle so he could lean the muzzle on the floor.

"I caught this guy breaking into my quarters!" Sulu gestured sharply at the suited figure between them. The joints of his suit creaked with the sudden movement. "I was trying to stop him when he went down this access ladder." Apparently seeing something on Chekov's face, he asked, "Why? What's the matter?"

"I was chasing the saboteur."

Sulu's outline pulled sharply upright with surprise, helmet light rebounding off the opposite wall. "You saw him?"

"I shot him." Chekov waved his rifle toward the tracked-up blood on the floor, wondering if they'd be able to clean all this up before the first shift crew came on duty. All he knew now was that his socks were wet, and the sleeve of his tunic was starting to feel clammy as the blood in the fabric cooled. "He must have used the same access ladder before you voided the atmosphere. Damn—the vacuum will have boiled the blood away and ruined the trail." He flexed his hand again; the fingers moved stiffly, coldly. "I can tell you one thing, though—whoever he is, he isn't human."

The prisoner's bark of surprise sounded more like a squeak over the helmet communicator. Stumbling back from Sulu in the doorway, the stranger tried to turn and lumber away, his helmet light vanishing from Chekov's sight as soon as his suit was turned. Chekov passed the rifle to his right hand again, and in two long steps caught the storage hook on the back of the suit and jerked the fugitive off his feet. Pain seared across his back and shoulders with the effort, and he was swaying on the edge of gray when he jammed the rifle under the environmental suit's breastplate so the occupant could feel the muzzle. "Don't even try it." He tried to keep his voice from sounding thick and muzzy, but he didn't think he succeeded too well. "Who is this guy?" he asked Sulu, blinking the helmsman into focus.

Sulu lifted his hands to shoulder height, the only way to shrug inside an environmental suit, and came a few steps closer. "I just chased him here. Your guess is as good as mine."

Chekov scowled down at the man below him. "I hate having to guess."

"Please—" The voice inside the suit was paper-thin, but hardly weak. "Gentlemen, surely we can reach some sort of compromise?"

"The security chief's on my side," Sulu pointed out. "I don't have to compromise." He clumped over to Chekov's side, tugging off his environmental suit gloves. "What were you doing in my room?"

"I-I was lost." The stranger squirmed a little under the rifle, but Chekov didn't let up the pressure, not sure he could bring the man down a second time. "I was looking for something. I lost my bearings in the hull breach—I didn't mean to cause any problems."

Somehow, Chekov wasn't convinced of their prisoner's veracity. "What's your name and rank?"

A little hiss of sound that might have been a laugh whisked past the suit's outer speaker. The prisoner's helmet thumped against the ground when he shifted position. "I'm afraid that's a little harder to explain—"

The lights came up with almost dizzying suddenness. New layers of heat and reflected long-wave light crumbled the visor's clean images. Chekov stepped away from their prisoner long enough to trap the rifle under his left elbow so he could reach up and pull off the visor without having to move his wounded arm. Even that small movement slammed a jolt of pain across his shoulders and made his vision dim.

He'd grown so used to interpreting the infrared signals through the visor that the dusty blue face staring up at him didn't even seem unusual until Sulu gasped with shock. Then the flaxen hair and pale antennae had their impact. "You're an Andorian!" Sulu pushed in front of him to throw an arm across his chest and catch him from staggering, and Chekov had to lean far to one side to keep the Andorian in view. "Who the hell are you?"

"My God, what happened?" The helmsman's voice came suddenly clear as he popped the seals on his environmental suit helmet and threw it to the floor. "You're bleeding all over your gun!"

Chekov tried irritably to elbow the helmsman aside, swaying only slightly against the crash of nausea that rose up to greet him. Sulu was right—the rifle's muzzle had channeled a thin drizzle of blood to the breast of the Andorian's environmental suit. "I'm . . ." He fingered the cold, wet fabric of his tunic sleeve, frowning. ". . . I'll be fine. . . ."

Then Chekov felt the deck spin out from under him, and he reached to grab at Sulu's arm to steady himself. He didn't even realize he was falling until his shoulder slammed against the helmsman, and he knocked them both to the floor.

"Oh, God, Pavel, don't be dead." Sulu squirmed out from under Chekov's limp body, trying not to roll him onto his back. The stench of charred clothes and skin clung to the corridor, a thin haze of smoke now vanishing into the ventilators. The floor beneath them was slippery with puddled blood, and Sulu briefly tried to tug Chekov out of it before he realized that it was still oozing out of the security officer's ruined shoulder. Despite the appalling pallor of his face, Chekov's chest rose and fell with steady breathing. Sulu's gaze slid aside from the sickening glimpse of scorched bone below the bloody flesh, and fell on the white-suited Andorian, trying to scuttle away.

"Hey!" The helmsman's pounce carried all the weight of his anguish and frustration, slamming the alien against the far wall with one arm twisted up behind his back. With his free hand, Sulu grabbed Chekov's blood-slicked phaser rifle and jammed it into the back of the Andorian's neck. "Don't move!"

The alien froze, only turning his head to regard Sulu with an ambiguous pinkish gaze. "Shouldn't you be doing something for your friend instead of assaulting me?" he asked in a not-quite-innocent voice.

"Assaulting you is what he'd want me to do." Sulu prodded him with the rifle. "Let's go. There's a communications panel down the hall. You're going to call sickbay for me, and then you're going to call the captain."

The Andorian's antennae cringed beneath his transparent helmet. "Oh, no, I don't think so—"

The double clatter of footsteps interrupted him. Sulu turned his head and sagged with relief when he saw a familiar, wiry figure striding around the corridor junction. "Dr. McCoy, over here!"

The doctor sprinted down the hall toward them. "Good God, what's going on here?" He dropped to his knees beside Chekov and reached into his medical kit. Aaron Kelly trailed behind him, an appalled look on his coffee-dark face. "Who the hell shot Chekov?"

"The guy who bombed the ship." Sulu swung around, bringing the Andorian with him by the simple expedient of not removing the phaser rifle from his neck. The alien groaned theatrically but didn't try to resist. "Is Chekov going to be all right?"

"He'll live." McCoy flipped the lid from a bandage canister, and a pale sheen of anesthetic foam hissed out over Chekov's seared shoulder. "But I can tell you right now, he's not going to be real happy about it."

The turbolift doors down the hall slapped open before Sulu could respond. A slim form in a red environmental suit vaulted out, followed by a defensive wedge of black-clad security guards. "What happened?" Kirk strode down the corridor toward them, his eyes jerking from Chekov's prone form to the white-suited Andorian. The alien visibly flinched beneath the captain's fierce scrutiny. "Is this the saboteur?"

Sulu shook his head. "No, sir. This is the guy I chased out of my room and down the maintenance ladder." He jerked his chin back at the security corridor, the acrid bite of scorched plastic and metal catching in his throat as he did so. Sulu tasted the underlying bitterness of burnt flesh and clenched his teeth against a lurch of sickness. "The guy who set the bomb was down here, shooting Chekov."

"And two other guards," added Aaron Kelly in a small, shocked voice. "He would have shot me, too, if Lieutenant Chekov hadn't stopped him."

Kirk snapped the bolts on his helmet and lifted it off sweat-dampened hair. The frown in his eyes told Sulu he was tallying all the information he'd been given.

"Did you see who did the shooting?" he asked the auditor.

Kelly shook his head numbly. "The lights went out before I heard the first shots." Sulu saw his dark throat tighten with a swallow. "As soon as the force barrier on my cell dropped, I ran. I just—ran and hid."

"Probably the most efficient thing you could do, Mr. Kelly," Kirk commented dryly.

McCoy finished spraying synthetic skin across Chekov's back, then looked up at the captain. "Jim, if you're done questioning this boy, I'd like to send him back to sickbay to get a transport sled for Chekov."

"He's free to go." Kirk handed his helmet to the nearest guard, then went down on one knee to examine the double trail of blood splattered down the corridor. "Bones, does all this blood look human to you?"

The doctor glanced down at the muddle of bloodstains on the floor. "That orange stuff sure doesn't." He pulled a scanner out of his medikit and passed it over the nearest dabble of orange.

Sulu blinked, unpleasant memories of past bar fights running through his head. "It looks like Orion blood to me, Captain."

"I thought so, too." Kirk rose to his feet and swung to face the security guards without waiting for McCoy's confirming nod. "Begin a shipwide search for an injured Orion, probably armed and dangerous. Include all maintenance ladders and access shafts, starting with this one. We know he went somewhere on it."

"Aye, sir." Ensign Lemieux lifted off her helmet and turned to face the rest of the guards. "Hrdina and Samuelsson, you take the access ladders. The rest of you, fan out on this deck." She paused, glancing at the silent Andorian while the guards scattered. "Should I put the prisoner in the brig before I leave, sir?"

"No." Kirk waved her away, his voice turning cold. "I have some questions I want to ask him."

The Andorian's head swung up abruptly. "I didn't have anything to do with it, I swear!"

"Anything to do with what?" Kirk stepped forward, giving the blue-skinned humanoid a flinty look. The alien skittered back, stopping only when Sulu nudged the rifle even more firmly into his neck.

"With bombing your ship." The helmet communicator flattened the Andorian's nasal accent into a whine. "I didn't do it, Captain. In fact, I'm the one who told your security chief where to find it!"

"I believe you didn't do it." Kirk took another step toward the quailing alien, then reached out to pop the bolts on the Andorian's helmet and lift it clear of his antennae. "But I don't believe you didn't have *anything* to do with it . . . Muav Haslev."

The Andorian jerked back so fiercely that the helmet tore out of Kirk's hands and went crashing to the floor. Sulu found himself wedged up against the wall, phaser rifle squeezed tight between his chest and the alien's back. He grunted and pushed the Andorian forward again, afraid he'd pull the trigger by mistake. The vinegar-sharp smell of alien sweat drifted over him.

"How did you know who I am?" Haslev demanded, his voice deeper but no less defensive now that he was speaking out loud instead of through the suit. Pale antennae quivered nervously above his damp flaxen hair.

Kirk snorted. "When two Orion ships conspire to

slow us down and board us, and then an Orion stowaway sabotages our ship so we can't get away, I begin to get the feeling I've got something on board the Orions want." He leaned forward to thump a gloved fist on the alien's breastplate. "Right now, Mr. Haslev, you have the distinction of being the one thing in the universe the Orions want the most. One missing Andorian weapons scientist, recently employed on a top-secret military research project."

"I wasn't employed there," Haslev corrected him indignantly. "I was in charge! They couldn't have done any of that work without me."

McCoy scrambled to his feet, eyebrows lifting in surprise. "If you're Muav Haslev, what in hell are you doing on board the *Enterprise?* I thought the Orions had kidnapped you!"

"Kidnapped? Is that what they're saying now?" Haslev sniffed with undisguised disdain. "I left of my own accord, thank you very much. The Andorian government undervalued my contributions to their research, so I went out and found someone who would pay me what I was worth."

Kirk reached out with both hands, and Sulu skipped prudently out of the way before the captain shoved the Andorian back against the corridor wall. "You sold Federation-level military technology to the Orions?"

"Why not?" Haslev squirmed for a moment, stopping only when Sulu poked him warningly in the ribs with the phaser rifle. His voice was aggrieved. "Their money spends just like everybody else's."

It was all Sulu could do not to take up the rifle and beat him with it. He restrained himself, watching Kirk step back with a grimace of disgust. "Selling any military technology to a neutral star system is a direct violation of Federation policy, Mr. Haslev," the captain said coldly. "We're going to have to arrest you."

"But it wasn't like anyone in the Federation wanted it!" Haslev's quartz-pink eyes widened in alarm. "No one even thought it would work—they said if we wasted any more research on it, they'd cut our funding! I *had* to go to the Orions. They were the only ones who believed in me."

McCoy snorted, stepping back as Aaron Kelly guided a medical transport sled down the hallway toward them. "If the Orions were so all-fired wonderful, what are you doing hiding away on a Federation ship?"

"We had a disagreement over an item in my contract," the Andorian admitted, the fine lines of his cheeks darkening to a brilliant indigo. "They wanted to kill me; I didn't want to die."

That seemed reasonable enough, whichever side of it Sulu considered. Kirk's mouth twitched slightly, as if he thought so, too. "Orions can be like that," he said smoothly. "What technology did you sell to them, Mr. Haslev?"

"I don't think I should tell you," the scientist said after a thoughtful pause. "Unless, of course, you promise not to arrest me."

Sulu saw Kirk's gloves clench into fists at his sides. "The only thing I can promise to do, Mr. Haslev," the captain said between his teeth, "is ship you back to the Andorians as soon as possible."

Haslev sighed. "You Starfleet people are all so short-sighted," he complained. "You just don't recognize true genius. I knew it would be like this when I came on board."

"How *did* you come on board?" McCoy glanced up

from sliding Chekov onto the transport platform. "I don't remember any intruder alerts going off."

"No, there was one," Sulu said suddenly. Memories of chaotic alarms and red alert sirens swept through his head, but it took him a moment to pin down the time and place. "It was right after we left Sigma One, during that radiation burst."

"But Chekov said one of the auditors set off that alarm." Kirk turned to glance at Aaron Kelly, hovering behind McCoy like a dark, worried shadow. "Was that you?"

Kelly nodded sheepishly. "I don't really know what kind of alarm I tripped, sir—I just banged on the nearest security panel until something went off."

"How convenient," commented Haslev. He saw Kirk's glare and added hurriedly, "For me, of course. I wondered why no one had been looking for me."

"Where have you been hiding?" Kirk asked.

The Andorian blinked pink eyes at him. "I'm not sure I should tell you that, either."

Sulu gave Kirk a meaningful glance across Haslev's shoulder. "We can always leave him out as bait for the Orion saboteur," the helmsman suggested.

"That's not a bad idea," Kirk agreed. Haslev jerked upright, his short antennae fluttering with outrage.

"You wouldn't dare!" He glanced from Kirk's grim face to Sulu's impassive stare. "Oh, all right. If you must know, I've been hiding in your turbolift shafts."

"Is that what's been causing all these damn lift delays?" McCoy grunted with annoyance. "How'd you manage to keep from being crushed?"

A smirk curled Haslev's pale lips upward. "I've found all the computer codes on board this ship ridiculously easy to manipulate. You really should consider hiring someone like me to update them."

McCoy snorted. "I don't know about you, Jim, but I've heard just about enough from this guy. If you don't mind, I'm going to take your security chief off to sickbay."

Kirk removed one glove and rubbed a tired hand across his face, deliberately turning a shoulder to Haslev. "How is he, Bones?"

"Lucky," the doctor replied promptly. "Fortunately for him, it takes a phaser more than a few seconds to burn through a human shoulder blade. He's going to need some skin regeneration, probably a bone graft, and a ligament reattachment as well."

"Get on it," Kirk said. "I want to talk to him as soon as he's awake."

"I am—awake, sir." The wavering voice was almost unrecognizable except for the accent. Sulu cast a worried glance at the medical sled, seeing nothing beyond the back of a tousled dark head. Kirk hurried around the other side of the transport, crouching beside the wounded security officer. "Sir, the saboteur—"

"—is Orion, we know." Kirk rested a hand on Chekov's good shoulder. "Did he say anything while he was down here?"

"No, sir." The Russian took a steadying breath. "He's armed—with at least one phaser, set on high heat, to avoid setting off the weapons detectors— that's how he got Davidson and Tate—" His head lifted slightly. "He escaped—down the access ladder—"

"We've already started a shipwide search. Don't worry, we'll catch him." The certainty in the captain's voice seemed to reassure Chekov as much as the words. The security officer relaxed back onto the medical transport with a sigh, and McCoy towed him down the corridor. Sulu watched them go, his eyes widening in surprise when a familiar tall figure stepped out of the turbolift and skirted carefully around the sled.

"Spock." Kirk's head lifted alertly. "What's the problem?"

"There is no problem, Captain. I merely have some information that I did not wish to transmit to you over ship channels." The Vulcan stopped a few paces away from Haslev and regarded him calmly. "Muav Haslev, I presume?"

The Andorian's antennae quivered in vexation. "Does everyone in the universe know who I am now?" he demanded querulously.

"The wages of treachery, Mr. Haslev." Kirk lifted an eyebrow at Spock. "Can you give me this information in front of our—er—guest?"

"I believe so, Captain." As usual, Spock's lean face betrayed no emotions, but Sulu got the distinct impression of urgency. "I have been calculating the probable arrival times of the Orion ships *Umyfymu* and *Mecufi*. Based upon our last contact, I estimate they will overtake our current position in approximately three hours thirteen minutes."

Kirk thoughtfully rubbed a thumb across his mouth. "And how long does Mr. Scott think our hull repairs will take?"

"No less than five hours, Captain, even with all available engineers assigned to the task."

"Hmm." Kirk swung back toward Muav Haslev, whose blue face had faded to ashy violet. "Well, that settles it, Mr. Haslev. We're throwing you off the ship."

"What?" Haslev's antennae flexed in shock. "You can't do that!"

"On board the *Enterprise,* I can do anything I want to." Kirk glanced over at Sulu, one corner of his mouth lifting with amusement. "Mr. Sulu, I want you to get an interstellar shuttle ready for the trip back to Sigma One. Plot a course that will take you wide of the Orions." The captain gave Haslev one last ironic look. "We're going to send our golden goose away before the foxes get here to fight over it."

Chapter Thirteen

"I KNOW JUST THE THING you need to give you extra
help on your job. Do you have any idea what a Mark
IV Defense Com goes for on the open market? I can
get it for you at cost."

Chekov tried to align his jacket shoulders so they
didn't feel so awkward over McCoy's restrictive sling.
He wondered if Haslev appreciated how lucky he was
that Chekov didn't have a free hand to clamp over his
mouth all the way down to the shuttle bay.

"Come on—uncuff my hands."

Probably not.

"Shut up," Chekov said, not turning to look at his
prisoner, "or I'll shoot you."

"Pavel—" The rebuke in Uhura's tone was obvious
despite the long whistle of their turbolift plummeting
down to the secondary hull. In a slightly-too-big new
uniform, without her usual elegant touch of gold at

ears and throat, she looked smaller and more fragile than usual. "Maybe you ought to let somebody else escort Mr. Haslev to Sigma One with us."

"There isn't anybody else." Chekov lifted his left arm to let her step around in front of him, recognizing by the way she tugged at his jacket that she'd finally tired of watching him fumble to dress himself. "The captain needs all the able-bodied guards to track down the saboteur, and Dr. McCoy won't let me do anything even if I stay on board. I might as well sit on a shuttle and hold a phaser on *him*—" He jerked his chin in Haslev's direction. "—for the next four days so all the healthy people can stay at home."

Uhura twisted her mouth into a wry grimace while she slipped his belt off and rolled it up between her hands. "Does that mean if I call Dr. McCoy, he'll tell me you were released from sickbay and returned to active duty?"

No. It meant McCoy would tell her Chekov had been released and sent home to sit around and do nothing for the next five days. Chekov suspected she knew that already. "He released me," he sighed, feeling boyish as she half-fastened the collar of his jacket and left the rest to hang open. "If I really wanted to ignore doctor's orders, I'd stay on board and run around after Orions. As it is, sitting on a shuttle is no different than sitting in my cabin. Please—" He pulled at his jacket again, resigned to being uncomfortable until the sling came off. "Just let me do this."

The turbolift doors coasted open on the vast pod of the landing bay, and Haslev asked meekly, "Would it help if I said I was sure I could take care of myself for the trip?"

Chekov ushered Uhura out the door. "No."

Two rows of shuttles tracked like gleaming metal peas down the long open space. Chekov glanced around, then located the *Hawking* among the large interstellar shuttles near the landing bay doors. Uhura angled for the craft without pausing, her footsteps echoing through the bay ahead of Chekov's. "If I were being a good officer," she complained, "I'd tell Captain Kirk you assigned yourself to this security detail and make sure he didn't let you come."

Then thank God she could be convinced to just be a good friend. "Thank you."

They rounded the *Hawking*'s blunt nose to find the sleek side door already open. A supply sled bobbed there under the weight of two technicians, loading food and water into the hold for the four-day trip to Sigma One. Chekov steered Haslev toward the boarding ramp when the Andorian tried to wander the other way, urging him to march up it with a hand at the small of his back.

"You're just not into basic compassion, are you?"

Chekov pushed him into a seat. "Sit down."

"Hey!" Sulu poked his head out of the open cockpit, his own uniform looking too pressed and new-made to have ever been worn before. It occurred to Chekov that his friends must have abandoned nearly everything they owned to the hull breach. "Chekov, what're you doing here? Who's taking care of my lizards?"

The lieutenant didn't look up from fastening Haslev's wrist restraints to the bolts on the arms of his chair. Just thinking about the breach made his heart labor. "Nobody."

"That's not funny." Sulu made a tragic face. "I paid a lot of money for those guys."

And somebody had no doubt paid a lot of money for that Orion saboteur. "If the ship blows up before we get home, Sulu, it won't matter who was or wasn't watching them."

"That's one way to look at it." Sulu feigned whispering to Uhura as she settled into her own chair. "What's put him in such a good mood?"

"The whole point of moving Haslev," Uhura explained, answering Chekov instead of Sulu, "is so the saboteur won't have to try to cripple the *Enterprise* anymore."

Haslev crumpled his antennae against his skull with a groan. "Does that mean he'll be coming after *us* instead?"

"Probably." Nodding an okay to the technicians ready to dog the outer hatch, Chekov slid into a seat at the front of the row. "But if we blow up before we get home, the lizards still won't matter."

Sulu blew a low whistle and backed into the cockpit to get ready for takeoff. "I just love it when you're being Russian." He ignored Chekov's scowl to toss a look at Uhura. "Does this mean he gets to ride up front with me?"

"Please—take him." Haslev only cringed a little when Chekov turned to glare at him across the empty shuttle. "For my sake, at least—I'm afraid of what will happen if you leave him back here."

The *Enterprise*'s huge hangar doors peeled open in stately silence. Chekov sat beside Sulu in the navigator's chair, absently rubbing his thumb over a dark indicator light while their shuttle drifted forward to be enveloped by blackness and distant stars. It felt strange not to have a real job on this mission; Sulu had downloaded whatever navigational data he needed from the *Enterprise*'s main computer, and Haslev could hardly be considered much of a threat. In fact, sitting there with his shoulder aching and his sling chafing at the back of his collar, Chekov felt more like excess baggage than an officer. He sighed and pulled the phaser from his belt to toss it up onto the panel in front of him.

Sulu glanced aside from his piloting with a smile. "You're the one who said you wanted to come."

Chekov snorted. "I just wish I could have come with both arms."

"No, you don't." Delicate engine gantries swept across the viewscreen as Sulu lifted them clear of the *Enterprise* and started their turn. "If you had both arms, you'd just be grumping about how you'd rather be back on the ship helping track down the saboteur. I know you."

Yes, he did. It was galling sometimes. "Don't mind me," Chekov grumbled, shifting in his seat to watch the ship pass by beneath them. "I'm just feeling useless, that's all."

Sulu didn't contradict that observation, which didn't do much for the lieutenant's temperament. Chekov kept his back half-turned to the helm, calculating their speed without really meaning to by mentally clicking off the seconds between one exterior weld and the next. Then the edge of the primary hull etched a shattered arc through the darkness below them, and Chekov's hand formed a fist inside his sling. "I thought they'd be further along with the breach repair."

"So did Mr. Scott. They're still tearing out the sections with concussion damage, though. He says she'll be warp ready by the time we get back."

Engineers and equipment crawled along the edges of the breach like slow mites, trailing clean, new metal behind them wherever they repaired. Chekov counted

171

the number of dark portals on either side of the breach, and guessed that three living sectors were still without power. He wondered where Kirk would manage to bunk all those crew.

"Speaking of getting back—" Sulu made some small adjustment to the readings on his panel. "You didn't really leave my lizards all alone, did you?"

"No." Actually, he had. But he'd left them with a soap dish full of fish food from the bio lab, a bathtub full of clean water, and a sponge to play with. They'd probably be more comfortable than Chekov would for the next four days.

"Thanks," Sulu said with a quick, automatic smile. He piloted a little longer, then asked, "How long has McCoy got you in that sling?"

Chekov glanced back at Sulu, found the helmsman intent on his piloting, and turned back to the viewscreen. By then, the wounded *Enterprise* had passed behind them, out of sight. "Two weeks."

"Did he have to do a lot of work on you?"

"Apparently." Bone and muscle grafts at least, and something more complicated involving nerves that Chekov hadn't really wanted to hear the details of.

"Will you ever be able to play piano again?"

He slid Sulu a sidelong scowl, and the helmsman returned his glare with a look of counterfeit surprise. "Well?" Sulu challenged, laughing a little. "You've got to help me out here—It's kind of hard to have a conversation when all you're contributing is the impression that I'm interfering with your sulk."

Chekov clenched his teeth against an unfairly sharp response when he heard Uhura come into the cockpit behind them. "Who's sulking?" she asked, with the innocent interest of someone not completely aware of what she'd walked into.

Sulu jerked a terse nod at Chekov. "Who else?"

There was nothing like being ganged up on by your friends. Twisting as far as he could in his seat, Chekov tried to distract the conversation by leaning around Uhura and glaring back toward the passenger compartment. "Should we really leave Haslev alone?"

She glanced reflexively behind her, but obviously wasn't concerned. "Why not?" A brilliant smile flashed across her dark features. "Maybe the saboteur will sneak in and kill him while nobody's looking."

Fear and annoyance flashed through him in equal measure, and Chekov sank back in his chair to look spaceward.

Uhura rapped her knuckles on the back of his chair. "Don't do that."

He tipped his head back to scowl at her. "Do what?"

"Don't lock us out like this every time something goes wrong." The sudden intensity of her gaze made him feel like squirming and turning away. "Pavel, what's the matter with you?"

He looked at Sulu to find the helmsman watching them from the corner of his eye, and tried to summon enough anger to deflect their intentions. "I've lost three guards in as many days," he said, sounding more stressed and weary than he intended. "I feel like I'm deserting my post by leaving the ship while there's a saboteur on board, but there's not a damned thing I could do to help if I stayed. Considering that the Auditor General already thinks I'm a sorry excuse for a commanding officer, I guess all of this has just put me in a bad mood." He fumbled to straighten the sling around his neck, deciding that was an obvious enough problem not to need mentioning.

Sulu finished bringing the shuttle up to warp speed,

then swiveled away from his panel. "That's not what she means."

"You've been acting strange since before anything went wrong on board," Uhura said, moving to lean against the console between them. "In fact, you haven't been yourself since we got back from Sigma One." She reached out to tug at Chekov's empty jacket sleeve. "Did something happen in that jail you didn't tell us about?"

If only it were that simple. "What's the matter? Haven't you two got anything better to do than sit around and worry about me?"

Uhura smiled, the quiet, gentle smile that always made Chekov wonder if this was what it was like to grow up in a family with bossy older siblings. "Sometimes, you give us a lot to worry about." She pulled on his sleeve again. "What's wrong?"

The purr of the warp engines seemed louder than normal in the attenuated silence that followed. Chekov caught himself studying the rivets in the decking, but couldn't make himself raise his eyes. Not if he was going to talk about this. "Did you hear about the *Kongo?*"

Sulu shifted a little in his seat. "They had a containment field failure," he said finally. "The dispatch said they clipped a cosmic string near Perseus." The quality of his silence hinted that he knew more, but wasn't sure how much to say.

"They lost the whole aft quarter of the ship," Chekov said for him, still not looking up. Grief-edged memories crowded his vision, and he tried to keep his words at arm's length so he could explain all this without being harmed. "They had thirteen engineers trapped in the Jefferies tubes when the field collapsed, another thirty on duty in the main room below. The string tore the gantries, and when the bridge tried to free the nacelles—" His voice tangled suddenly in his throat; he cut off the words until he could wrestle them back under control.

Uhura surprised him by reaching across to brush his cheek. "You knew someone on board," she said softly. "Didn't you?"

He nodded, and this time it was hard to keep the anger out of his words. "The science officer. He was my friend at the Academy." He dragged a hand across his eyes, frowned with embarrassed irritation when it came away wet. "He and another officer went EV to manually jettison the nacelles. They knew the radiation exposure would kill them, but they didn't think they had time to take a shielded shuttle—they wanted to free the engines before the drive pulsed and killed everyone in the tubes."

Sulu nodded slowly, and Uhura rubbed at her arms as if the shuttle had grown unaccountably cold. "That was incredibly brave of them," she said.

"It was also incredibly pointless!" Chekov surged out of his seat, wanting to pace away from them, away from the ugly things he'd been feeling these last two days, but only made two strides before the closed cockpit door stopped him. "An antimatter wave from the warp core killed the engine room staff and destroyed their major equipment. The bridge couldn't know what was going on with the drive, but—" He leaned his head against the door and closed his eyes. "The engines had pulsed when they first hit the string. There was no one to go for, no one to save. They went outside and died for nothing."

"It wasn't nothing."

Chekov turned at Sulu's tone of gentle surprise. "What did they gain?" he demanded. "They didn't even get the damned nacelles blown free! Now, their ship might be irreparable, over one hundred of their crew are dead—my God! Core heat burned them out of existence before they even got close enough to see the lock! Tell me what you think they gained!"

Uhura dropped a hand to Sulu's arm when the helmsman opened his mouth to protest. The worried crease between her brows struck Chekov with a guilt almost strong enough to override his anger. "Would you rather they never tried?" she asked him, head cocked. "Believing there might still be people in there, would you rather they had taken the safe route and waited to prepare a shuttle?"

"I would rather they hadn't died at all." Even as he said it, he knew it was stupid.

Neither of the others laughed, though. Sulu only ducked his head in quiet sympathy, and Uhura asked, "What if they'd jettisoned the nacelles and saved those people? Your friend still would have died, wouldn't he?"

Being that close to an engine in flux? Undoubtedly. Chekov nodded.

"And would that have made a difference? Would you feel any better knowing he'd managed to accomplish something by what he did?"

Chekov stared at her, all sorts of conflicting answers roiling about inside him. It was the pointlessness, yes; the fearful suddenness, too. Underneath all that, though, he was tortured with a fear of dying badly, of staying on in a career where his own life might end just as cheaply.

He opened his mouth, not sure what answer he was willing to give, just as darkness gripped the little room, and the song of the shuttle's warp engines died.

"Oh, what now?" Sulu groaned.

As if in answer, a clap of brittle thunder pealed through the rear of the shuttle, kicking the little ship to its heart and slamming them all to the floor.

"Isn't there anything I could do to help?"

"No, Mr. Kelly." Kirk glanced at the auditor, waiting patiently near the rear of the turbolift. "I appreciate your offer, but you'd really do best to keep out of the way." *You also shouldn't follow me up to the bridge,* he didn't add. *But I don't know where else to send you.*

Kirk had spent the morning filling in for Chekov as security chief, unwilling to leave a crew of ensigns in charge of catching the saboteur while their lieutenant had his shoulder reconstructed. It was a job the captain had hoped would be well over by now. Instead, one frustrating blind alley had followed another, and he'd finally had to leave Deck Seven for the bridge. At least there, he could make things happen, get things done.

"I just know I have a lot to be grateful for," Kelly volunteered as the turbolift began its vertical climb for the command center. "If Lieutenant Chekov hadn't shown up when he did, that saboteur would have killed me—he nearly killed the lieutenant. I just want you to know I appreciate that."

Frustration eased a little of its iron grip. Apparently, being a Federation auditor didn't mean you'd had all of your humanity beaten out of you, after all. "Thank you, Mr. Kelly." Kirk nodded somewhat graciously, but still couldn't bring himself to smile. "Why don't you see if the relocation teams need help on Deck Three? We've got a lot of crew needing new cabin assignments." And it seemed the sort of thing an auditor just might be able to streamline and still stay out of trouble.

Kelly flashed a boyish grin. "Thank you, Captain." He stepped back against the rear bulkhead as the turbolift doors flashed open. "I'll do that."

Kirk hoped someone would be on Deck Three to appreciate Kelly's help. "Mr. Bhutto," he called, stepping clear of the turbolift and trotting down the steps. "Any sign of our Orion friends?"

Bhutto glanced up from her navigation panel, shaking her head. "No, sir. No ships detected within sensor range."

Kirk pursed his lips. "Then they're slower than I thought." He paused by the command chair, studying the empty viewscreen as though his eyes might detect enemy approach before sensors could. "Spock, have we had any luck using the ship's internal systems to find our saboteur?"

"Negative, Captain." Spock straightened from his science station, rotating his chair to meet Kirk halfway when the captain turned to face him. "I suspect the saboteur has taken refuge in an area of enhanced heat flow on the ship, to conceal his own physiological temperature from our instruments."

Kirk started to lower himself into the command chair, then paused and cocked a look at Scott. "Does that mean he's hiding near the warp engines?"

The engineer rocked back in his seat, arms crossed and chin high. "Captain, we've searched every nook and cranny in engineering—for bombs *and* for saboteurs." He shook his head firmly. "I can guarantee you, he's not in my engine room."

"The amount of heat flow needed to obscure the ten-degree difference between human and Orion body temperatures need not be large, Captain." Spock lifted one eyebrow in his universal expression of thought. "Any unit of shipboard equipment that consumes a significant amount of power—for example, one of my sensor arrays—would produce enough Joule energy to accomplish the objective."

Sometimes, sorting through Spock's explanations was almost as challenging as the problem at hand. "So," Kirk paraphrased, settling into his chair, "he could be hiding anywhere on the ship." At Spock's nod, the captain dropped his chin into his hand, considering. "But wherever he is, he's near some power source?"

"That is what I would surmise."

That was something, then. Kirk rapped the intercom button with the side of his hand. "Kirk to security."

"Security. Lemieux here."

"Ensign Lemieux, focus your search teams on all ship sectors whose power consumption exceeds—" He glanced at Spock, throwing his hands wide for suggestions.

"Fifteen kilojoules," the Vulcan supplied.

"—fifteen kilojoules," Kirk went on, nodding his thanks to the science officer. "Contact engineering for specific equipment locations."

"Aye-aye, sir. Lemieux out."

"Captain!" The communications officer's voice jerked Kirk around in his seat. "I've lost our tight-beam contact with the *Hawking.*"

Kirk's hands tightened on the arms of his chair. "Is the signal being jammed by an Orion ship?" he asked.

The young lieutenant flicked anxious eyes across his boards, calling up readings with quick touches of his hands. "No, sir. The cause appears to be equipment failure on their end." He lifted worried eyes to Kirk. "It could just be a malfunction, sir."

"It could be, Ensign." Kirk pushed to his feet, suddenly unable to stay passively seated. "But considering how resourceful our saboteur is, I wouldn't bet the farm on it. Scotty—" He roamed the edge of the railing until he could lean across to his engineer. "Can we engage warp drive yet?"

"No, sir." The engineer was emphatic. "We haven't even got closure on the hull breach yet, much less reinforced it for warp stress."

"Well, how about impulse drive? How fast *can* we travel?"

Scott's brow knotted with concern, and Kirk knew the engineer could read his captain's intentions as clearly as if Kirk had shouted them. "With incomplete shielding around the breach," Scott said, "we're limited to about 0.1 light speed. Any faster than that, and she'll take damage from micrometeorite impacts, maybe even ruin what we've got of the repair."

Oh point one. Kirk drummed his hands against the railing, calculating Scott's projected velocity against how long the *Hawking* had been gone. "Eighty-seven minutes before we could rendezvous," he said aloud. He pushed off from the rail just to turn and lean back against it. "Dammit, that's too long. If the Orions haven't gotten here by now, something must have distracted them." He glared at the empty viewscreen, stomach roiling. "And I have a very bad feeling I know what that something is."

Chapter Fourteen

"WHAT WAS *that?*" Uhura's voice crept out of the darkness, quiet with dismay. Beyond the sound of her voice, Sulu could hear the distant hiss of gas exploding out of a ruptured line.

"It sounded like an explosion." The helmsman kicked himself out of the cramped space between his chair and the instrument panel, already feeling the bone-deep shiver that meant they had fallen back into normal space. A quick glance at the warp-field monitor showed him the strobing red glare of failure lights. "Oh, God, not the magnetic containment housing—"

"Are we going to lose control of the core?" Chekov asked.

"I don't know." Sulu found the emergency light switch and slammed a hand down on it with a lot more force than it needed. The dim glow of self-powered spotlights showed Uhura already leaning over the communications panel while Chekov doggedly tried to free his loosened jacket from an instrument panel it had tangled with. "I'll have to go back and look at it."

"I'll go." The security officer tore the cloth loose with a sudden fierce jerk and rolled to his feet.

"No, you won't." Sulu grabbed Chekov's good arm to stop him. "You need two arms to get down the access tube—"

"I can manage—"

"We've lost subspace radio capability." Uhura broke into their argument without ceremony, looking up from her board with a frown. "I've activated the emergency distress beacon, but even at light speed, the *Enterprise* won't receive our signal for another hour."

Sulu cursed and thrust Chekov into the pilot's seat. "Our impulse engines should still be functional. Reverse our course—get us back to the *Enterprise* at maximum impulse velocity."

For once, Chekov didn't argue, merely punching commands into the helm computer with single-handed determination. Sulu spun past Uhura and ran for the back end of the shuttle.

Ice-cold mist met him when he ducked out of the cockpit, rising from crystal rivulets of liquid nitrogen spreading across the shuttle's floor. Sulu felt his boots stiffen as he sprinted through the superchilled fluid, occasional droplets splashing up to burn through the cloth of his trousers. *Space is about two hundred degrees colder than that,* his mind reminded him bleakly. He gritted his teeth and tried not to think about it.

The nitrogen fog cleared away at the back of the passenger bay, burned off by darker curls of smoke snaking through the opened emergency locker in the rear bulkhead. Sulu skidded to a stop, staring at Muav Haslev. The Andorian had somehow worked himself free of his wrist restraints and was already sliding into one of the shuttle's orange-and-gray environmental suits.

"About time you got here," Haslev complained, then yelped in alarm when Sulu shoved him aside and yanked open the door to the engine compartment. More nitrogen fog billowed out, carrying the smell of scorched metal with it. "Hey, don't do that! If the radiation shielding is ruined, we could die!"

"Shut up." Sulu dove into the narrow access tube leading back to their miniature warp core, coughing at the smell of burnt metal and melted wiring that clogged his throat. The trickle of emergency lighting showed him the dark bulk of the toroidal magnetic lens, wrapped around the warp core to focus its antimatter drive. As Sulu wriggled closer, he could see the effect of the explosion: a fist-sized hole blown through the housing's thick outer shell, with shattered metal petaling away from the impact site. Gashes in the tunnel walls showed where the rest of the exploded metal had gone. A cascade of liquid nitrogen poured out from broken coolant lines inside the magnet, forcing him to straddle the center line of the access tunnel to avoid it.

Sulu's pulse hammered in his throat while he leaned forward to peer through the breach, trying to see if the core shields inside the housing had been destroyed by the blast. The dim gleam of transparent aluminum was barely visible through the silvery fog, but the phosphorescent fire on its inner surface told him it was still intact. He slumped back against the tunnel wall in relief, then cursed when something blunt and metallic smacked into his back.

"Hey!" Chekov's voice echoed down the tunnel from the passenger bay, sounding furious. "What do *you* think you're doing?"

"Getting ready to evacuate." The tinny sound of Haslev's reply told Sulu the Andorian had already donned his suit helmet. "I figured when I heard the phaser—"

"Phaser? What phaser?" Chekov's voice rang down the access tunnel. "Sulu, do you see a phaser inside there?"

"I think I just found it." Sulu wriggled around to tug at the object that had poked him. Tape tore away from the corrugated metal wall and the familiar shape of a phaser pistol fell into his hand. Under a crystal film of ice, its power indicator was dead black. Sulu tucked it into the belt of his jacket and crawled back out to the passenger bay.

He emerged to find Uhura and Chekov staring at him through the mist with identical expressions of fierce concern. "Don't worry," he said at once. "The shielding's still intact. There's no radiation leaking out."

The fine lines around Uhura's eyes smoothed out with her sigh of relief, but Chekov's worried frown didn't fade. "What about the containment housing?" he asked.

Sulu shook his head, tossing the phaser at him. "The saboteur set this to blow a hole right through it. We've lost all the coolant in the torus. The magnetic field strength is probably decaying already." He closed the door to the access tunnel, wishing he could shut away the lurking danger behind it just as easily. "It's only a matter of time before the warp field goes out of control." His gaze met Chekov's through the filmy mist, seeing the grim knowledge darkening the other man's eyes. "I don't think we can make it back to the *Enterprise* in time. We're going to have to evacuate."

"Well, I'm ready." Haslev shrunk back a step when Chekov swung around to glare at him. "What's the matter with you now?"

"Did it even occur to you to call us when you heard that phaser?" the Russian demanded hotly. "We could have disarmed it before it damaged the housing!"

Haslev grimaced. "And then continued with our voyage to Sigma One? No, thank you. I'm much happier with the situation as it stands."

"We'll see how happy you are if the explosion catches us before we get outside the blast radius." Sulu ignored the alien's squeak of dismay, shouldering past him toward the opened emergency locker. Uhura was already there, sorting through the environmental suits stored inside. "How did you get free anyway?"

The Andorian's voice turned sulky. "It doesn't take an engineering genius to figure out the principles behind a mechanical lock," he pointed out. "Engineering geniuses can just do it a lot faster than other people."

Chekov snorted in disgust. "So can common criminals."

"What I can't figure out," Sulu said, waiting for Uhura to hand one of the orange-and-gray suits out to him, "is how the saboteur knew we were going to take this shuttle."

"I don't think he did," Chekov said grimly. "I think he was trying to sabotage the *Enterprise*. For all we know, he may have rigged every shuttle in the bay." The security officer strode across the mist-filled aisle to join them. "A containment field breach in a core this size would be enough to take out the entire ship if it blew inside the hangar."

185

"We've got to get back to the *Enterprise* right away." Sulu glanced down at the communications officer, puzzled by her sudden stillness. "Uhura, what's the matter?"

"This." Uhura stepped out of the locker, face numb and dark eyes shadowed with dismay. She held out her hand to show Sulu the shard of bright-edged metal cupped in her dark palm.

"That looks like shrapnel from the containment housing." His stomach lurched with dread as he guessed what must be wrong. Behind him, he heard Chekov curse in soft, vehement Russian. "Oh, God. It didn't explode into the suit locker, did it?"

"It must have. I've found some of it embedded in every suit so far." Uhura's fingers curled around the metal fragment, tightening recklessly around its arrow-sharp edges. "As far as I can tell, not a single one of them is space-worthy."

Chekov reached past Uhura to jerk one of the buried suits off its storage rack. Jagged slivers of metal shook loose from the tattered fabric, shattering around his feet in a nitrogen-cooled shower. He slung the suit across the aisle, diving in for another. "Pull them all out!"

Discarding her own suit, Uhura turned to obey while Sulu pushed Haslev back from the locker to make more room. "What are you doing?" the Andorian asked Chekov.

"The blast can't have destroyed everything." The lieutenant twisted free an undamaged sleeve and tossed it onto the seat behind him. "We can take pieces from all the different suits to make up a few good whole ones." He threw another ruined piece aside. "You've got two hands—get in here and help us!"

Pieces tumbled into unsteady piles on the deck as they sorted, the heap of shrapnel-littered wrecks rising higher than Chekov cared to think about. Still, he couldn't help keeping mental tally of every unscarred sleeve and helmet, and despair sank deeper and deeper into his heart with every useless suit discarded. Before Uhura even crouched among the parts to count them out, Chekov knew they had only five sleeves, two trouser arrangements, eight breastplates and ten helmets to choose from.

The communications officer looked up from her counting, eyes dark and tragic. "There's only enough here for two suits."

"Three," Chekov corrected her. He couldn't believe how calm and certain his voice sounded. "Counting Haslev's."

Sulu glanced darkly at the Andorian fidgeting by the airlock. "So what do we do now?"

Chekov hefted a suit torso and shoved it into Sulu's arms. "You suit up and get out." When the helmsman turned to stare at him, Chekov bent to pass a breastplate to Uhura so he wouldn't have to look at his friend.

"Chekov—"

Not that Uhura's huge, frightened eyes were any easier to face. "No," she said thinly.

Chekov took her hand and gently looped it around the suit to make her hold it. "You haven't any choice."

"Sure we do." Sulu pushed between them, hugging his empty suit like a shield as he confronted Chekov. "We can argue about which of us gets to stay."

"And waste time we don't have." Chekov tugged at

his sling to remind Sulu of its reality. "I can't move my arm," he said plaintively, trying to keep his voice from shaking. "It will take me forever to suit up, and I won't be able to work the controls EV—"

Sulu threw his partial suit to the ground. "Bull. It doesn't take physical strength to move around once you're outside." The anger in his voice and stance bled so rapidly into concern that Chekov almost felt his friend's fear as a physical pain. "I could help you suit up," Sulu pleaded. "I know it couldn't—"

"Sulu, don't." Chekov reached up to clamp a hand over Sulu's mouth, and aborted it to grasp his friend's shoulder at the last minute. "Someone has to stay," he said carefully, "and there's no good or fair way to decide who. Please—" He tightened his grip, both in warning and entreaty. "Don't make me knock you unconscious to put you in that suit."

"Well—" Haslev danced forward to drag on Sulu's arm with one hand, pulling Uhura to her feet with his other. "You heard the man—he's volunteering. Let's go!"

Sulu jerked himself out of the Andorian's grasp. "You're not welded into that suit," he snarled. "We could still take you out of it."

Haslev pressed his antennae down into his hair, but fell silent. Leaving him to Sulu, Chekov turned to drag suit trousers over to Uhura. "Get dressed," he said gently.

Her face was smooth and calm despite the tears tracking down her cheeks. "We'll send somebody back for you."

"I'm counting on it." He wiped her face with his fingers, heart nearly caving in with despair. "I don't want to die," he admitted in a whisper.

She echoed his gesture by reaching up to take his

own face in both small hands. "And I don't want to leave you."

"I could have hours before the containment field decays." It was both the truth and a lie—the truth because probability allowed for it; a lie because he didn't believe it for a moment. He brought her hands down to fold them in his own. "If nothing else, I'll patch one of these suits and follow you as soon as I can. I promise."

Sulu stooped grudgingly to collect sleeves for his suit. "I just want you to know," he said, frowning, "I hate this plan."

Chekov managed a small, almost heartfelt smile. "I'm not in love with it myself."

He helped them suit up as best he could with only one hand. Uhura only nodded miserably at his reassurances, and the bleak silence with which Sulu stepped into his own gear told Chekov how out of control the helmsman must feel with the situation. If he could have thought of some way to defuse the fear crowding among them, he would have. Instead, he did what he always did; he fell back on the practical things that needed doing no matter how uncertain the future. Retrieving his phaser from the helm console at the front of the shuttle, he held it out to Sulu butt first. "Take it with you," he said. Then, nodding at Haslev. "And don't trust him. He's not worth it."

Inside his helmet, Sulu's face looked gray and grim behind ghost reflections of his surroundings. He reached for the phaser without lifting his eyes, closing his hand instead around Chekov's wrist, and pulling the lieutenant into a quick, fierce hug.

Chekov closed his eyes, fear crowding his chest and making his voice uncharacteristically gruff. "I'll see you soon," he promised.

"You'd better."

Then, there was nothing more to say. They pushed apart by silent consensus, and Sulu turned without hesitating, herding Uhura and Haslev into the airlock. Chekov watched, hand pressed to the portal, as the atmosphere hissed out of the small chamber and the outer door rolled silently aside. It looked cold outside. And dark. And empty. He managed to stay brave long enough for the outer door to seal and hide him from their sight. Then he sank to his knees and leaned his head against the airlock, wondering what in hell he was going to do.

The stars burned in silence, their fires cold and distant across the engulfing blackness of interstellar space. Sulu stepped out toward them, gritting his teeth against the sudden lurch of weightlessness when he left the *Hawking*'s airlock. He let the momentum of his final step carry him slowly away from the shuttle, keeping his gaze nailed to the steady shimmer of a nearby nebula until his stomach adjusted to the sense of perpetual falling.

"Sulu." Uhura's quiet voice emerged from the suit's helmet communicator, close as a whisper in his ear. "Can you hear me?"

"I can hear you." The helmsman let his arms and legs float up to the position they normally found in space—elbows flexed, knees bent as if for sitting. He began to reach up to his chest panel with his right hand, then remembered he still held the phaser in it and lifted his left hand instead to activate his jets. Compressed gases exploded silently from valves in the hardened back of his suit, kicking him toward the nebula he'd chosen as a reference.

"Set your thrusters to maximum velocity," he told

the others. "They should last long enough to get us outside the blast radius."

"What if they don't?" Haslev asked apprehensively.

Sulu took a deep breath, anger at the Andorian bursting through his fierce control for a moment. "Then we'll kick you back toward the shuttle and use the momentum to go the rest of the way!"

"Sulu." There was no reproof in Uhura's voice, only concern and warning. Personal feelings had no place in a deep-space evacuation—their lives were balanced too precariously to allow any emotional reactions to cloud their judgment.

"I know." Sulu didn't glance back at her, keeping his face turned toward the shimmering starscape around them. He forced himself to identify as many systems in it as he could, so he wouldn't have to think about the darkened shuttle disappearing behind them. He found Deneb, first and brightest, with blue-white Spica trailing quietly behind it. Further overhead, Antares gleamed an unmistakable ruby red, with Beta Centauri and Achernar flanking it—

"Sulu!" This time it was Uhura's voice that crackled with emotion, disbelief mingled with elation. "I think—I think I hear the *Enterprise!*"

The helmsman gasped and ducked his chin, pressing his communicator up to maximum reception. A hiss of ominous static overlay the subspace radio, so close it had to be coming from the damaged warp core of the shuttle. Beyond it, he could just hear the rising whistle of a familiar hailing frequency. A jumbled mutter followed it.

Sulu groaned. "I can't make out what they're saying!"

"Something about losing contact with us." Uhura paused and Sulu held his breath, afraid even so slight a noise across their communicator channel would interfere with her reception. "And something about proceeding on impulse power—" The distant voice faded, drowned out by an increasing roar of static from the *Hawking*. Sulu heard Uhura's teeth snap in frustration. "That's all I could manage to get."

"Proceeding under impulse power." The helmsman tried to subdue a leap of desperate hope. "I wonder if they meant us or them?"

He heard Uhura pull in a startled breath. "Could they move the *Enterprise* with the hull breached?"

"If they went slowly enough, they could." Somehow, the stars no longer looked so impossibly distant and cold to Sulu. "And if Captain Kirk guessed we had a problem with the shuttle, I'm betting that's exactly what he'd do."

"Yes. Yes, he would." Uhura paused. "But can he get here soon enough?"

Sulu frowned and used his small wrist jets to swing himself around. Uhura and Haslev were only odd-shaped shadows against the surrounding stars, their faces barely illuminated by the interior lights of their helmets. Behind them, the *Hawking* had receded to an equally small patch of darkness in the sky. He did a crude mental triangulation off Deneb, Beta Centauri, and Achernar, comparing their positions to the final glimpse he remembered of them through the shuttle's viewscreen.

"It looks like the shuttle made it about a tenth of the way back to the *Enterprise* before we evacuated," he guessed. "Even with the hull breach, the *Enterprise* can probably move at triple our impulse speed. They should be in transporter range in about—" Sulu glanced back at the *Hawking*, willing its magnetic shielding to stay intact that long. "—an hour."

"I hope we have locator beacons built into these suits." The sudden intrusion of Haslev's voice startled Sulu. The Andorian had been silent for so long, Sulu had almost managed to forget he was there. "Otherwise, how will your ship find us with their transporter beam?"

"We have beacons," Sulu said shortly. He hit his wrist jets again and let the slow momentum of his turn carry him around to his original position. It was too hard to watch the distant shuttle, knowing that at any moment it could explode into an inferno of surging antimatter.

"Well, how do you turn them on?" Haslev persisted. "I can't find the switch for mine."

Sulu didn't reply, staring at a small bluish star midway between the unmistakable bright fires of Spica and Procyon. It had been invisible until now, perhaps hidden under the dark red dust of his reference nebula. Unlike all the stars around it, it seemed to be growing in intensity.

After another moment of silence, Uhura answered for Sulu. "The locator beacon is activated automatically, Mr. Haslev, whenever the ventilation system in the suit comes on." Her voice altered, as if she'd read something in the helmsman's body stance. "Sulu, is something wrong?"

"Maybe." As Sulu watched, the small star slowly brightened until it rivaled Spica's glare. "We've got a ship coming in from one eighty-three mark seven."

"The *Enterprise?*" Hope and disbelief mingled oddly in Uhura's voice.

Sulu shook his head, then remembered she wouldn't be able to see it. "Not from that quadrant, and not that fast. Someone else must have heard our distress call—someone closer than the *Enterprise.*"

He turned his head to meet her troubled gaze through the space that separated them. "We won't be able to tell who they are until they come out of warp speed. By then, they'll be close enough to catch our suit beacons."

"So what?" Haslev sniffed. "Whoever they are, they're coming to rescue us, aren't they?"

"Maybe." Minutes crawled by, slow as their creeping progress away from the shuttle. Sulu never took his eyes off the blue fleck of fire, now brighter than anything else in the sky. It braked out of warp speed in a last nova-bright burst, then resolved into the battered contours of a hauling ship, blunt-nosed and moving faster than any cargo ship had a right to. He groaned. "That's what I was afraid of. It's the *Umyfymu.*"

Chapter Fifteen

"THE ORION DESTROYER that stopped us before?" Uhura bumped into him when he maneuvered his suit around to watch the military ship. "What do you think they'll do?"

"I don't know." The Orion destroyer hovered just behind the *Hawking,* and Sulu guessed it was probing at the shuttle with invisible sensor beams. He absently put out a hand to stop Uhura from bouncing away, firing one wrist jet to keep them on their original course. "If they're scanning Federation frequencies, they'll know we're here. I don't know what they'll do about it."

"Why, pick us up, of course." The surprise in Haslev's voice seemed genuine. "The Orions want me."

Sulu glanced over Uhura's shoulder, frowning at the Andorian as he drifted closer. "I thought you said they wanted you dead."

"Well, yes," Haslev admitted. "But that was before I—er—absconded with the results of my work. Now, they just want me back working for them again." He shrugged with his antennae inside the helmet. "Otherwise, they'll be out all the money they spent."

"And Orions aren't known for being generous." Sulu watched the *Umyfymu* shear suddenly away from the shuttle, and winced. "I think they just discovered the problem in the warp core."

"Do you think they beamed Chekov out?" Uhura asked.

"They might have, if they thought he was Haslev." Even as he said that, the dull ache in Sulu's gut told him he didn't believe it. The Orion ship circled the shuttle, its running lights blinking as haphazardly as any tramp freighter but the smooth curve of its trajectory a dead giveaway of powerful thrusters under its rusty shell. "I just hope they don't decide to blow the shuttle up before it explodes."

"But that would make it explode anyway!" Uhura protested.

"Hey, no one ever said Orions were smart." Sulu's fingers tightened uselessly around his phaser, his palm damp with sweat inside his glove. He watched the *Umyfymu* come closer, breath rasping in his throat.

"Well, at least they're not blowing the shuttle up." Uhura's gloved hand tightened tensely around Sulu's wrist. "They'll be in beaming distance in another minute or two, won't they?"

"Yes." The grip on his arm gave Sulu an idea. He tugged Uhura around to his other side, then reached out for Haslev. The Andorian didn't try to evade him, merely gave him a puzzled look as they drifted closer.

"What are you doing?"

"Making sure we all get beamed over together."

Sulu wrapped a gloved hand around Haslev's upper arm, then lifted the phaser pistol and carefully aimed it at the alien's head. "And making sure we have something to bargain with once we get there."

"Hey!" Haslev squirmed inside his grip, but the Andorian's greater strength gave him no advantage in space without gravity for leverage. "You can't do that—"

A brilliant blast of light interrupted him, stabbing through the darkness toward them. For one horrible moment, Sulu thought it was the shuttle finally exploding. Then he saw his suit's polarizing filters slam down across his face plate and realized he was seeing the deadly radiance of a phaser blast. It skated overhead, missing them by only a few kilometers.

Sulu tightened his grip on Haslev's arm, fingers digging fiercely into the insulated fabric of the Andorian's suit. "I thought you said the Orions wanted you alive!" he shouted across the sudden crackle of subspace static as the *Umyfymu*'s shields shimmered into place.

"They do! They have to!" Haslev's face was hidden behind his own polarizers, but his voice was numb with shock. "I stole everything from them when I left—my notes, my computer models, the prototype device—"

Another Orion phaser blast cracked the interstellar night, all the more terrifying for its silence. Sulu closed his eyes and tensed himself for annihilation, then opened them again a moment later, surprised to find himself still alive.

"That wasn't anywhere near as close as the first shot," Uhura observed in a voice that sounded unnaturally calm.

"It wasn't?" Sulu scowled as the Orion ship swerved

away from them in an almost evasive maneuver. "What the hell—"

The answer came to him an instant before he saw the returning flare of light, exploding out from somewhere behind them. Sulu cursed and pulsed his wrist jets to swing them in that direction. The familiar silvery gleam of the ship looming behind them made his throat tighten. Despite the ugly gash across her disk, there was no mistaking that silhouette.

"It's the *Enterprise!*" He heard astonishment and relief melt through the frozen surface of Uhura's voice. "How did she get here so fast?"

"By taking a little damage." Sulu lifted the hand she clung to and pointed at the blackened craters near the hull breach, where the ship's incomplete shields had let micrometeorites through. The iridescent shimmer of the starship's defenses weakened noticeably across that stretch. "God, I hope the Orions don't notice that. If they concentrate their phasers on it—"

"I don't think Captain Kirk is going to give them time to notice anything." Uhura ducked her head reflexively as another blinding phaser blast knifed past them. "I just hope he knows we're out here."

"It doesn't matter if he does." The grim realization sank into Sulu as he spoke. "He can't beam us on board with the ship's shields up, and he won't endanger the whole ship just for three people. He'll fight this battle just as he would if we were still on board—"

"But one of the three people is *me!*" Haslev wailed. "Your captain can't leave me out here to die!"

"I don't see why not." His sense of humor came to Sulu's rescue at that last, releasing the tense knot lodged in his throat. "You have to admit, it would solve a lot of problems."

The Andorian swung around to glare at him, but

even as he opened his mouth to speak, he paused, glittered briefly—

—and materialized inside an unfamiliar transporter room, with Sulu and Uhura beside him.

Kirk braced himself against the bridge railing, folding double as the *Enterprise* lurched and bucked under another rake of Orion phasers. Stressed hull supports groaned in tandem with the higher wail of internal ship alarms. "Damage report!" Kirk shouted, not even waiting for the deck to settle beneath him.

The lieutenant at the engineering console scrambled to his knees beside his chair. "We've lost partial screens across the lower decks, sir. Mr. Scott has a crew working to restore them now."

"Orion shields are showing phaser damage, too, Captain," Mullen reported from the weapons station. "Particularly in the forward hulls. Should we concentrate our assault there?"

"No!" Kirk pushed upright, still gripping the rail with one hand as he glared at the viewscreen to track the *Umyfymu*'s looping flight. "That forward radiation shielding is just for disguise—they're sacrificing it to draw our fire. Keep hammering at her central hull." He half-turned to Goldstein at communications. "See if you can raise the Orion commander. I want to know what the hell he thinks he's doing firing on a Federation vessel."

"Aye, sir!"

Phaser fire slashed across the viewscreen, and another impact rocked the bridge. Kirk almost expected the flooring to buckle from the blast.

"They're focusing their shots on the hull breach, sir," the engineering lieutenant reported grimly. "We're losing shield integrity there."

"Bhutto!" Kirk leapt forward to slap the back of the navigator's chair. "Swing the ship around! Keep that area out of the Orions' line of fire. Spock——" The science officer was already bent over his sensors. "Any sign of that second Orion ship?"

The Vulcan's eyes were the only thing that moved while he studied his screens. "Sensors detect a very distant warp trace in sector four fifty-nine, Captain." He glanced aside to Kirk. "Either the *Mecufi*, or the unidentified sensor ghost we noted earlier. In either case, the reading shows no signs of approaching us."

"Keep an eye on it." Kirk's hands clenched rhythmically at his sides. "They could be waiting in reserve, hoping to join the battle when we don't expect them." He couldn't help shooting a keen glance back at the viewscreen, asking Goldstein, "Any luck with that contact, Ensign?"

"Coming through now, sir. I'll inset it on the main screen."

A small block of light and color exploded in the lower right-hand corner of the starfield. Kirk recognized the thick jade features and woven beard of *Umyfymu*'s commander, his image glaringly backlit by a host of electrical fires. The Orion's bejeweled teeth looked almost purple in the harsh lighting. "I presume you called to surrender, *f'deraxt'la*."

Kirk tightened his grip on the back of his command chair. "I called to remind you that firing on a Starfleet vessel is an act of war. The Federation will not tolerate Orion aggression against a defenseless starship——"

"Defenseless!" The Orion's grunt of laughter made his teethwork flash. "Not exactly defenseless," he snarled, slamming a smoking panel with one hand. "Besides, little mammal, this is not an act of war—this is an act of punishment."

Kirk drew back, disgusted. "Punishment for what?"

"You received stolen military technology from an agent of the Orion government! In Orion penal codes, such possession is classed as piracy." The commander twisted his mouth into a grimace and leaned closer to the screen. "What does *your* government do to pirate ships, *f'deraxt'la?*"

Kirk scowled. "Mostly, we chase them back across the Orion border."

"Really?" The Orion sounded genuinely surprised. "Well, we blow them up." He jerked his attention aside, ears pulling back in what could only be Orion pleasure when a growl of excitement swelled from somewhere off-screen. "I understand your screens are failing across the spot of damaged hull," he remarked, his smile growing as he turned back to Kirk. "Are you sure you don't want to surrender?"

Kirk bit off the first thing he thought to say, and made a chopping gesture behind his back at Goldstein. "Get him off my screen."

The Orion's image shattered and dispersed to blend with the stars again.

Spinning his empty command chair to face him, Kirk vented some of his frustration by slapping a hand on the intercom button. "Scotty."

"Engineering, Scott here."

"Isn't there anything we can do to shore up the screens across that breach?" On the screen, the *Umyfymu* swept around to begin another approach.

As if he could see what faced Kirk so clearly, Scott said, "Not with the Orions pounding away at it, Captain."

Damn.

"I've tried to keep the breach turned away, sir." Bhutto kept her attention tight on her panel, plotting

201

against the Orions' position on the astrogator even as she spoke. "They move a lot faster than we do right now."

Kirk nodded, angry at himself for taking his frustrations out on his crew. "I know." He dropped into the command chair and let momentum turn it to face the front of the bridge. "Ensign Mullen—how much power can we shunt to starboard phasers?"

The ensign flicked a glance at his boards, lifting his eyebrows with a shrug. "As much as you want, sir. We've taken no damage in any of our phaser banks."

Kirk actually let himself smile. "Good." He thumbed the intercom switch again. "Scotty, I want all the power you can spare directed to the starboard phasers."

"Whatever you say, sir."

"Ensign Mullen, cancel all commands to the starboard banks from your console—return fire with port phasers only."

Mullen nodded shortly, a thin frown of incomprehension between his eyes, but he did as he was told. "Starboard banks locked out, sir. Portside ready to go."

Kirk swung to face behind him. Spock was already waiting, hands in lap, for his commands. "Mr. Spock, please program our starboard phasers for continuous wide-beam emission. Phase-shift their frequency to depolarize the Orion phaser strikes, and make sure you cover the area above the starboard phaser banks as well as the hull breach."

Spock offered his captain a look of dry reproach. "This *is* standard procedure when using phasers as a depolarizing defense system, Captain."

"I *know,* Spock, but it's been a while since we tried this trick." He quirked one corner of his mouth into a wry little grin. "I just wanted to make sure you remembered."

Spock, as expected, didn't seem amused.

A tense buzzing from communications caught Kirk's attention even as Spock turned to his panel. "Mr. Goldstein?" He twisted an alarmed look over one shoulder. "Problems?"

"Yes, sir—" Goldstein looked up with one hand to his earpiece, blue eyes bleak and uncertain. "We've just lost two of the suit locator signals, sir. We're no longer in contact with the shuttle crew."

Alone on board the *Hawking,* Chekov shouted a string of pungent oaths, kicking a helmet in frustration after ten wasted minutes of trying to get out of his sling one-handed.

The strap around his neck was twisted into a constricting rope by the time he fell into one of the empty passenger seats. McCoy, damn him, had been smarter than Chekov gave him credit for. Without being obvious, he'd strapped on Chekov's sling so that it couldn't be undone without a second hand. A belt across his chest pinned his arm to his side; he couldn't reach the buckle to loosen that band, and he couldn't lift off the neck strap unless he could raise his arm. Desperate fear burned through him again, and he kicked the seat in front of him for lack of anything more constructive to do.

If he hadn't given Sulu his phaser, he could have tried to burn through the chest strap with a low heat setting. As it was, he didn't even have so much as a dinner knife with which to attack the webbing. Even the twists of shrapnel littered among the environmental suits were too brittle with nitrogen-cold to be useful. If only—

He stopped, turning in his seat to frown at the wreck behind him. Silver-white pools of liquid nitrogen still drizzled from behind the environmental suit compartment. It boiled away with a secret hiss, kissing a hollow trail of frost along the deck where it passed. Reaching out with one foot, Chekov stepped gently on one of the ice-whitened scraps of metal, and it splintered into dust beneath his boot.

True hope speared through him for the first time since the explosion. He bounded across the aisle to snatch up his jacket and loop it around his hand. It made an awkward bundle, but he could move inside it well enough to fumble a piece of shrapnel off the floor without freeze-burning his fingers. Jacket fabric crackled as it fought to equalize temperatures with the metal, and Chekov tried not to think about how quickly the cold would eat through to him as he squatted beside the cabinet door to scoop up a thin puddle of nitrogen.

Contact with his body heat evaporated the liquid faster than it could run down the chest strap's width. Glossy ice still hissed along the nylon fibers, though, and the ephemeral touch of nitrogen on his skin sliced across his nerves like a painless knife. A second meager dousing froze a band wide enough to form its own stress fracture; he barely had to twist the strap to shatter the frozen fibers.

Much as he appreciated the need for pampering his arm just now, Chekov still felt better once he'd struggled the sling over his head. Being strapped down made him feel too much like an invalid, too helpless in a situation already out of his control. He carefully rotated his shoulder joint while he scooted suit pieces around with his foot. He'd lied to Sulu, a little, at least; he could move the arm well enough, but it was weak and wouldn't last long. The muscle across the back of his shoulder burned with fatigue after hefting nothing heavier than one of the intact suit torsos. So perhaps his justification had been only half a lie. After all, he probably wouldn't be able to lift his arm at all by the time he'd cannibalized even one useful environmental suit.

The torso he squirmed into was scarred across the front, a finger-deep gouge angling from shoulder to hip while still managing to miss the suit's more vital functions. He felt comforted by the shell's bulky weight, almost believing he could leave this floating deathtrap if he had to, maintain a minimal atmosphere, possibly even survive. Fitting the one good sleeve onto the body of the suit, he stayed gloveless long enough to kneel in the bottom of the locker and search for a repair kit not blown apart by the explosion.

He couldn't find one.

The alloy patches from countless suit repair kits peppered the floor; two-part sealant pooled among them and was already hardening where both parts had run together. Smoothing out a tear between unsteady fingers, he scooped up a gobbet of sealant and smeared it thickly on the suit trousers laid out beside him. It took two patches to cover the tear, and another fingerful of sealant to fix it all into place. The next hole was even bigger, though, and he was only halfway down its length before the puddles of sealant on the floor had thickened beyond the point where he could scrape them up. Then he had to crawl away from the cramped workspace to scrub his hand clean on the remnants of his sling. He didn't have enough sealant to finish fixing even one environmental suit; the last thing he needed was to glue his fingers together, as well.

A shriek of sirens tore past him from the front of the ship. Jerking upright, fear bolting through him like lightning, he listened to the computer's dispassionate singsong without being able to breathe. "Core temperature one thousand seven hundred degrees Centigrade. Containment decay irreversible; core breach imminent. Estimated time to breach: twenty-three minutes forty-three seconds."

Chapter Sixteen

SULU SPUN AROUND, blinking as his eyes tried to adjust from interstellar space to the sudden glare of arc lights. He found himself confronting a circle of uniformed and blue-visored forms, and pressed his phaser firmly to Haslev's helmet. "If you try to beam us away, I'll shoot him," he warned through his external suit communicator.

A ripple of ironic laughter answered him instead of the Orion growls he expected. "Feel free to do so," a dry voice said. "It will save us the trouble of arresting him and taking him home for trial."

Sulu jerked in surprise, realizing that what he'd taken for visors were actually bright blue faces. He heard Muav Haslev's agonized groan across the helmet channel.

"You're Andorians!" Sulu reached up with his free hand to unlock his helmet and tug it off his shoulders, so they could see his Starfleet collar. "Is this Federation ship?"

"Passenger transport *Shras,* currently on paramil tary assignment with the Andorian Reserve Fleet. The nearest Andorian stepped forward, bowing wit the old-fashioned courtesy of his race. He was a ta man, with a long and bony face. "I'm Captain Po Kanin."

"Good." Sulu swung toward the technician sittin behind the transporter console. "We left a Starflee officer stranded on that shuttle out there. Beam hir over at once."

"Please." Uhura lifted off her own helmet, a flare c hope lighting her eyes. "If you heard our distress cal you know it's urgent."

The Andorian glanced uncertainly at his captair "Sir?"

"Starfleet officers hold automatic command autho ity over all planetary reserves," Captain Kanin tol him, one antenna flexing in gentle reproof. "C course, we will oblige the lieutenant comman er's request. Scan for the shuttle's coordinates, an lock—"

Sulu's feet kicked out from under him withou warning, staggering him back against the transporte chamber's wall. He saw Uhura catch at Haslev whe he stumbled onto his knees. Bulkheads groane around them with the recoil from a photon torped strike, and the crew of the *Shras* broke into shouts c alarm; several scrambled for the exit.

"Captain!" A nervous voice crackled across th ship's intercom. "We're being fired on by the Orio police cruiser *Mecufi!*"

"Shields up! Take evasive action immediately!" second thunderous blow rocked the *Shras,* and Po

Kanin let out a hissing curse. "How did they find us?" he demanded, turning on the gray-faced officer next to him. "I told you to plot a course that would make us look like a sensor ghost!"

Sulu struggled to his feet, made clumsy by the rigid metallic fabric of his suit. He pushed himself off the shuddering wall toward Muav Haslev. "Take off your helmet!" he ordered, slapping at the release buttons on his shoulders. "As long as you're using the suit ventilator, its distress signal is still going out—"

The alien yelped in dismay and flung the helmet away. His face was ashen with distress. "Why didn't you tell me?"

"I had other things on my mind." Sulu swung around in time to see the Andorian captain stride through the doorway with his crew, obviously headed for the bridge. The helmsman's mouth hardened with determination. "Come on. Let's see if we can still convince them to rescue Chekov."

Uhura threw him a puzzled glance as the Andorian ship shuddered under a third glancing blow. "But the shields are up! There's no way we can beam Chekov on board now."

"No, but we can dock and pick him up." Sulu tossed the phaser over to her. "Here, you take this. We might still need to use it on Haslev for bargaining."

"You can't do that!" Haslev's pale antennae quivered with apprehension. "You heard what they said— they'll let you shoot me!"

"You'd better hope they were joking." Sulu stepped off the transporter pad and headed for the door. Uhura prodded Haslev with the phaser, forcing him to follow.

Outside the transporter room, one narrow corridor ran along what looked like the entire length of the ship, anchored at either end with manual access shafts instead of turbolifts. Sulu guessed the passenger transport had been modeled after a Starfleet courier: perhaps five decks high and only wide enough for two rows of cabins on its passenger decks. He pounded past silent doorways to the forward access shaft, feeling the ship shiver as it was pushed to its highest warp capability.

"They're trying to run away!" Uhura crowded Haslev into the access shaft, and pushed him to climb up the ladder rungs behind Sulu. "They're going to leave the *Enterprise* to fight the Orions by herself!"

"Why not?" Sulu asked breathlessly, pulling himself up past another empty passenger deck. He heard Haslev's reluctant footsteps climbing after him. "You heard the Andorian captain say he'd been hiding from us as a sensor ghost. No one can accuse him of abandoning a battlefield if no one knows he was there in the first place."

Uhura's voice echoed in the ladderway. "But *we* know he was there."

"Exactly what I'm going to point out to him." Sulu heaved himself up the last of the rungs and out onto a long teardrop-shaped bridge. A small cluster of uniformed Andorians milled about near the main viewscreen, ignoring their posts to watch something there. Otherwise, the bridge, like the rest of the ship, looked deserted.

Sulu reached down to pull a panting Haslev out of the shaft, then stepped back when Uhura scrambled up after him. "Looks like they only brought a handful of crew on this trip," he commented.

"And a worthless handful at that." Uhura used her phaser to push Haslev away from the access shaft, her dark face carved with determination. "Let's go. We don't have any time to waste."

Haslev turned reluctantly toward the front of the bridge. "You know, it might already be too late."

"Shut up." Sulu strode past him, staggering a little when another photon torpedo exploded near the *Shras*. He scowled. "One of the Orions must be chasing us—that was too close to be a miss on the *Enterprise*."

"Then what is everybody doing standing around?" Uhura toggled her suit's external speaker, lifting her amplified voice across the chaos of shouts and ship alarms. "All hands to battle stations! Repeat, all hands to battle stations *immediately!*"

The Andorian crew members scattered like fragments from an exploding nebula, clearing the space in front of the viewscreen. Sulu saw Pov Kanin swing his captain's console around to stare at them in astonishment. Behind him, the curving viewscreen was dominated by the sleek, predatory shape of the Orion police cruiser *Mecufi*. Sulu's scowl deepened. The steady angle of the sensor image told him that the *Shras* was simply trying to outrun her pursuer.

"Is this what you call evasive action?" Sulu crossed to the helm panel in two strides and yanked at the shoulder of the Andorian manning it. "I'm a Starfleet pilot," he snapped, stripping off his bulky gloves. "Let me take this helm before we get blown to Sigma One!"

The crew member threw a quick look at her captain, then scrambled out of her seat. Sulu slid in behind the panel, scanning its layout, then tapping in a swift series of flight maneuvers. The *Shras* slewed abruptly sideways.

"What—" Kanin's voice broke off as another photon torpedo exploded brilliantly across the screen, far off the port side of the ship. The *Shras* barely quivered in response. "What are you doing?"

"Getting us out of torpedo range, I hope." Sulu glanced over at the navigation panel, not trusting the gray-faced navigator to give him an accurate estimate of distances. The *Mecufi* had overshot them when they turned, and was now turning herself to cross over her previous path. Sulu waited until she'd found her new heading, then spiraled the Andorian ship off on a completely different course. The *Mecufi* shifted again and again while Sulu continued the random corkscrew motions, each time losing ground in the chase.

"The Orions would be better off to stay on one course," Kanin observed, leaning across his console to watch Sulu's maneuvers.

Sulu spared him a tight smile. "Don't worry. They'll realize that in a moment. And when they do—" He made one more course alteration, and this time saw no response from the Orion ship. His smile widened while he laid in the course he'd intended to follow all along. "Engineering, give me every ounce of speed you've got."

"Affirmative!"

The *Shras* slowly accelerated, moving away from the Orion cruiser. It took the pursuers several long moments to realize this wasn't just another evasive swing, and by then, the *Shras* had flashed out of torpedo range. The image of the *Mecufi* dwindled behind them, disappearing when the scanners hit the end of their range.

"That should keep them off our backs for a while." Sulu set the ship's scanners around to the front, then glanced over his shoulder at Pov Kanin. "I've set our course to three forty-nine mark four." The Andorian's bony face slid from relief to worry when he recognized the heading. "I don't think you want to be brought up on desertion of battle charges when you get back to Andor."

"But—" Kanin's dark pink eyes narrowed in honest dismay. "But we rescued you!"

"And then abandoned our ship, not to mention our friend in the shuttle. Saving our lives isn't going to make us grateful enough to forget about that." Sulu glanced over at the navigation board, watching the coordinates roll back to familiar numbers as they drew closer to the *Enterprise*. Faint flickers in one corner of the viewscreen showed the starship still battling with the Orion destroyer *Umyfymu*. "We're within hailing distance of the *Enterprise* now. Uhura, can you run the comm and cover Haslev at the same time?"

"No, but I can make Haslev run the comm for me." Uhura nudged the Andorian physicist toward the communications station, waving the technician there out of his seat. "Come on, get moving."

"But as soon as we start broadcasting a signal, the Orions will know where we are!" Haslev protested.

"No, they won't. We'll use a coded tight-beam channel to the *Enterprise*. The Orions will never even know we sent it." Uhura prodded him again, this time with the phaser. "Hurry up. We've got to let Captain Kirk know who we are before the *Enterprise* fires at us."

"Oh, this is just great. If the Orions don't manage to kill us, your friends on the starship probably will." Haslev sat down with a theatrical groan, antennae drooping in dismay. "Why did I ever think it was a good idea to stow away on a Starfleet ship?"

Uhura gave him an exasperated look. "Probably

because anyone else would have killed you by now, just to shut you up. Now, start calling."

"Captain!" Goldstein's excited voice cut across the tense hum on the *Enterprise*'s bridge. "I'm receiving a coded message on Federation frequency! It's being sent tight-beam, sir."

Kirk swung his command console to face the viewscreen, trying not to hope for too much. "Put it on-screen, Ensign."

An unfamiliar bridge, stark with battle lights, shimmered into focus at the lower corner of the viewscreen. The edges of the picture glimmered with coding static, ensuring that no one could break into the channel.

"This is Captain James T. Kirk of the—" The captain stopped himself as soon as the picture steadied on familiar Starfleet environmental suits and equally familiar faces. "Sulu, Uhura—where are you?"

"On the Andorian Reserve Fleet ship *Shras*." Sulu's face was tense and slick with sweat, his hair ruffled from being recently inside an environmental suit helmet. Behind him, a slim Andorian in the uniform of a planetary reserve captain fidgeted in a command chair near Uhura, looking unhappy to be there at all. "Our current heading is three forty-nine mark four, approximately twenty thousand kilometers from you and closing."

"That corresponds with the position of our sensor ghost, Captain," Spock said quietly from behind Kirk. "And if my readings are correct—"

The *Enterprise* rocked with the force of a nearby torpedo burst, and Kirk swore as Mullen looked up nervously from the weapons console. "Damage to the aft phaser banks, Captain."

Too close, too close. "Alter course to one sixty mark six," Kirk snapped at the helmsman. "Bring our port phasers into range. Fire!"

"—the *Shras* was recently attacked by the Orion cruiser *Mecufi*, and driven away," Spock finished calmly.

"Or ran away." Kirk gave the Andorian captain an eagle-hard look and saw the man flinch with a lavender blush. He was definitely *Shras*'s commander, then, and not particularly proud of what he'd done. "I presume that was before you took over the helm, Sulu?"

"Aye, sir. The Orions are still chasing us, but we've managed to make it out of their firing range. I'm laying in a course that will make us look like a sensor ghost to them now." Sulu took a deep breath. "Sir, Chekov is still on board the *Hawking*. Request permission to dock and remove him."

"You left Chekov in the middle of a battle zone?" Kirk decided this wasn't the time to tackle the question of what Chekov was doing on the shuttle to begin with.

Uhura and Sulu exchanged careful looks, and the helmsman shrugged as if to some question Uhura hadn't asked. "We didn't have enough environmental suits for everyone, sir," the communications officer finally replied guardedly. "Most of them were pierced with shrapnel from the explosion—"

"—that destroyed the magnetic shielding," Muav Haslev added from off-screen, his voice bright and helpful, "and left the warp core totally destablized."

"Haslev!" Sulu glared to his right, apparently at the

Andorian scientist, and Uhura hissed something sharp that Kirk didn't quite hear.

"Hey," Haslev complained, "just because you two are willing to die for your friend doesn't mean I am, too."

"Nor I!" The Andorian commander jerked his shoulders back, antennae rigid with outrage. "We are not going to dock with a ship whose containment field could explode at any moment!" He scowled across the channel at Kirk. "Captain, you cannot legally command us to engage in such a suicidal action simply to rescue one missing crewman."

If he had one brave man for every coward he met in the line of duty, Kirk would reckon himself a very lucky man. "It's true," he said tightly, "I can't *command* you to do it, Captain. I can ask—"

"And I can refuse!"

"Yes, you can." Kirk swung his gaze to Sulu, seeing the helmsman's eyes glittering with the same frustration Kirk himself felt. A distant bang shuddered through the *Enterprise*'s deck, and Kirk heard a flurry of alarms wail into life at the engineering station. There wasn't even time left for talking, much less planning an unlikely rescue. "I'm sorry, Sulu. It doesn't look like there's anything we can do."

Sulu clenched his teeth into his lower lip, but nodded stiffly. "Aye, sir," he said in a wooden voice. "I'll await your orders for battle deployment—"

"You mean we're going to stick around and fight with the Orions?" Haslev demanded incredulously. He lumbered on-screen to tug at the Andorian captain's arm, his own environmental suit looking two sizes too big for his effete frame. "Can he make us do that?"

The older Andorian's eyebrows drew together in

annoyance. "The Reserve Fleet's first duty is to aid and support all actions of Starfleet," he said unhappily. "The *Shras* will perform that duty to the utmost."

"Well, I'd rather we didn't," Muav Haslev admitted frankly. The renegade physicist looked back at the viewscreen. "Kirk, let's cut a deal. If I can save your crewman, will you let me out of the rest of this fight?"

"No," Kirk snapped, appalled to even be asked. "But if you save him voluntarily, I'd have to mention that in my report to Starfleet. It might influence your trial."

"Assuming I live long enough to get one!"

"It's my only offer, Haslev." Kirk braced himself while the *Enterprise* swung on swift evasive action. The viewscreen flickered with radiance when a photon torpedo exploded harmlessly above the bridge, nearly overwhelming the incoming signal. "Take it or leave it."

"You Starfleet people are all so adamant," Haslev complained. "Oh, all right—it's a deal."

"How are you going to carry out your end of it?" Sulu burst out, obviously overwhelmed with skepticism. The look of painful hope on Uhura's face helped Kirk understand the helmsman's anger. "How the hell are you going to save Chekov?"

"You'll see." The renegade physicist clapped his hands together, blue face bright with satisfaction. "You'll *all* see."

"See what?" Kirk demanded.

Haslev took a deep, expectant breath, antennae quivering. "Exactly what the Orions paid me for."

Climbing to his feet, Chekov stood for a moment in the *Hawking's* cluttered aisle, torn between clambering up front to verify the computer's report on the warp core, and running for the airlock wearing only half a suit. Death was suddenly a very real presence and not just a frightening possibility. He looked to the airlock door, and his blood ran as crystalline as the nitrogen trails around his feet. Technically, he had the minimum suit required to survive a limited vacuum exposure. He could lock down the joints that should have serviced the suit's legs and left arm, and that would preserve an atmosphere inside the torso and helmet—enough to service his internal organs and brain, although he'd surely lose the unsuited limbs to cell damage and freezing. What was the point of abandoning the shuttle if that were the best he could look forward to?

No! He moved to poise his hand above the airlock controls, trembling. Living was worth any price. For him, it always had been, and always would be. Surviving at all would be miraculous—he couldn't afford to be stingy about the details. Punching the controls to cycle air back into the lock, a sudden rigidity along his muscles startled a gasp from him and locked him immobile. Then, panic was smothered by joy when a familiar silver spray engulfed his vision, and the itching thrill of the transporter beam erased the walls around him.

The new room shimmering into being around him wasn't the *Enterprise*'s transporter room, though. Walls threatened too close on either side, the transporter's fading whine was too loud and close in his ears—and he materialized with only one foot on solid deck. He toppled heavily to his right, unable to catch himself under the weight of the half-suit when his foot came down in some smooth, rounded basin, and he flipped to fall face forward over the edge.

If it hadn't been for the hard shell of the suit, the fall

would have knocked the wind from him. As it was, his face plate cracked against black marble without breaking, and he hung there a moment, fighting to regain his bearings. The deck was a Starfleet deck—another shuttle, he realized, just as he pushed up on one elbow and recognized the molded marble basin beneath him.

"Sulu's lily pond—?"

All other questions were knocked from his mind by a powerful jerk on the back of his suit. He slammed against the far wall without even touching the ground, and his head snapped against the back of his helmet with a silent thunder of pain. Sagging into half-darkness, he gasped when a powerful fist caught the front of his suit and heaved him into the wall again.

"How?!"

Chekov grabbed blindly at the bellowing mammoth in front of him, locking both hands on a forearm that he couldn't even fit his fingers around.

"How were you able to use it?" Lindsey Purviance pressed so close to Chekov that the rust-orange blood from his torn left side smeared the environmental suit like rotten oil. "Tell me what you carry that lets you use the trans-shield anode, *f'deraxt'la,* or I'll snap every bone in your body trying to find it."

Chapter Seventeen

SULU STARED INTENTLY up at the Andorian viewscreen, trying to catch *Hawking*'s fugitive patch of darkness among the stars. He found it hovering in the lower left corner of the viewscreen, overshadowed by the distant white fires exploding between the *Enterprise* and the *Umyfymu*. At this distance, there was no way to tell if Chekov was still aboard.

"What is our position relative to the Orion police cruiser?" Captain Kanin demanded for what must have been the third or fourth time.

Sulu checked the intersecting isopleths on his helm panel, rubbing at the frown of concentration that had gathered between his eyes. He had to maintain a fragile piloting balance: staying inside transporter range of the *Hawking* but out of its probable blast radius, all the while mirroring the *Mecufi*'s course so closely as to look like a sensor ghost to the Orions. The police cruiser was prowling slowly around the section of space where their warp trail had ended, trying to flush them out with random phaser shots through the interstellar darkness.

"We're still about seven thousand kilometers away from the Orions." Sulu lifted his gaze back to the viewscreen, wishing he could somehow tell from the *Hawking*'s shadowed exterior whether Muav Haslev's new technology had worked. It seemed as if the physicist had been down in the transporter room with Uhura for hours, but Sulu knew better than to trust his sense of time in a crisis.

Kanin shifted nervously in his command console. "And our distance from the other ships?"

"Almost fourteen thousand kilometers." Sulu's head jerked around when he heard the unmistakable metallic scrape of bulky environmental suits against the access shaft. Haslev's flaxen head emerged from the ladderway first, antennae waving triumphantly.

"It worked!" The renegade physicist pointed both his thumbs together at Pov Kanin, who stiffened in his chair. Sulu guessed it was an Andorian gesture of contempt. "The beaming technique all your stupid admirals said would never be feasible—I made it work!"

"You *think* you made it work," Uhura corrected, climbing up onto the bridge after him. "We won't know for sure until we get confirmation from the *Enterprise.*" Despite her guarded words, an underlying note of optimism warmed the communications officer's voice.

"You managed to beam Chekov in through their shields?" Even as he asked the question, Sulu felt the same quiver of disbelief that he'd experienced when Haslev first told them what he'd made for the Orions. Of all the lessons drilled into you in Starfleet Academy, one of the most basic was: never transport anything through a ship's defensive shields. The problem wasn't the ability of the beam to go through, but the mess that came out at the other end. Sulu swallowed hard, remembering the red smear that had been Sweeney and Purviance and Gendron.

"I think we got him through." Uhura ducked past Haslev and headed toward the ship's unmanned communications station. "I'm going to contact the *Enterprise* on a tight-beam channel to be sure, but I made Haslev test it on one of our spare suit batteries before we sent Chekov over. The control panel reported coherent reception of the beam at the trans-shield cathode—"

"Trans-shield *anode*," Haslev corrected her sharply. "You have to call it an anode because it attracts the subspace bosons of the transporter beam the same way an anode attracts electrons. That's why the beam can pass through—"

"Did you bring the battery back, to see if it was all right?" Sulu demanded, breaking into the physicist's lecture without ceremony. "Before you sent Chekov over?"

"No," admitted Uhura, tapping open a hailing frequency to the *Enterprise*. "I was afraid to wait too long—it took Haslev forever to reprogram the transporter, and then we had to patch in an extra power unit to make the beam strong enough to go through."

"And furthermore, the technique doesn't work that way!" Haslev snapped, giving Sulu an annoyed look. "The anode device can only *receive* a transporter beam, not create one. To get the battery back, we'd need another trans-shield anode on this ship. And right now, the only one in existence is on your ship."

He lifted a finger and aimed it at Sulu. "In *your* cabin."

"In my cabin?" Sulu's eyes widened when he remembered the multiple break-ins. "So that's why you kept trying to get in there!"

Haslev looked indignant, but before he could reply, Uhura swung around from the communications panel. "Sulu, I'm not getting any response from the *Enterprise,*" she said, frowning. "Not to my hailing, not to my questions about Chekov, nothing."

Sulu glanced up at the screen, trying to find the spider-web explosions of light that marked the distant battle between the *Enterprise* and the *Umyfymu.* "Try scanning all open Starfleet channels," he suggested.

"Scanning." She ran one hand across the communications board, listening intently to the monitor in her ear, then gasped in alarm, "Oh, my God! All I'm getting is the automatic distress signal from the computer—it says it's lost all communication with the bridge!"

The stars burned away as a flare of subspace static seared across the *Enterprise's* viewscreen. Kirk shot a startled glance upward as the bridge lights dimmed and every alarm on every station screamed. "What in God's name?" He couldn't even hear himself above the howl.

Spock's hand closed on his shoulder from behind. "We appear to have been hit by another subspace radiation pulse," the Vulcan shouted, mouth close to his ear.

"How?" Kirk half-stood, turning so that Spock could read his lips if nothing else. "Where did it come from?"

Spock shook his head. "Unknown, Captain. All controls have been rendered inoperable."

Kirk broke away from his first officer to lean over the helmsman's shoulder. The navigation deflector alarm nearly deafened him, and Kirk reached across to deactivate it even as he shouted, "Do we have helm control?"

The pilot only shook his head, struggling with his own blaring panel.

Other alarms died, one by one, leaving Kirk's ears ringing wildly. "Cut impulse drive!" he ordered engineering, just as a phaser hit staggered him against the forward console. "Dammit! Do we still have shields?"

"I can't tell!" Mullen sounded desperate. "My panel's showing no contact with ship's defenses."

"Shields and other automatic systems should not have been affected by the radiation surge," Spock offered. "However, with starboard phaser banks no longer under our control, the depolarizing defense will degenerate into random phaser bursts in one minute fifty-three seconds."

Well, Kirk thought grimly, *at least we'll die with precision.* "Mr. Goldstein, how about communications? Can we send a tight-beam signal on manual control to the last known location of the *Shras?*"

Goldstein picked up his earpiece and turned to his panel. "I can try, sir."

Kirk forced himself to move calmly back to his command chair, not looking up at the hissing viewscreen until after he was seated, his hands clenched on the arms. Static still painted the screen an electric white, and Kirk frowned at the shrouded image for what felt like a very long time before asking, "Does that interference mean we can't transmit?"

Goldstein was silent for a moment, fighting with his board. "I think it's only affecting our reception, sir," he said at last. "But I really can't tell. My panel shows no response on any frequency."

"I suspect our own equipment is at fault, Captain." No longer drowned out by alarms, Spock spoke more calmly from his science console, emergency lights sliding long crimson shadows across his face. "As it did before, the subspace radiation pulse has superimposed its interference patterns onto our viewscreen. Based on our current levels of power consumption, however, I believe the signal transmitter is still operational."

Kirk nodded and turned to face the screen again, staring at it fiercely in the hope he could pierce the interference by sheer force of will. *"Shras,* this is the *Enterprise* calling. A subspace radiation pulse has damaged our helm and shield control, and has left us at the mercy of the Orion destroyer *Umyfymu.* We need immediate diversionary action on your part. Last recorded location of the Orions—" Kirk shot a quick glance at the helm panel, "—was heading two sixty-five mark seven, distance seven thousand kilometers and closing—"

A brilliant burst of torpedo fire shook the ship, staggering several crewmen from their stations. Kirk clung grimly to the helm, eyes narrowed against the scorching light. "Repeat, we need immediate diversionary action! I'm counting on you, Sulu—Kirk out."

Sulu didn't wait for Kirk's image to fade—he was already punching a new course into the helm computer. "Engines, warp three." He sent a blistering look at the hesitant Andorian engineer when he felt no response from the ship. *"Now!* Or I'll have Uhura shoot you for disobeying Starfleet orders."

The *Shras* jerked abruptly out of her hovering circle, darting off toward the brilliant firefight in the distance. Sulu watched the navigation screen intently, gauging their distance from the approaching battle zone. He sensed that Uhura had come to stand behind him.

"Sulu, this bothers me," she said quietly. "How could the *Enterprise* get hit with another subspace radiation pulse? The last one was at Sigma One, and we're light-years away from there by now. Doesn't that seem odd?"

"Very odd."

Uhura paused. "Do you think it's some kind of new weapon the Orions have?"

The sharp metallic squeak of environmental suit joints brought Sulu's head around. Muav Haslev was wriggling in his seat, a distinctly guilty expression on his pale blue face. Several disjointed slivers of information suddenly locked together in Sulu's mind, and the picture they formed seared him with anger. Swinging around from the helm console, he leaned forward to glare at the physicist. "It's not a weapon," Sulu accused. "It's Haslev's trans-shield anode!"

The Andorian's wince confirmed his guess, and Sulu snorted in disgust, turning away to meet Uhura's puzzled frown.

"A burst of subspace radiation must be created as a side effect of someone beaming over to the trans-shield anode," Sulu explained. "The first pulse at Sigma One came from Haslev, beaming on board the *Enterprise.* This one—" He glared up at the embattled ships still dwarfed by distance on the screen. "This one came from us, beaming Chekov over to the ship."

Uhura spun to stare at Haslev. "Is that true?"

"Well, basically—" The physicist rubbed sheepishly at one antenna. "There are still a few flaws in the anode system, I admit. But the radiation effects are merely transient—"

"In the middle of a battle, even a transient instrument failure can be fatal!" Uhura's normally soft voice was stiff with outrage. "Why didn't you warn us?"

"Because you were the ones who insisted I use the thing!"

Behind them, Captain Kanin cleared his throat. "If the radiation effects are transient, can't we just wait for the *Enterprise* to get its defenses back?" he suggested uneasily.

"No." Sulu went back to calculating vectors on the helm console, preparing for battle as the explosions in the sky drew nearer. "Last time this happened, we lost helm control for almost three minutes right after the subspace pulse faded. If that happens to weapons control this time, the *Enterprise* will be annihilated. We have to go help them."

"But this is idiocy!" Captain Kanin protested, his voice thick with disbelief. "How can we rescue a Constitution-class starship from anything? We're only a passenger transport—we don't even have any weapons!"

"No, but the *Mecufi* does." Somewhere behind them, Sulu knew, the second Orion ship would have noted their sudden appearance on sensors and flung themselves into pursuit. "If we time this right, we can get them to provide Captain Kirk with just the diversion he needs."

Chekov scrabbled to brace his feet against the wall behind him, trying to lift himself high enough in his environmental suit to keep from choking on the collar.

"Tell me!" Purviance roared. His bloody fist rebounded against the suit's breastplate, and Chekov felt the panel snap with frightening ease. "I know you have some extra component. I want the trans-shield anode—give it to me now, or I'll tear it from your steaming organs!"

Chekov's feet slipped on the wall yet again, and his shoulder wrenched with agony against the joint of his suit. "Give you what?" he gasped, teeth clenched and eyes closed. "I don't know what you're talking about!"

Purviance tightened his grip on the suit's front handle and banged Chekov against the wall in warning. "How did you get back on board?"

"I don't know!"

"Liar!"

"How did *you* get here?" Chekov shot back. One foot caught on some irregularity in the wall behind him, and he brought his left hand down to his side on the pretext of balancing himself. "They found your genetic material in that transporter accident—you couldn't have survived."

A growl of laughter roiled out of Purviance, and he brought both hands up to Chekov's suit. "They found Lindsey Purviance's genetic material in the transporter remains," the Orion pointed out. "One human hand was enough to guarantee that. You couldn't have told two bodies from three in that mess, so three sets of DNA let you make your own assumptions. When Gendron sent that transporter tech away, I thought I was going to have to kill myself. It's a good thing your guards are so willing to do what their senior officers tell them to, or I might never have gotten Sweeney into the transporter room."

It was all Chekov could do not to swear at the Orion. "I'm afraid I don't cooperate so well."

"We'll see." All-too-human-seeming eyes narrowed to brutal slits, and Purviance leaned close to breathe white steam against the face plate. "I want to leave this rat hole with my prize, Lieutenant Chekov, but my people's transporter can't reach past your screens. If you come in but I can't go out, then you must have some secret I need." He reached down to grip Chekov's thigh in one beefy hand. "How many bones is this secret worth?"

None, so far as Chekov was concerned. Never taking his eyes off Purviance's face, he braced himself against the wall and swung at that face as hard as he could. His fist collided with Orion muscle knotted as hard as human bone, and he knew in that very instant that striking out had been a mistake. Purviance smashed the visor on his helmet in a single-fisted blow, and Chekov was suddenly pinned to the rear of his helmet with a huge Orion hand clamped across his lower face.

"For that," Purviance purred in a deadly whisper, "I break your jaw."

Chekov twisted away from the suddenly fierce grip, letting his suit take his weight as he kicked out at anything he could hit. He felt one foot contact soundly on living body, and this time the Orion crumpled with a roar of pain and rage. The grip on Chekov's suit abruptly vanished, and Chekov toppled to the deck beside Purviance, tumbling as far from the Orion as he could in the crowded shuttle compartment.

Blood, dried to a thick burnt-orange, matted the saboteur's uniform from elbow to knee. He hadn't had the benefit of McCoy's skilled treatment after last night's firefight, and Chekov knew that was all to his advantage. Rolling to his knees, he seized the edge of Sulu's lily pond and twisted his whole body into the swing. A stray environmental suit battery spun away from the basin, and the pond smashed into the Orion just as he rose to all fours. He went down again with a grunt of surprise, and Chekov lurched to his feet to hit Purviance a second time, and a third. On the fourth blow, the cast marble burst apart with a dull, fractured boom, and a glitter of silver scattered to the floor among the pieces. Electronic components. This trans-shield anode thing? Molded into the body of the lily pond? But why?

Chekov decided to consider the mystery later. All that mattered now was that if Purviance wanted this anode badly enough to have stolen the pond from Sulu's room, Chekov couldn't afford to let him have it. Ducking around Purviance's groaning form, he scooped up the largest piece of the device and scrambled with it for the door.

The main shuttle compartment was empty, the hatch to the outside closed. Their shuttle was still in the *Enterprise*'s hangar bay, though—Chekov could see bulkheads, other shuttles through the forward viewscreen. That meant a certain safety waited for him if he could get outside this craft. He skidded to a stop in front of the door to the outside, only to be plowed to the deck by a massive force from behind him before he could even open the hatch.

When visible light flashed across the *Enterprise*'s viewscreen—tearing apart to reveal a static-charged starfield and the *Umyfymu* arrowing straight down the *Enterprise*'s throat—Kirk nearly jumped to his feet in alarm and surprise. "Phasers?" he demanded.

"Negative, sir," Mullen shouted back even as the hull rang with a photon torpedo launch many decks below. "I've launched torpedoes to compensate, but the Orions are evading most of them."

"Unlike us." He saw the deceptively warm glow of another phaser shot just before the *Enterprise* rocked from the hit. "Dammit, Sulu, where are you?"

"Captain," Spock said, "I am having no success at reprogramming weapons control through the main computer. I suggest phasers be manually activated by their respective crews. Their aim may be less accurate, but even misguided phasers—"

"—are better than none at all," Kirk finished for him. "Do it, Mullen."

"Aye, sir."

Kirk felt his heart flutter with anxiety as the *Umyfymu* skimmed just beyond the *Enterprise*'s screens, her phasers swinging wide when the *Enterprise* rolled to compensate. "That still leaves us with the problem of our unshielded hull."

"Indeed." Spock sounded unconcerned, but thoughtful. "Manual control cannot align the phasers precisely enough to depolarize incoming fire."

Kirk nodded, his mind already rushing ahead of Spock's words. "Then we'll just have to get the Orions to fire somewhere else. Ensign Mullen—" He turned to lock eyes with the young security officer. "Load another photon torpedo in the port tube—then order it to detonate just outside the *Enterprise's* shields."

Mullen hesitated, his hand poised above his board. "Just outside *our* shields, Captain?"

"That's right. I want it to look like one of the Orions' torpedoes blew a hole in our port side."

Mullen grinned and nodded excitedly. "That way they'll transfer their attack to our strong port shields, away from our weaker starboard ones!" One hand flashed across his panel while the other cradled the torpedo launch controls. Kirk swung his chair to face the viewscreen just as the deck shivered and Mullen announced, "Torpedo away!"

The detonation was almost instantaneous. Plasma fingers roiled across the edges of their screens, shimmering blue and red and amber, then faded to a flickering corona that lingered just long enough to draw a bloom of Orion phaser fire. Mullen yelped, "It worked!" and Kirk nodded with dark satisfaction.

"The Orions may be tricky," he said, "but that doesn't mean they can't be tricked." Damage reports still chattered over the communications panel, though, and warnings and telltales lit half the boards on the bridge. "Let's just hope that buys us enough time for the *Shras* to get here."

Chapter Eighteen

MUAV HASLEV GROANED, watching as the viewscreen of the Andorian bridge filled with the light of distant battle. The sector of space between the *Enterprise* and the *Umyfymu* now resembled a tiny nebula, bright with debris and the streaky afterglow of photon explosions. "Commander Sulu, if you take us in there, you're going to get us killed!"

"No, I'm not." Sulu began feeding a complex series of instructions into the helm buffer, preparing for the light-swift maneuvers to come. "That is, not unless you distract me with annoying comments in the middle of piloting. Uhura, I'm going to need you on navigation."

"I'm there." The communications officer tugged the gray-faced Andorian navigator out of his chair and slid in beside Sulu. Her coffee-dark eyes scanned the screen, her face smooth with the expression of taut calm that emergencies always brought out in her.

"Orion police cruiser *Mecufi* now in firing range."
Sulu threw the ship into a twisting roll as a phaser shot
seared past them. "Distance three thousand kilometers and closing."

"Exactly where we want them." Sulu scanned the
complex parabolic equations spiraling across his
screen, verifying his calculations one last time, then
spared a swift glance for the engineering station.
"What's the maximum speed you can give me?"

The Andorian's antennae flattened tensely. "Warp
four if you need it, but only for a few minutes."

"All right. Wait for my mark." Sulu stared up at the
viewscreen, watching the individual shapes of the
Enterprise and the *Umyfymu* slowly resolve out of the
glare. The path he planned to follow between the two
ships wove through multiple coronas of torpedo explosions, lit from within by the occasional opalescent
fire of phaser blasts. The helmsman kept his gaze fixed
on the deceptively awkward shape of the Orion destroyer, his fingers hovering over his board.

"Orion police cruiser *Mecufi* now two thousand
kilometers and closing," Uhura said tensely.

"Warp four—*now!*" Sulu kicked in his first preprogrammed maneuvers, and the *Shras* leapt into the
battle zone. The viewscreen flared with static as they
burst through a photon corona, then cleared again to
show them the nearly invisible shimmer of the
Umyfymu's warp trail just ahead of them. Faster than
human reflexes could have sent it, the little Andorian
transport shot into a looping spiral around the larger
ship, close enough to set off all the Orions' proximity
alarms.

"*That* should give the *Umyfymu* something else to
shoot at besides the *Enterprise*." Sulu clenched his
teeth when the *Shras* rose with a bone-jarring swoop

to avoid the destroyer's sudden barrage of phaser fire. "Now, let's see if we can get the *Mecufi* to shoot back at them for us." He fought the pull of transient gravity fields long enough to slam the helm computer into its second preprogrammed maneuver. This time, the little ship slewed sideways and darted swiftly in between the two Orion ships. It hung there for a long breathless moment, recklessly inviting enemy fire.

Uhura looked up from the navigation monitor, dark eyes wide and solemn. *"Mecufi* one thousand kilometers and closing."

"Sensors show they've fired photon torpedoes," one of the Andorians added. Sulu heard Muav Haslev groan again. "Torpedoes approaching vector ninety-five mark six—"

"Phaser fire coming in from the *Umyfymu!"* warned a second Andorian. The ship sensors began to scream with damage alarms. "Port shields are hit—"

"Do something, helmsman!" roared Captain Kanin. "The Orions are going to destroy us!"

"Oh, no, they're not." Sulu took a deep breath, then set his last course into the helm. The *Shras* shuddered in protest when its warp drive spun it around, slinging it back toward the *Umyfymu*. At the last possible moment, the Andorian ship sheared off to skim just below the destroyer's fake cargo holds, where her phasers couldn't follow them. They hurtled out the other side, viewscreen sensors automatically swiveling to stay fixed on the ships behind them. Sulu grinned when he saw the iridescent flash of a photon torpedo, far back on their warp trail.

"What are you so happy about?" Haslev demanded waspishly. "The *Mecufi* just fired photon torpedoes at us!"

"But they fired them *before* we ducked under the

Umyfymu." Sulu watched the screen, keeping his attention on the *Mecufi.* The police cruiser banked abruptly, veering away from the corona of torpedo debris bursting out from the *Umyfymu's* flanks. "The wonderful thing about photon torpedoes," he told Haslev, "is that they can't tell one ship from another."

"It's a good trick," Uhura agreed. "But you know you can't pull any trick twice on an Orion. So what fancy maneuver are we going to use on the *Mecufi?"*

Sulu frowned, watching the *Mecufi's* shark-sleek silhouette round the crippled hulk of its sister ship and arrow after the *Shras* through the darkness. "One that Chekov once told me about," he said, reaching out to toggle the main viewscreen back to a front-angle shot. Deep in the funneling stars around them, he knew, there still waited the ominous patch of darkness that was the *Hawking.* "It's called Russian roulette."

Purviance crashed atop Chekov with the force of ten men, and the lieutenant felt bone snap along the outer wall of his ribs. An instant later, pain slashed liquid-bright through his lung, and he lost the last of his breath in a anguished cry when Purviance planted a knee in the small of his back and arched him painfully upright.

I'm dead. Chekov was surprised at how calmly that certainty came to him. Purviance would simply break his spine, take the trans-shield anode, and do whatever he damn well pleased to the *Enterprise.* Whatever this anode thing was, it was important enough for six people to have died for. Chekov decided he might as well save what he could of this mission before he became number seven.

The anode shattered into a million multicolored

pieces when he smashed it against the deck. Purviance froze, and Chekov squeezed his eyes shut tight, waiting for the killing blow. Instead, the Orion abruptly released him, and he fell flat, gasping, and still pinned.

"You *fool!*" Purviance wailed. "That anode was irreplaceable!"

Chekov hugged his arms to his sides, struggling to breathe without letting pain knock him senseless. "Then you're trapped here," he wheezed, "just like me. Your people can't beam you out, and Captain Kirk will never let you leave this ship alive."

The weight on Chekov's back lifted, and he heard heavy footsteps retreat to a few meters behind him, slow and uncertain. "I don't think your Captain Kirk will have the luxury of making that decision."

Almost immediately, phaser fire cut across Purviance's voice, sharp and feral in the shuttle's close confines. Chekov remembered Haslev saying that he'd heard a phaser just before the *Hawking*'s containment housing exploded, and he knew with sudden terror what Purviance planned to do.

"You can't!" he cried, struggling to his knees. "Purviance, you'll destroy the entire ship, yourself with it!" It seemed as though the deck lurched unevenly when he stood, arms wrapped around his chest, and staggered toward the rear of the shuttle. "This won't accomplish anything!"

Purviance loomed in the doorway to the shuttle's engine compartment, planting his arms on either jamb to block himself in place. "It accomplishes what I was sent for," he snarled. "At least some small part of it. I keep you from getting the anode, and I keep you from telling anyone the hellish thing ever existed."

He leered down at Chekov as though amused at the smaller man's tenacity at trying to stop him. "The only real difference between you and me, Lieutenant, is that I never planned to live to the end of my mission. It would have been nice, but I never thought it necessary." He leaned down close to confide, "You people certainly gave me a run for my money."

Purviance was still smiling when the shuttle's containment housing blew. The explosion sounded infinitely louder without two compartments' distance to dampen the sound; Chekov recoiled from the blast without thinking even as a shock wave of pressure, shrapnel, and liquid nitrogen slammed Purviance from behind and threw both Orion and human halfway down the shuttle's main aisle.

A searing rush of phaser fire skimmed past the *Shras*. Sulu angled the little ship into a random spiral to evade it, trying to throw off the *Mecufi's* tracking systems without altering *Shras's* course toward the crippled shuttle.

"Helmsman." Captain Kanin's voice held an uneasy note. "What exactly is this maneuver called Russian roulette?"

Sulu shrugged, not taking his eyes from the viewscreen. "The original version is a game played with an old-style explosive projectile weapon. You put a single projectile in the six-projectile chamber. Then the players take turns aiming the gun at their heads and firing." He punched another swerve into the helm as the *Mecufi's* phaser shots swung closer. "Since the gun holds only one projectile, the lucky players don't get shot."

The foreboding in Pov Kanin's voice deepened. "And how were you planning on doing this with spaceships?"

"By making the Orions chase us around that damaged shuttle out there until it explodes." A tiny mote of darkness appeared in the corner of the screen, parallaxing across more distant stars. Sulu blew out a tense breath of relief. Part of him had been terrified that the *Hawking*'s unstable core might have already blown, unnoticed in the light and fury of battle.

Muav Haslev groaned, sinking into the empty communications station with melodramatic despair. "You mean we're going to get our antennae roasted after all?"

"Maybe." Sulu punched a new and more complicated set of instructions into the helm. The *Shras* launched herself into an obscure and jittering orbit around the abandoned shuttle, maintaining a more or less constant distance from it without ever quite keeping to a predictable course. Sulu heard Uhura gasp, and glanced over at her screen to see the red trace that was the Orion cruiser cutting across their arc to catch them. The larger ship didn't seem to notice it had come within a hundred kilometers of the *Hawking*. "And maybe not. If I can keep the Orions taking shortcuts like that, they'll always be closer to the shuttle than we are."

"But meanwhile, they're catching up to us!" Kanin protested. "And even if the shuttle explodes, what guarantee do we have the blast won't catch us, too?"

"None," Sulu admitted honestly. He winced when a photon torpedo exploded close enough to rattle the hull through the shields. "That's why I called it Russian roulette."

Haslev opened his mouth to say something, then yelped instead when an insistent whistle erupted from his panel. "Someone's calling us!"

"Inset it on the main screen," Uhura advised. She cast an exasperated glance at Haslev when no boxed

239

image appeared against the swirling stars. "It's the small yellow button, next to the frequency control."

A scowling green-skinned face rippled into view across the starfield, and Sulu recognized the double-plaited black beard and scowling bronze eyes of Police Commander Shandaken. The boxed signal pared off the Orion's nonessential surroundings, but the trickle of sweat steaming down his bare chin, and the fierce roar of Orion voices in the background, told Sulu this chase had pushed the police cruiser to its limit.

"Surrender, Andorians!" Shandaken snarled. "We're faster than you, and we have weapons. It's only a matter of time until we catch you."

"Or until you blow up," Sulu said softly. Uhura threw a warning look at him, and he realized Captain Kanin had activated the communications monitor on the ceiling to reply.

"You are violating Federation laws, Orion." The Andorian captain's voice was polite, but his antennae quivered with outrage. "You have no legal right to attack this vessel."

"We do if you are helping Orion criminals to escape." A straggle of uneven teeth appeared through Shandaken's dark beard, the expression Orions considered a smile. "Of course, if you were to beam the traitor-weasel Haslev over to us, we might be willing to make a compromise."

"What kind of compromise?" Kanin asked.

Shandaken's smile widened. "We could blow off only your front hull instead of your entire warp drive."

Pov Kanin stiffened, face flushing indigo with anger. Sulu's respect for the Andorian rose a notch. "I must consult on this decision," he said tightly. "My ship is presently under Starfleet command."

"Don't vacillate for long." Shandaken lifted one beefy fist to show them the chronometer he wore on his thumb. "You have one standard minute to think it over."

The *Enterprise's* viewscreen glowed blinding blue in response to the torpedo strike the *Mecufi* had landed on *Umyfymu's* hull. Plasma-shrapnel corkscrewed in all directions, and the Orion destroyer heeled over onto one side, her lower shields blowing out with a silent shower.

Kirk clenched one fist in restrained victory. "*Good,* Sulu!" He swung to face Mullen. "All phasers, full power—target that unshielded area!"

"Aye, sir!"

"Fire!"

Phaser strikes glowed darkly along the destroyer's belly, and the ship rocked as if in a tempest. When the first crystalline sprays of frozen gas jetted from her seams, Kirk waved at Mullen to hold off. He was interested in stopping the Orions, not killing them. "Spock—sensors?"

"Scans indicate extensive damage to the *Umyfymu's* hull, Captain. They appear to have lost both phaser and photon torpedo control, as well as their warp drive."

Kirk nodded, watching the listing ship for any movement. "Is there anyone left on the bridge?"

"Hailing them now, sir," Goldstein reported. "Contact coming through on main screen."

This time, Kirk let Goldstein fill the viewscreen with the Orion's image. He wondered as soon as the visual came on if this had been a mistake. Half the *Umyfymu's* bridge lighting appeared to be inoperative, but enough remained to clearly display a stack of burned Orion bodies among the ruined control boards. The Orion commander, his knotted black hair thick with blood, scowled at Kirk with slitted eyes.

"Well, Commander," Kirk said, suppressing his sympathy. "I believe it's my turn to ask for your surrender."

"Never." The Orion spat a bloody string between his feet. "Orion military officers would rather die than surrender to inferior mammals."

The sentiment almost pulled a smile from Kirk. "Speaking as an inferior mammal, Commander, may I point out that we currently have you at our mercy? Your hull won't withstand another phaser attack—"

"And your shields won't withstand the explosion of our warp core," the Orion returned with a snarl. "Since you can't run faster than we can follow, we have you at *our* mercy should we choose to self-destruct."

Kirk turned his back to the screen and motioned Goldstein to cut their audio link. "Spock," he said, glancing at the science officer, "will the blast from their warp core really take us out?"

The Vulcan glanced briefly at the screen, then came to stand at Kirk's level with his back to the Orion's image. "Quite possibly, Captain. At this distance, I estimate only a 34 percent chance of antimatter impact from the explosion. However, there is an 86 percent probability of damage from secondary radiation effects."

Kirk leaned on his fist with a sigh. "Not good enough odds to gamble with."

"I believe we have what Dr. McCoy would describe as a Mexican standoff."

"Yes—" Turning back to the viewscreen, Kirk nodded for Goldstein to return their audio. "Commander," he called to the Orion. "Are you willing to agree to a cease-fire instead of a surrender?"

The Orion worked his mouth sullenly, thinking. "Would the cease-fire terms include handing over to us the traitor-weasel Muav Haslev?"

As far as Kirk was concerned, anyone who wanted Haslev was welcome to him. He wasn't sure he was free to make that promise, however. "What happens with Haslev will depend on the Andorians." He glanced back at Goldstein. "Get the *Shras* on-line. I want to—"

"Sir," Goldstein cut in, "the *Shras* won't respond to our signal. I'm picking up contact between them and the *Mecufi,* sir, and—" He looked up in surprise, eyes wide. "—and the *Mecufi*'s just announced its intention to destroy them!"

Chapter Nineteen

MUAV HASLEV SWUNG AROUND as Shandaken's image faded from the Andorian viewscreen, leaving the sleek silver menace of the *Mecufi* in its place. "You can't send me over to them!"

"Not with all our shields up," Sulu agreed, settling the *Shras* into a less jarring orbit while the Orions' phaser fire ceased momentarily. "At least, not real successfully." He shot a speculative look at the physicist. "You know, I don't think the Orions quite understand how your trans-shield anode works, Haslev."

The Andorian squirmed a little in his seat. "It's so hard to explain complicated technologies to non-scientists—"

Uhura lifted one eyebrow. "Especially, when you have to tell them their expensive new transporter device will send a radiation pulse through their ship every time they use it?"

"That's only a temporary problem—" Haslev jumped at the sound of the Orion's hailing whistle, then put an unsteady hand out to transfer it to the main screen.

"Time's up," Shandaken said without ceremony. "Are you going to beam the weasel over, or do you prefer him to be annihilated along with—"

The inset viewscreen image shivered into static as a stronger signal cut into the channel, cutting off the Orion's growling voice. When the image resolved again, it showed the familiar determined face of Captain James T. Kirk.

"Mecufi." The confident ring in Kirk's voice sent a surge of relief through Sulu. He knew it meant his captain had taken control of the situation. "This is the USS *Enterprise*. The Orion destroyer *Umyfymu* has just agreed to a cease-fire with us. I advise you do the same."

"Impossible!" Shandaken's image was gone, but his voice sounded shaken. "Orion military officers do not negotiate with criminals and traitors! You're lying, *f'deraxt'la!*"

"Am I?" Their abbreviated view of the bridge swung dizzily when Kirk turned toward the communications station. "Mr. Goldstein, patch in the Orion commander."

Once again, the viewscreen image rippled, this time replaced by the smoke-blurred image of an Orion in military bronze and black. The captain's medallion that dangled from the Orion's ear dripped bright orange blood onto one burly shoulder.

"Shandaken, *dgr'xt en,*" he snarled. *"K'laxm f'dactla en str'ln axltr'dn. Pr'dyn dgreilt jarras'tla en axm b'rerr—"*

Sulu glanced over at Uhura, seeing her eyebrows

tighten with concentration while she listened to the growl of Orion speech. "He's telling them to give up," she translated. "He says he wants them to go back to Orion, where they can all be charged with high treason—"

Sulu cursed and slammed a sudden change of course into the helm. The *Shras* leapt into a jagged roll, kicking most of the Andorians out of their seats.

"What are you doing?" Haslev squealed, staring up from the deck in dismay. "The Orions were going to surrender!"

"No, they weren't." Phaser fire seared past them in a sheeting wave, as painfully brilliant as a nova. Sulu twisted the *Shras* into a banking roll, trying to find a safe path through the destruction. "He wasn't telling them to surrender—he was telling them to commit suicide!"

"Orions would rather die than be humiliated for firing on their own ship. And, being Orions, they'll try to take us with them when they go." Uhura's voice was almost drowned out by the sudden scream of damage alarms. She looked up from her screen as the *Shras* rocked with a second glancing blow. "Orions closing fast. They've increased their speed to warp five."

Sulu grunted and sheered away from an explosion of torpedo fire, skimming the *Shras* so close to the crippled *Hawking* that he could see the ominous glow of decaying fields inside. "They can't maintain that speed for long," he said through gritted teeth. "It'll burn out their core."

Kirk's voice cut through the wailing alarms, although no image disrupted their screen. The *Enterprise* captain knew better than to transmit visuals during a battle. "Sulu, head for the *Enterprise!* We can cover—"

An erupting shriek of subspace radiation broke the contact and burned out the helm display in a shower of red-gold sparks. Sulu jerked his head up to stare at the main screen, cold fear exploding through his blood. He had just enough time to recognize the almost-invisible shimmer of uncontained antimatter exploding toward them from the *Hawking* before the shock wave slammed into their ship.

Chekov jerked erratically toward consciousness, catapulted out of darkness on bright-edged thrusts of pain. He tried to catch his breath, realized he was coughing, and spat his mouth clear of blood before struggling up on one elbow. *Not good,* he thought as muscles along his back and side clenched in anguished protest, *not good at all.* Sheeted with pain, the left side of his chest felt heavy and hot with congestion; Lindsey Purviance sprawled across his lower half, grotesquely pinioned with frost-burned shrapnel from the rear of his skull to his knees. Behind Purviance, liquid nitrogen skated silver rivers across the shuttle's floor and leapt into vapor shimmers wherever they brushed the Orion's still-warm corpse. The dancing sheet of light spilling upward from the remnants of the containment housing accompanied a whine furiously similar to the *Hawking's* dying song. The explosion of the engine housing wasn't powerful enough to have damaged the *Enterprise* herself, but from the front of the shuttle, the computer droned, "Core breach imminent. Estimated time to breach: seven minutes fifty-four seconds."

Chekov pushed weakly at the body on top of him,

afraid he could never dislodge it with a cluster of broken ribs and only one useful hand. But he had to get out of this shuttle and tell someone what had happened.

Authoritative pounding rumbled through the shuttle's small interior, and Chekov stiffened with a startled gasp. "Open up!" a muffled voice called from outside the forward hatch. "Starship security—let us in!"

Urgency gave Chekov the strength to heave Purviance aside with one hand and one leg, and he rolled to end up on all fours, coughing again, while the security guard outside shouted another round of warnings. For a horrifying moment, Chekov was afraid his haste would kill him. Then the fit subsided, and he found he could sustain himself on shallow, blood-tainted breaths long enough to stumble upright and make for the outer hatch.

He reached the door just as the guard forced it open with a portable override. "All right, I—Lieutenant Chekov!" Lemieux stepped back in surprise, bumping into the engineer behind her. "Sir, I didn't know you were here. We heard the explosion and came to find out what happened to—"

"Get everyone out of here." Chekov pushed Lemieux away from the door and climbed out into the bay. The closest undamaged shuttle still looked an impossible distance away; he could almost feel the core explosion building behind him. "That's an order!" he shouted, heading for the other shuttle. "Evacuate the bay!"

Lemieux nodded curtly, brows still knit in confusion, and cupped her hands to her mouth to bellow, "You heard the lieutenant! Everybody out of the bay!

Move it!" Then she trotted away with the engineer in tow, hurrying along anyone who hesitated for even an instant.

I hope I get the chance to commend her, Chekov thought as he keyed open the next shuttle's door. The interior smelled perplexingly of sweat, engine coolant, and burned polycarbons. Chekov realized the stench came from him when a touch of his environmental suit glove on the helm console left a smear of Orion blood behind. He paused long enough to wrestle off the glove and pitch it into the compartment behind him.

"Bridge to shuttle *Brahe.*" Kirk's voice demanded attention across a radio panel of blinking lights. "What's going on down there?"

Chekov woke up the *Brahe*'s small engines, then reached across the console to punch a stud in reply. "Bridge, this is *Brahe.*"

"Chekov?" The honest surprise in Kirk's voice almost made the lieutenant smile. "How in God's name did you get back on board?"

"I'm not exactly sure." He bent double over the helm to try to ease the torture on his ribs while the engines warmed. "Sir, we don't have much time. There's a field breach on one of the interstellar shuttles—I have to get it outside before it explodes." When this was over, he was going to crawl down to sickbay on hands and knees and beg Dr. McCoy to take him in.

"We can dump the bay atmosphere and open the doors," Kirk said. Chekov could almost picture the captain signaling the engineering station. "Unless you fly it out the door, though, I don't know how you're going to get it outside."

The helm signaled ready, and Chekov sat upright to take hold of the controls. "If you can get those doors open, sir, I can get the shuttle outside."

"For all our sakes, I hope so." The air in front of *Brahe*'s viewscreen rippled and thinned as the bridge initiated bay launch procedures. "Good luck."

Luck's about all that can save us. Chekov thought it best not to voice that out loud, though. After all, if the shuttle exploded while still confined within the *Enterprise*'s deflector screens, the great ship's warp nacelles might still be forfeit. That could prove just as disastrous as suffering the explosion in here. He lifted *Brahe* neatly off the deck and started her into a lumbering turn. Best not to think about variables he couldn't affect. First order of business was to get this time bomb outside; they could worry about how to either detonate or defuse it later.

The shuttle that came into Chekov's view looked placid and undamaged despite the core spikes washing across Chekov's sensor display. Elegant red script spelled *Clarke* across its blunt nose, and Chekov noticed for the first time that it was one of the lighter interstellar shuttles, one of only a few dozen tons. Perhaps not as impossible to push outside as he'd first feared. He idled *Brahe* around the rear of *Clarke* by agonizing inches, all the while flicking glances up at the closed shell doors, willing them to trundle open.

Brahe shuddered dully when her nose bumped *Clarke*'s rear bulkhead. Chekov felt his shuttle's frame tremble, felt its impulse engines growl with strain as he eased the throttle gently upward. When the moment of inertia broke, stress clanged throughout *Brahe*'s structure as the two shuttles leapt forward, and Chekov was jolted back in his seat with an involuntary bark of pain. *Clarke* stuttered and scraped across the deck, the silent vibrations of its resistance translating through *Brahe*'s hull into a deafening wall of thunder. Shivering like heat ripples outside the shuttles' trembles, the bay doors reared high and imposing. And stayed closed.

"Open, damn you," Chekov groaned. He didn't dare take his hands from the controls, or he would have pounded the helm in frustration. *"Open!"*

A black rift sliced up the center of the big doors. The band widened steadily, and Chekov realized it was his wished-for exit just as *Clarke* danced sideways and skipped off the end of *Brahe*'s nose.

"Govno!"

He fought the impulse drive into reverse, slewing *Brahe* around in a desperate attempt to keep from skating past *Clarke* and into open space.

"Chekov?" Kirk cut sharply across his attention, sounding tense and distracted. "Chekov, report."

Chekov ignored the captain's intrusion, and re-aligned the attitude controls as quickly as he could right-handed.

"Is the shuttle clear?"

"No!" *Brahe* caught itself with a fluid bump, drifting to half-face *Clarke*. "No, sir," Chekov said again, more evenly. "I'm working on it."

"We haven't got much time, Mr. Chekov."

"I know, sir." His shoulder burned with fatigue if he so much as flexed his fingers, and pain ate into his breathing in deep, steady stabs whenever he moved. If he'd had to do more than bumble a shuttle around the hangar bay on impulse, he'd never have been able to control the craft, and he wasn't all that confident he'd accomplish what he needed to anyway. Not for the first time, he wished Sulu were with him—to pilot, and to just be there, so Chekov wouldn't feel quite so alone.

He wondered forlornly if Sulu and Uhura were safe, outside the *Hawking*'s blast range and close enough to rescue. It seemed an eternity ago that he'd watched them leave the airlock.

No—no time for other worries now. Easing *Brahe* back into the main bay, he readdressed *Clarke*'s listing form, framing it on his viewscreen between the open hangar doors. *Clarke* presented its side to the starry outside, having turned a full one hundred eighty degrees in Chekov's first attempt to push it out the doors. He crept *Brahe* up to it again, this time aiming for the center point of *Clarke*'s squat profile. The first bump of shuttle against shuttle skidded *Clarke* awkwardly sideways; Chekov pulled back immediately, adjusting *Brahe* barely a meter to starboard before driving forward again. This time, the two crafts met with a deep, mating *clang*, and *Clarke* shuddered as though struck to the core while *Brahe* powered it the last long distance across the hangar bay and out into lightless vacuum.

Chekov felt the thunder of friction release them the instant *Clarke* dipped past the *Enterprise*'s gravity field and into free fall. He pushed up the acceleration without looking down at the helm. He didn't want to rely on readouts—he needed to see *Clarke* rush toward the stars ahead of him, needed to count the seconds in his own mind. It had been years now, but he'd been a ship's navigator once; he could feel where the screens sat like he could feel his own skin, having honed that sense over countless hours of commanding their distance, configuration, intensity, and use. Driving *Clarke* ahead of him, he increased velocity to as far from the bay as he dared, then slammed *Brahe* into reverse and left *Clarke* to continue its sublight tumble away from the *Enterprise*. If the starship's screens were still in action, Chekov wanted to be as far from *Clarke* as possible when the little shuttle impacted the deflectors and exploded.

He dragged *Brahe* straight back along their original escape course, aiming for the still-open hangar. Readouts flashed across the helm panel, and Chekov trusted their guidance as much as he dared. Twice, he switched the viewscreen aft to verify that the ship still hung behind him, but he didn't dare look away from *Clarke* for long. Not that he could have done anything more to save himself, or the *Enterprise*. He just wanted to face whatever was coming, whenever it happened; he couldn't stand not to know.

Still, the bloom of brilliant white that flashed across his screen when *Clarke* exploded caught him by surprise. He ducked his head without wanting to, and the first wave of raw energy knocked him out of his seat and bucked *Brahe* nose upward, rocketing them back into the bay.

Oh, God, Chekov thought, his mind crowded with fearful images of *Brahe* plowing through the bay's rear bulkhead. He struggled to his knees and slapped at the helm controls, trying to equalize engine output and kill the shuttle's momentum. The first telltales of deceleration sprang to life on the control board just as they crashed into something huge and unyielding out of sight behind the shuttle. Chekov had time for one only dismal thought—*I hope the captain got the screens down in time*—before *Brahe* careened over onto her side, and everything around him slammed down into darkness.

Chapter Twenty

"Sulu?" Hands patted gently at his cheek, as though afraid he'd break under too much force. "Sulu, can you hear me?"

Sulu groaned and dragged his eyes open to the twilight blue of low-power lighting. Moving figures blurred around him, but he focused on the only one he recognized. "Uhura?"

"Don't move." Smoke misted around Uhura's concerned face as she leaned over him, and Sulu's stomach knotted in alarm. He struggled up onto his elbows despite her effort to stop him.

"What happened to the ship?" he asked, searching the dim reaches of the Andorian bridge for the cascading whiteness of a ruptured nitrogen line or the smolder of burning electronics.

"The electromagnetic surge from the shuttle explosion blew out our control systems." More mist appeared when Uhura spoke, and Sulu realized it was only her frosted breath, dissipating into the cold ship air. "We've lost helm control, shields, and communications. Ventilation is running off emergency power, but we don't have heat or lights."

Sulu groaned again, rubbing the sore spot where his jaw had met some unyielding object. "What happened to the antimatter flare from the *Hawking?*"

"It washed out about fifty kilometers short of us." Uhura's eyes glimmered with the beginnings of a smile. "You were too busy cracking your chin on the helm console to notice."

"Too bad." Sulu managed to sit all the way up, then waited for his head to stop buzzing before he craned it toward the main viewscreen. The unpowered panel was frustratingly blank. "What happened to the *Mecufi?*"

Uhura shook her head, her fine-boned face turning grave. "It was almost a thousand kilometers closer to the shuttle than we were. Our sensors showed an antimatter flare eating a hole right through its hull. The ship broke apart after that." She raised a thin eyebrow at him. "Your Russian roulette maneuver worked."

"I'll have to remember to thank Chekov when I see him." Sulu used Uhura's offered hand to haul himself to his feet, then noticed the subtle thrum of the deck under his feet. "Hey, we're moving!"

Uhura nodded and scrambled up beside him. "The *Enterprise* has us in a tractor beam. Mr. Scott says they're going to pull us into the shuttle bay for repairs."

"Mr. Scott says?" Sulu blinked at her, wondering if his groggy brain had misconstrued the words. "I thought you told me we lost communications?"

"We lost *ship* communications." Uhura bent with

her usual grace, scooping a bowl-shaped plastic and metal object off the floor. Sulu frowned, then recognized it as her environmental suit helmet when she turned it right side up and tapped the communicator panel inside the chin. "The crystal chips in our suits survived the surge just fine. With our shields down, I didn't have any trouble using them to contact the *Enterprise.*"

"I would never have thought of that." Despite the ache in his jaw, Sulu's mouth twitched into an appreciative grin. "Have I told you lately that you're awfully good at your job?"

The communications officer's dark eyes warmed to rich mahogany with her smile. "Well, so are you. Most pilots would have gotten us killed if they tried playing hide-and-seek with an Orion destroyer."

"That's true," Sulu agreed immodestly. Uhura snorted and tugged at his elbow.

"Come on," she said. "We should be in visual range of the ship by now. There's a viewport on the next deck down." She slanted another concerned look at him. "Can you climb down the ladderway in that heavy suit?"

"Well, I'm certainly not going to take it off." Sulu grinned again at the puzzled look she gave him. "After all the sweating I've done since we left the *Hawking,* even I don't want to know what I smell like."

The *Enterprise* swam through the darkness toward them, phaser burns dark as bruises across her long platinum sides. Sulu's lips tightened into a soundless whistle as he scanned the damage. The worst destruction was concentrated near the unshielded area around the breach in the primary hull, but a long rippled impact scar also ran the length of the secondary hull, level with the shuttle bay. Even from here, Sulu could see suited crews of engineers crawling out to reinforce the stressed sections of metal.

"They're lucky that didn't cause another hull breach," Uhura said, watching quietly at his shoulder. The words made Sulu wince, bringing back the memory of his vacuum-shattered belongings and ransacked room. He'd been vaguely planning to collapse in the plant-scented warmth of his cabin after Kirk finished debriefing them. Now, all he had to look forward to was the cold comfort of emergency quarters.

The thought made him recall something else he'd forgotten, and he scanned the impact scar more closely. "That doesn't look like photon torpedo damage," he pointed out to Uhura. "I wonder if the Orion saboteur did it?"

"Well, he must have hidden in the shuttle bay at some point, to rig his phaser-bomb inside the *Hawking.*" Uhura's dark eyes widened as the tractor beam pulled the *Shras* around to face the massive landing bay doors, now splitting open to admit them. The back half of the shuttle bay lay shielded behind a vacuum barrier, but the transparent aluminum wall couldn't hide the torn and crumpled shuttles piled up along the rear bulkhead. "Oh, my God. Maybe the saboteur *did* rig all the shuttles."

"It looks more like he just wrecked them." Sulu counted the empty spaces along the walls while the tractor beam deposited them gently inside the landing bay. *"Brahe, Clarke, Kahoutek*—dammit, he took out all our good interstellar shuttles! If they haven't already caught him, I'll hunt him down and strangle him myself!"

Uhura gave him an amused upward glance as the bay doors slid closed behind them. "Sulu, I'm sure

Starfleet will give us new shuttles when we dock for refitting."

"That's not the point!" Sulu trailed her back toward the ladderway. He could already hear Haslev complaining about something on the deck below them as the Andorians gathered by the hatch. Outside, compressed air roared around them, rattling the ship's hull as it flooded back into the landing bay. "I liked the shuttles we had! I knew which ones handled best in microgravity, and which ones were good on atmospheric reentry—"

The rumble of the hatch door opening interrupted him, and Sulu dropped down the last few feet of ladderway with a thud. He followed Uhura out past the hesitant Andorians, as eager as she was to be back in the familiar air of the *Enterprise*.

"Sulu, Uhura." Captain Kirk emerged from the turbolift exit across the bay and strode to meet them, Spock just behind him. Despite the bruise darkening his forehead, the captain moved with his usual restless energy. "You're both all right?"

"We're fine, Captain." Sulu swung around to survey the destruction in the shuttle bay, more clearly visible now that they were out of the ship. "Did the saboteur rig more of the shuttles for explosion, sir?"

"No. Apparently, he only had time to sabotage one other besides the *Hawking*." One corner of Kirk's mouth turned up in rueful amusement as he glanced back at the mess. "Chekov did the rest of this, trying to *stop* the saboteur."

"*Chekov* did?" Uhura and Sulu exclaimed together. They exchanged puzzled looks. "I guess we must have beamed him into the shuttle bay," Uhura said blankly. Her eyes darkened with concern as she glanced at the wrecked shuttles. "Is he all right, sir?"

The captain nodded. "A little battered, but that's usually what happens when you get into a fist fight with an Orion. Dr. McCoy's standing by to take him to sickbay as soon as the engineers cut him free."

Uhura looked dismayed. "You mean he's trapped inside one of those shuttles?"

"Yes." Kirk smiled at her, a quick, understanding smile that lit his eyes to gold. "I'm sure he'd be glad to have your company while he's waiting, Commander."

She threw him a grateful look and turned toward the turbolift. "Thank you, sir. You'll have my full report in the morning."

"Good." The captain swung to face the clatter of feet coming off the *Shras*. "Captain Kanin." Kirk stepped forward and gave the Andorian officer the polite bow his race favored. "We're grateful for your assistance with the Orions. Your ship's courageous performance in this battle will be duly noted in my report to Starfleet."

"Thank you, sir." Kanin returned the bow, antennae flushing pale lavender with pleasure. "Most of the credit must go to your pilot, however. He did an excellent job evading the Orions."

"Yes." Kirk rubbed at the bruise on his forehead, casting an amused look back at Spock. "We could have used him aboard the *Enterprise*." His amusement faded to a steely smile when his glance fell on Muav Haslev, now handcuffed to a stocky Andorian security guard. "Ah, Mr. Haslev—the cause of all this havoc. We have a visitor who would like to speak with you." He nodded at Spock, and the Vulcan crossed to speak into the nearest intercom.

"I'll have you know that none of this was my fault," Haslev protested. "If you hadn't decided to send me back to Sigma One—"

"—the *Hawking* would have exploded right here, and we would all be dead now," Sulu finished sharply.

The Andorian physicist glared at him. "Listen, you're the one who started all this—"

"Little weasel!" The distinctive roar of an Orion voice crashed over the argument like a storm wave. Sulu swung around to see the bulky form of the Orion military commander emerge from the turbolift and stalk toward them, flanked by a brace of security guards. The white swath of bandage taped across his bearded face didn't make him look any less dangerous. "You *lied* to us!"

Haslev tried to sidle back, his antennae curving defensively downward. "Um—when, Commander Ondarken?"

"You told us your trans-shield anode would make any transporter beam go through a shield." The Orion shoved through the group around Haslev, Andorians scattering before him with yelps of alarm. "But when we tried to beam our agent out with it from this ship, nothing happened." He came to a halt, looming over the gray-faced physicist. *"Why?"*

"Um—" Haslev's antennae quivered. "Well, there were a few minor details about the trans-shield anode I didn't have time to explain."

"Such as?" Ondarken's bronze eyes narrowed to slits.

"Well, in the first place, you can only beam *to* the anode, not away from it." Haslev swallowed. "And I'm afraid you can't beam the transsshield anode itself anywhere—you have to carry it to your intended destination."

"Not to mention the fact that it creates a subspace pulse on board ship every time you use it," Sulu added.

"What?" Kirk's exasperated voice rose over the Orion commander's growl. "Using the trans-shield anode was what made all our instruments go out?"

"It's only a minor flaw," Haslev quavered, shrinking when Ondarken leaned over him with bared teeth. "I'm sure I can iron it out with just a little more research—"

"I am afraid not, Mr. Haslev." The note of certainty in Spock's quiet voice sliced off the physicist's spluttering. "Constance Duerring's original theory of transporter electrodynamics clearly states that energy is generated whenever a transporter beam encounters a force shield." The Vulcan thoughtfully steepled his long fingers in front of his chin. "In most cases, the energy is absorbed by the random rearrangement of molecules within the transported objects. Your anode device prevents that by diverting the energy to the surrounding subspace boson field, where it is re-emitted as low-frequency radiation." Spock lifted a quizzical eyebrow. "Really, Mr. Haslev, you should know that you cannot evade the first law of thermodynamics. Energy can be neither created or destroyed, only transformed."

"Exactly so," Pov Kanin agreed, his lean blue face creasing with a smug smile. "That's why the Andorian government refused to fund Haslev's transporter research to begin with." He needled a malicious glance at the Orion commander. "We never thought other governments would be obtuse enough to believe Muav Haslev's wild proposals—"

Ondarken growled, spinning around to face the Andorian. "What did you just call me, weasel?"

"Let me elaborate—"

"Gentlemen!" Kirk stepped between them, apparently oblivious to the fact that either of the high-

gravity aliens could have crushed him where he stood. His voice rang with stern authority. "We're here to decide on the fate of Muav Haslev, not to squabble with each other." He glanced at Kanin, ignoring the renegade physicist's squeak of alarm. "The Orion commander has asked for permission to extradite Mr. Haslev so that his government can try him for treason."

"I must refuse," the Andorian captain said politely. "On the grounds that Mr. Haslev committed treason against *my* government first."

Kirk's mouth twitched up into a smile. "That certainly seems reasonable." He turned to face Ondarken when the Orion commander growled in protest. "I'm sure that when Mr. Haslev has finished serving his prison sentence on Andor, they'll be more than willing to let him face charges on Orion, as well."

"If he's still alive by then." Pov Kanin ignored Muav Haslev's piteous groan from behind him. "Now, Captain Kirk, may I have your permission to find temporary housing for my crew on board your ship—and a secure cell for my prisoner?"

"Permission granted." Kirk glanced at Spock, amusement glittering in his eyes. "I'll have my first officer arrange it for you, Captain Kanin. Perhaps he can explain the first law of thermodynamics to Mr. Haslev along the way."

"Thank you." Kanin motioned to his crew to follow the Vulcan, pausing only long enough to cast a silent look of triumph at Ondarken before he went along. The Orion commander scowled after him, anger rumbling wordlessly in his throat.

"I believe that concludes our business here, Commander Ondarken," Kirk said crisply. "Unless you would like to stay to answer some questions about how your agent got on board—"

"What about our stolen property?" The Orion glared down at Kirk. "What about the fate of the other criminals?"

"Other criminals?" Kirk followed Ondarken's glance to Sulu, and his mouth hardened. "Commander, my helmsman was carrying out Starfleet orders when he diverted your companion ship's fire toward your ship."

"Not that!" howled the Orion in frustration. "What he did before, on Sigma One! He received the stolen property from Haslev's conspirator, the human plant merchant who helped him escape from us. That's how the trans-shield anode got smuggled aboard this ship!"

"Oh, my God." Sulu felt his stomach contract in shock when he realized what Ondarken meant. "The trans-shield anode must have been hidden inside my lily pond!"

"Not that black marble thing Chekov kept calling a swimming pool?" Kirk looked equally stunned. "Oh, my God! That's what he was trying to tell me—" He turned to meet the Orion's scowl with a grim look of his own. "I'm afraid your stolen property is gone— blasted out into space along with the shuttle your agent rigged to destroy the *Enterprise*."

"Agent? What agent?" Ondarken tried to arrange his bushy eyebrows into an expression of surprise. "I deny all agents—"

"Of course you do." Kirk motioned the security guards forward. "Escort Commander Ondarken to the transporter room and see he gets back to his ship."

"Aye, sir." Lemieux tugged at one beefy forearm,

unintimidated by the glare she earned. "Let's go, Commander Ondarken."

"My government will pursue the criminals on board your ship!" the Orion warned, shouting over his shoulder as he was led away. "We will sue for extradition and punish—"

The turbolift doors cut off his diatribe midword, and Sulu felt his tense shoulders relax at last. He heard Kirk sigh, and suddenly realized how tired the captain looked. It was a mark of Kirk's force of will that Sulu hadn't noticed it at all during the confrontation.

"Sir?" he asked tentatively. "May I have permission to see if Chekov is still in the bay?" Something deep inside him wouldn't believe the Russian was really alive until he saw him.

"Let's both go." Kirk headed down the vast shell of the shuttle bay, toward where engineers were rolling aside the multisectioned vacuum barrier. The volatile smell of spilled lubricant mingled with the sharp ozone scent of metal being hit by phaser torches. Bright lights among the shuttles showed where engineers still worked to cut them apart. Medical aides picked their way through the morass of twisted metal, a gravsled steadied between them. A single environmental-suited figure scrambled after them, her dark face vivid with concern.

"The engineers must have just gotten him out." Kirk lengthened his stride to meet them. "Bones! Is Chekov all right?"

McCoy looked up from the blanketed form on the medical sled, his face lighting with a crooked smile. "Well, considering that I thought we were going to need a can opener to get him out, he's doing pretty well. Some broken ribs, a whole raft of bumps and bruises—" He glanced down as Chekov made a bubbly mutter. "—and one punctured lung. Nothing I can't fix."

Kirk paused beside the gravsled, Sulu crowding at his heels. Chekov looked awful—face red-purple with bruises where it wasn't crusted with at least two colors of dried blood. His chest moved with painful shallowness beneath the blanket, thick, liquid gurgles catching in his throat with every breath. Sulu felt his own throat tighten in sympathy.

The security officer squinted up at Kirk. "I heard—Orions."

"The commander of the *Umyfymu* came over to talk with the traitor-weasel Haslev." Kirk's voice turned wry. "And to demand his stolen property back."

"The lily pond—" Chekov coughed, then found his voice again. "I had to break it—I'm sorry, sir—"

McCoy heaved a weary sigh. "Oh, not this again."

Kirk flicked an amused smile at Sulu. "I told you he was worried."

"Hey, Pavel, that's okay." Sulu crouched down beside the Russian, wishing there was some part of his friend that looked safe to touch. "I don't need it now that my lily's dead."

"But the lizards—" Chekov's voice held the stubbornly worried tone of someone fighting off shock. "We have to get them some other container—they can't stay in my bathtub forever—"

McCoy tugged meaningfully on the edge of the gravsled, scowling at Sulu until the helmsman climbed to his feet to back out of the way. "They can at least stay there until you get out of sickbay."

Uhura rose up on tiptoe to peek at McCoy over Sulu's shoulder. "But, Doctor—"

"No buts!" He stabbed a stern finger at Sulu, who

backed up into Uhura in surprise. "You two go back to your cabins or something—find a home for those damned lizards!" He scowled down at Chekov when the security chief opened his mouth to protest. "You shut up and pass out before I sedate you."

"Bones—"

"And *you!*" He fixed his fiercest glare of all on Kirk, and Sulu felt better when even the captain looked contrite. "If you know what's good for you, you'll get up to the bridge and start back to Sigma One before these three can get us into any more trouble!"

Chapter Twenty-one

CHEKOV LOOKED UP from his bathroom floor when he heard Sulu enter the outer cabin.

"Anybody home?"

It occurred to the lieutenant that sitting on the floor of his bathroom in the dark—his dress uniform jacket tossed across the sink and his hand trailing in a bathtub full of warm water—was perhaps not the most dignified situation in which to let himself be found. After running around a hull breach in his stockinged feet, though, not to mention being cut out of an environmental suit by an engineering ensign with a phaser torch, he figured he probably didn't have any dignity left worth worrying about. Besides, it wasn't like Sulu was one of his security guards; he and the helmsman had known each other a long time. "I'm in here."

Sulu appeared in the doorway like a slim shadow, the light from the outer cabin silhouetting him until his face was too dark to see. "You okay?" he asked quietly, and Chekov nodded.

"Just thinking." He prodded a floating sponge with one finger and sent it drifting lazily across the bathtub, its load of passenger lizards chirping merrily. If his right arm hadn't still been confined in a sling, he might have tried to reach their fish food from the floor. Trussed up as he was, though, the effort just didn't seem to be worth it.

"What are you thinking about?" Sulu asked, taking a seat on the floor across from him. He pulled up both knees to rest his chin in his hands. "The wonderful, exotic dinner Uhura and I have planned for you now that we're back at Sigma One?"

"No." Considering everything that had happened since they left the space station, Chekov found the suggestion oddly amusing. "I'm thinking about what a terrible week this has been."

"Hey—" Although Sulu reached out to kick him in playful admonishment, the concern in the helmsman's voice was real enough. "You promised the memorial service wouldn't put you in a bad mood."

"It didn't." Chekov shook the water off his hand, and the lizards nearest his movement froze into a heartbeat of silence. He waited for them to start singing again before saying, "Really—I'm glad I went."

With a final toll of one hundred forty-three dead, the memorial service for the *Kongo's* crew had taken all morning and had been held in one of Sigma One's docking bays for lack of another place that could hold all the crew, Starfleet personnel, and station workers who wanted to attend. Chekov had gone to the huge gathering alone, a little afraid to confront the emotions he'd kept tightly locked inside since first hearing about the accident. On board the *Enterprise,* he'd been a solitary mourner among people who could only view the tragedy from sympathy's comfortable distance. Today at the service, he'd been surrounded by people who had also lost friends, lovers, valued colleagues; it had been easy to touch them, talk with them, cry with them.

"I got to meet the *Kongo*'s chief engineer," he told Sulu. She hadn't been at all like Montgomery Scott—small, thin, almost fragile in her paleness. "We talked a lot about Robert, and what happened the day he died."

Sulu nodded, looking a little uncertain about how he should respond. "Did she know him well?"

"Well enough." He wrapped his arms around his knees and looked across the darkness at Sulu. "She was supposed to go with the party that tried to unbolt the nacelles. Robert convinced their captain he could do her work just as well, and there wasn't any need to send her along." Bracing his free hand on the side of the bathtub, he pushed to his feet. "She had her children with her at the service."

Sulu stood along with him. "So he didn't do it for nothing," he said, following his friend out into the main cabin when Chekov went in search of his duty jacket. "If nothing else, he did it for her."

"I think so, yes."

Sulu snatched the jacket out from under Chekov's hand when the lieutenant reached for it, earning a warning glower. "You *think* so?"

"All right." Chekov took the jacket back with an irritated tug. "Yes, she was grateful for what he did. And I'm glad something good came out of his sacrifice."

"That's better." Sulu took over Uhura's unofficial

job of fastening Chekov's collar and straightening his jacket shoulders. "All points considered, I still like you better when you're grumpy instead of depressed."

Sometimes, Chekov decided, trying to have meaningful conversations with your friends just wasn't worth the effort. "I don't know why I put up with you," he grumbled, heading for the door.

Sulu swung into step beside him, grinning in that bright, disarming way Chekov found so damnably hard to ignore. "Because my charm and wit enrich your life?"

"No, that can't be it."

"Because I feed you?"

"I *know* that isn't it." He held open the door and waited for Sulu to move out into the hall. "Maybe," he suggested with a smile, "it's because you're not going to argue with me when I tell you I'm keeping your lizards."

Sulu blinked at him. "Are you keeping my lizards?"

"We can talk about it on the way to Sigma One."

Chekov hesitated in the doorway to the restaurant, not sure if he should follow Sulu any farther inside. He should have expected something like this, he realized. The junglelike profusion of blossoms and vines was just the sort of thing Sulu would love in a restaurant, and the copious lack of anything resembling a table probably struck Uhura as quaint. Chekov thought it all looked more like the sort of equatorial rainforest where security officers were routinely killed by natives, poisonous insects, and carnivorous plants.

"So, where are you planning to keep them?" the helmsman asked, slowing only enough to catch Chekov's empty sleeve and pull him along behind.

"You yourself said they can't live in your bathtub forever."

If it weren't for Sulu being with him, Chekov probably could have returned to the *Enterprise* and claimed that he wasn't able to find the restaurant. That's something he'd have to keep in mind for future dinner dates. "I thought maybe you'd let me use that old fish tank of yours."

"The one in my quarters?" Sulu asked. He felt among the foliage as though searching for some sort of doorway in the green. "The one that went the way of all my other possessions when the hull breach evacuated Deck Six?"

That did throw a bit of an obstacle into Chekov's plans. "How about visiting a pet store before we leave the station?"

Sulu grinned and pulled aside a swatch of jungle. "That sounds a little more reasonable."

The dining area beyond the living drapery was bigger than the lobby but no less tropical. Small, simple tables stood like quiet mushrooms among the green riot, and long trains of flowers snaked across the floor from every angle. Weaving among the plant-life, they came up behind the restaurant's only human patron, and Sulu announced without prelude, "Chekov's keeping my lizards."

Uhura leaned back to grin up at them, twirling a flower between her fingers. "I thought you said all that chirping would keep you up at night," she said to Chekov.

He shrugged as he slid into the empty seat across from her. "I was wrong."

"Well, keep them with my blessing." Sulu sat with as much energy as he did everything, slipping a flower out of the vase at the middle of the table and sniffing absently at it. "I don't need them if I don't have the lily pond. Besides—" He returned the flower in an obvious attempt at nonchalance. "I'm going to be too busy organizing a free-fall gymnastics group to spend much time with lizards."

Chekov smiled, but didn't comment. So much for last week's all-consuming hobby.

"Have you thought about what you want to order?" Uhura asked them both, helping herself to another part of the arrangement. "I was beginning to think you weren't coming."

Chekov tipped the flower vase far enough to see down the throats of various orchidlike blossoms, but couldn't take the prospect of eating them very seriously. "If I'd known you were going to feed me houseplants, I probably wouldn't have." He let the vase rock upright again. "What is this—the only restaurant on Sigma One where it's socially acceptable to eat with one hand?"

This time it was Sulu's turn to grin with evil pleasure. "Actually, you're not supposed to use any hands at all. But the Tellerites understand that humans have underdeveloped snouts, so they give us a little leeway."

Chekov made a face that a Tellerite would probably have considered inadequate. "That's disgusting."

"And *that's* cultural arrogance," Uhura countered. She nipped a trio of petals off the flower in her hand. "Some people consider sturgeon eggs and fermented cabbage disgusting, too, you know."

Chekov shrugged, and Sulu waved over a passing Tellerite waiter. "Maybe we can find some local cole crop for him to torture," the helmsman suggested to Uhura. "That should keep him happy."

The Tellerite swung past their table without slowing down, pitching three menu cards among the litter of leaves and petals. Chekov watched Sulu and Uhura eagerly scoop their menus out of the foliage, then caught his with one finger and slid it close enough to look at without actually lifting it off the table. Nothing in the long list of flowers and ivy looked much like food to him. "How late do you think the human restaurants are open on Sigma One?"

"Do you really want to risk running into some of the humans hanging around this station?" Uhura reached across to duff him on the shoulder with her half-eaten flower. "You know Aaron Kelly's looking for you."

Chekov frowned across at her, not sure at first that they were thinking of the same person. "Aaron Kelly the auditor?"

Sulu laughed, and Uhura explained, "I ran into him on my way to the restaurant." Her dark eyes twinkled with humor. "He said he feels a special kinship with Starfleet after everything that's happened on this mission. He wanted to thank you and show his appreciation."

Chekov couldn't help uttering a gruff sound of disgust, even though it earned him an admonishing finger-shake from Sulu. "Don't snort," the helmsman told him. "Kelly's decided you walk on water after you saved his butt in that brig shootout with Purviance. He went over the captain's report of the mission and has decided to preempt John Taylor's recommendation to the Auditor General—they're not going to try to restructure security after all." Chekov raised his eyebrows, and Sulu grinned. "You and your department are safe."

The security chief rocked back in his chair, feeling smug. "Maybe I should break auditors' noses more often."

"Chekov," Sulu said with a sigh, "I think you're taking the wrong lesson away from all this."

The disjointed rustling of larger-than-Tellerite bodies among the greenery broke across their conversation. Chekov saw Sulu flick a startled glance toward the back of their little clearing, and Uhura's eyebrows lift with surprise, just as Kirk's voice assured them, "This is all just a misunderstanding—don't anybody worry." Then Sigma One security guards closed in on all sides.

"Oh, no—" Chekov stood when one of the dozen or so black-clad patrol officers motioned to him with her phaser. "I thought we had this sorted out," he said, lifting his free arm so another of the guards could dart forward and pat him down.

"Lieutenant Pavel Chekov, you are under arrest for disturbing the peace, assault with a deadly weapon, possession of a firearm in a restricted civilian area, and violation of bail without appropriate legal bond. You have the right to remain silent—"

Chekov cast Kirk a helpless look over the closest guard's head, and the captain spread his hands in distressingly contrite chagrin. "I've tried to explain that the Orions who filed those original charges won't be around to make the court date," he said. "But—"

"But—" Sigma One's security chief turned the reader card in her hand as though to display whatever was printed on it, even though she took it back too quickly for Chekov to see. "There's still the matter of bail violation. No matter where your Orions are, only a Federation judicator can dismiss outstanding criminal charges. Until those original charges are dropped, I have a legal obligation to hold you in custody pending receipt of appropriate bail."

"But Lieutenant Purviance—" Even as he said it, Chekov realized they had a slight problem. "Never mind."

Kirk nodded with a rueful grimace. "Exactly."

At least, the station chief looked equally unhappy as she accepted the wrist locks and belt restraint passed forward from the back of her squad. "Whoever posted bail for you, sir, he wasn't Lindsey Purviance. In fact, Lieutenant Purviance was murdered several hours before your release."

"But I *thought* it was Lindsey Purviance!"

She nodded and opened the wide belt restraint. "No matter what you thought, sir, I'm afraid it's still jumping bail."

Kirk stepped in to catch at her wrist before she could fasten the belt around Chekov's waist and cuff down his hands. "Is that really necessary? He's got one arm in a sling, for God's sake."

"We were told he was dangerous," one of the other guards volunteered. "Our report said he beat an Orion military officer to death on board your ship."

Sulu burst out laughing, and Uhura elbowed him sharply. "He had his arm in a sling when he did that, too," the helmsman pointed out, ignoring a warning glower from Chekov.

Kirk fixed stern hazel eyes on his helmsman, and Sulu fell silent even though he didn't look any less amused. "You're not helping," the captain said coolly. Chekov had to agree.

"I hope they get a judicator in port before we're scheduled to leave," Chekov said to Kirk. The guards locked his left hand to the belt, then hesitated over his right as though unsure whether to remove the sling or not. He wasn't about to offer them any advice.

"Don't worry," Uhura said gently, "we've got three more weeks here—somebody's bound to show up before then."

He knew she meant that to be reassuring, but somehow the concept of spending three weeks in Sigma One's tiny brig didn't do much for his morale. He wondered if Sulu could be talked into a judicious jailbreak.

"I'll have you out within an hour." Kirk grinned when they all turned to look at him, and Chekov recognized the smug gleam in his captain's eye. "You're a dangerous commodity," Kirk said with no small amount of relish. "If Max Petersen won't remand you to my custody, I'll just give him a tour of the *Enterprise*'s shuttle bay." He angled a mock-threatening look down at his security chief, and his smile widened. "Then I'll threaten to leave you here when we ship out."